Bayard Tuckerman

Life of General Lafayette

Vol. 1

Bayard Tuckerman

Life of General Lafayette
Vol. 1

ISBN/EAN: 9783337333690

Printed in Europe, USA, Canada, Australia, Japan

Cover: Foto ©Raphael Reischuk / pixelio.de

More available books at **www.hansebooks.com**

LIFE

OF

GENERAL LAFAYETTE

WITH A CRITICAL ESTIMATE OF HIS CHARACTER AND PUBLIC ACTS

BY

BAYARD TUCKERMAN

IN TWO VOLUMES

VOL. I

LONDON

SAMPSON LOW, MARSTON, SEARLE, & RIVINGTON
Limited
ST. DUNSTAN'S HOUSE, FETTER LANE, FLEET STREET, E.C.

1889

PREFACE.

ORIGINAL materials for a study of Lafayette's character and public career exist in abundance. The six volumes of correspondence and papers published by his family give a full account of his thoughts, political views, relations with public men and private affairs from his own point of view. Mme. de Lafayette's and Mme. de Lasteyrie's family biographies describe his early life and domestic relations. Besides this published matter, the Historical Societies and private collections in America contain many letters of Lafayette of a private nature which afford much additional information.

On the other hand, there is no lack of contemporary testimony by friends, opponents, and enemies. For the period of his first adoption of the American cause may be mentioned the Deane papers, the reports, diary, and letters of Franklin, the State papers and reports of Ver-

gennes, the Memoirs of Madame de Campan,
of Beaumarchais, the Diplomatic Correspondence, the de Kalb papers in Knapp's Life of
de Kalb, Mme. de Lafayette's life of the Duchesse de Noailles, the Memoirs of the Comte
de Ségur, the reports of Lord Stormont, many
French memoirs, the correspondence of Mirabeau and the Comte de la Marck, and collections of papers in the library of the State
Department at Washington and of Congress.
For his military career in America and com-
ments on his personal conduct there: the
writings of Washington, Hamilton, Franklin,
Madison, John Adams, the ordinary and secret
journals of Congress, letters of Generals Greene,
Wayne, Knox, Sullivan, Steuben, the Corre-
spondence of the American Revolution by
Sparks, Niles's Principles and Acts of the Rev-
olution, Moore's Diary, the Annual Register,
British Blue Books, Walpole's Last Journals,
Wraxall's Historical Memoirs, the Correspond-
ence and Reports of Generals Howe, Cornwallis,
Clinton, and Carleton, Rivingston's Gazette,
Gentleman's Magazine, d'Estaing's reports, the

Rochambeau papers in the Library of Congress, Heath's memoirs, letters of Colonel Laurens, and many unpublished letters of Revolutionary characters in Historical Societies. Accounts at second hand and criticisms are to be found in nearly all biographies and histories dealing with the period, such as Marshall's and Irving's Washington, the lives of Greene, Knox, and Sullivan, Dawson's and Carrington's Battles, Stedman's, Gordon's, Ramsay's, Moultrie's histories of the war, Lossing's Field Book, Thatcher's Military Journal, Chevalier's Histoire de la Marine Française. Lafayette's labors in Europe on behalf of the United States are described in the papers of Vergennes, Franklin, Jay, Adams, Jefferson, and the Diplomatic Correspondence.

For Lafayette's career in France the sources of information are without end. The general left among his papers a full account of his conduct and views. To compare with this, the most obvious works are the Diary and Correspondence of Gouverneur Morris (1888) and the Correspondence of Mirabeau and Lamarck.

The two latter works contain the most severe
opinions of his character and acts, and need to
be corrected by other accounts. About three
hundred publications might be enumerated
having Lafayette for their principal subject.
A large number of political pamphlets, favorable and hostile, were issued by Royalists,
Girondists, Jacobins, Bonapartists, and Liberals.
The writer has made a study of a valuable collection of these. The period was extremely
rich in personal memoirs, which afford views
of Lafayette from many stand-points. Berville
and Barrière's collections of memoirs are essential. The Memoirs of Mirabeau, of Ségur, of
de Staël, of Ferrières, of Bouillé, of Madame
de Tourzel, of Sieyès, of Malouet, of Joseph
Bonaparte, are equally important. The *Moni-
teur*, Camille Desmoulin's *Révolutions de France
et Brabant*, and several other newspapers contain much material. The examination of
contemporary caricatures has furnished the
writer with impressions of changing public
opinion not otherwise obtainable. The kindness of friends and the politeness of owners of

unpublished autograph letters have supplied
accurate details regarding points which must
otherwise have been difficult to pass any judgment upon. The best critical remarks on Lafayette's character are to be found in an essay by
Sainte-Beuve. Lafayette's character and public
acts have been estimated by the most eminent
writers on French history; their varying opinions have been compared with each other and
with original evidence. Among these are the
English histories of Carlyle and Alison, and
the French works of Thiers, Michelet, La-
cretelle, Deux Amis de la Liberté, Louis Blanc,
de Tocqueville, Montgaillard, and Taine. Ste-
phens's History of the French Revolution pre-
sents the old Tory view of Lafayette. Other
important critical works are C. K. Adams's
Democracy and Monarchy in France, von
Sybel's History, and Vaulabelle's Histoire des
Deux Restaurations.

In this examination of Lafayette's career and
character an attempt has been made to arrive
at impartial conclusions, to point out the mistakes as well as the successes of his career, the

failings as well as the qualities of the man. Lafayette has suffered, perhaps, as much from the exaggerated praises of his admirers as from the bitter attacks of his enemies.

BAYARD TUCKERMAN.

THE BENEDICK,
    NEW YORK, Dec., 1888.

CONTENTS.

VOLUME I.

LIFE OF GENERAL LAFAYETTE.

CHAPTER I.

The News of the American Revolution in France. — Lafayette's Determination to join the Insurgents. — His Youth, Family, Education, and Marriage. — His Negotiations with United States Commissioners. — Overcomes all Obstacles and sails for America.

TOWARD the close of the year 1776, the Duke of Gloucester, the brother of George III., in the course of his travels arrived at the town of Metz, in France. The old Comte de Broglie, distinguished in the Seven Years' War, was stationed there in command of the garrison, and he invited some of his officers, passing the required time of service far from the pleasures of Versailles and Paris, to meet the royal visitor at dinner. The duke himself was something of a rebel, being at that time in banishment for having defied the authority of his brother by marrying the Countess of Waldegrave. He had lately received news from England regarding the conduct of some of His Majesty's colonies in America, and naturally made it the subject of conversation at the dinner-table. He related how these colonies had resisted various paternal injunctions of the home government, had declined to be taxed without representation, had driven the British soldiers ignominiously out of a town called Boston, and had even gone so far as to declare their independence of His Majesty altogether.   Such a relation, by a brother of George III., to officers belonging to the proudest aristocracy, and subjects of the most absolute sovereign in Europe, would seem to have deserved no other notice than the hope that the rebellious *canaille* would be sufficiently punished.   But nothing can illustrate more significantly the dangerous condition of France at this period, when the mutterings of angry discontent with arbitrary power were audible in every class, from the starving peasantry to the spendthrift court, than the interest and sympathy excited by this account of a distant people struggling for their political rights. One of these officers had been listening with particular attention.   He was just nineteen years old, tall and thin, with a long nose, retreating forehead, and reddish hair; his solemn expression of countenance, and rather awkward manner, contrasting with the frivolous grace of other young men of his rank and age.   He was a marquis of long and noble descent, connected by marriage with a family reputed to be the greatest at the court of France, and having at his own disposal an income of more than thirty thousand dollars a year.   He listened intently to all that was said, his grave face grew animated as his eager questions were answered, and he rose from the table resolved to abandon the pleasures which rank and wealth had to bestow in the gayest court and capital of the world, to leave even the young wife who had given him one

child and was soon · to give him another, that he
might risk life and fortune in the cause of the threatened people of whom his French schooling had probably not even taught him the existence. In his own
words, "When first I heard of American independence, my heart was enlisted!"

From the account given by the Duke of Gloucester,
it is not likely that the true merits of the case were
exposed, nor was the French mind prepared to appreciate the practical simplicity of the points in dispute.
But one idea was plain enough, — the insurgents were
fighting for liberty; and this word, so seldom in the
mouths of those who possess the benefits it represents,
is sufficient to rouse the deepest feelings of men who
daily feel the hand of oppression. Not only in Paris,
but throughout France, and in the principal cities of
Europe, arose a spontaneous cry of sympathetic approval at the news that an oppressed people was
rebelling against its sovereign. The courage of the
insurgents, or Bostonians, as they were called, was
lauded to the skies by men who longed but feared to
follow their example.

The young Count de Ségur wrote that the first
cannon-shot fired in America in defence of freedom
resounded throughout Europe with the rapidity of
lightning. At Spa, where were gathered many
travellers — voluntary delegates, as Ségur called them
— from all the monarchies of Europe, all were
unanimous in admiration of the men who had
dared to resist tyranny. The fashionable English

game of whist had to give way to another called Boston.

In Paris, the news awakened violent emotions. Idle nobles and officers saw an opportunity for military service and glory; statesmen, an opportunity to humiliate England and wipe out the disgrace of the last peace. And the people in general, suffering under the accumulated abuses of generations of arbitrary and corrupt government, welcomed, in the example of America, a proof that tyranny, ruinous taxation and oppression need not endure forever. These feelings took the form of devoted attentions to Franklin and the other American envoys, of loud applause at the theatres of every passage which referred to liberty or resistance, of animated discussions of the rightful functions of government. The fever took possession of the highest ranks of society, making American affairs the principal subject of conversation, introducing Franklin medallions, snuff-boxes, and fans, even into the palace of Versailles. Mme. du Deffand, writing to Walpole, d'Alembert to Frederic the Great, declared that the American insurgents occupied the attention of the philosophical and intelligent world.

Of the powerful sentiments which resulted in the French alliance, Lafayette's early and brilliant efforts made him the exponent. He was by no means a young man from whom great things were expected, nor was he known to possess other advantages than those of wealth and powerful connections at court. His family was ancient and distinguished. In 1421, the Marshal de La Fayette won the battle of Beaugé, which resulted in the death of the Duke of Clarence, and prevented Henry V. of England from taking entire possession of France. In 1503, Antoine de La Fayette, a captain in the army of Louis XII., was taken prisoner by the Spaniards. For a brief period, one of the obstacles in the way of Cardinal Richelieu's complete ascendency over the mind of Louis XIII. was Mlle. de La Fayette, a charming young girl of seventeen, beautiful and. virtuous, about whom Mme. de Genlis has written an historical romance. The melancholy king sought in her sweet society some measure of the social happiness and confidence which his elevation denied him. But Mlle. de La Fayette, although she returned the king's affection, had from childhood intended to become a nun. The king would not resist her resolution, yet begged her to delay its execution until after his departure for the army. The young girl watched from a window the royal carriage roll out of the courtyard, and turned away with the words, "Alas! I shall see him no more." But Louis, on his return, visited her at the convent, and remained so long "glued to her grating," according to Mme. de Motteville, that Richelieu took alarm and put a summary end to the friendship.

In 1633 was born Marie Madeleine Pioche de la Vergne, destined to confer on the family distinction of a more lasting kind by beginning the modern novel of real life. She married François Motier, Comte de La Fayette, Seigneur de Nades, and lieutenant in the Gardes Françaises. An old French song which describes the first meeting of the affianced couple, represents the count as awkward and embarrassed to a degree which excited the merriment of the family circle gathered together for the occasion. Mlle. de la Vergne, however, expressed her opinion that the count would make a good husband enough, *quoique peutêtre bête.* The song concludes with the prediction that the husband

> Ira à sa terre,
> Comme monsieur son père;

and his wife will write

> Des romans à Paris,
> Avec les beaux esprits.

Mme. de Lafayette seems to have made a good wife and mother, as times went, notwithstanding the dissimilarity between her husband's tastes and her own. She had shown uncommon intelligence from childhood, and her very superior acquirements had caused her to be called *précieuse* by Scarron before Molière's ridicule cast discredit on the term. She became one of the literary ornaments of the reign of Louis XIV., continued for many years a friend and correspondent of Mme. de Sévigné, and was exceedingly intimate with the Duc de la Rochefoucauld, who had improved her mind, she said, as she had improved his heart. Until the publication of her novels, the ponderous romances of Scudéri, Calprenède, and Gomberville, with their endless, pointless tales of French, Persian, Grecian, and Indian princes and princesses, had supplied the want of readers of fiction. But before even Mrs. Behn had composed her trivial tales, and a hundred years before the great burst of genius in England which produced the works of Richardson, Fielding, and Smollett, Mme. de Lafayette published the "Princesse de Montpensier," "Zaïde," and the "Princesse de Clèves," which form so happy a beginning of the most popular department of modern literature.

Michael Louis de Mottier, the father of our Lafayette, was killed in the Seven Years' War, waged by Frederic the Great of Prussia, assisted by England, against Russia, Austria, and France, and which, extending to the Western Continent, resulted in the loss of Canada, and the extinction of French power in America. The marquis fell at the battle of Minden, under command of the Marshal de Broglie, on the thirteenth day of July, 1757. Although only twenty-four years old, he had already distinguished himself, was colonel of the Grenadiers of France, and chevalier of Saint Louis. It is said that his death was caused by a cannon-shot from a battery commanded by the same General Philips against whom his son fought in Virginia in 1781. He was a poor man, but had made up for that by marrying Mlle. de la Rivière, daughter of the Marquis de la Rivière, from whom his son inherited the fortune which he used so well. Hardly a month had elapsed after the young colonel's death at Minden, when, on the 6th of September, 1757, at the Château of Chavaniac, his wife's home in Auvergne, was born his only child, who received the name of Marie Paul Joseph Roche Ives Gilbert de Mottier.

The education of an aristocratic French child under the *Ancien Régime* was chiefly conducted by a dancing-master. Whether boy or girl, the object of all instruction was a capacity to shine in the drawing-room, to be an ornamental and pleasing article of furniture. The most important accomplishments consisted in a graceful bearing, a genial manner, a habit of easy conversation which never allowed a subject to be discussed so seriously as to fatigue the weakest mind of the company or to provoke the least heat of discussion. It was indispensable to adapt one's bow to its object, from the servile inclination of the body to a prince of the blood, through all degrees down to the insulting nod vouchsafed to a *roturier*. It was necessary to know how to compliment appropriately, to pick up a fan correctly, to offer an arm with enough, but not too much, politeness. To utter a successful *bon mot* was the highest and most coveted of triumphs. Boys and girls were bred for a life to be passed in a drawing-room without occupations or interests beyond it. A *gentilhomme* should have no use for his hands except to hold a sword, nor for his mind except to converse agreeably. To draw up an arm-chair was a footman's duty; to superintend property or regulate expenditure was the intendant's affair.

These accomplishments were not simply the ornaments of life — they made up the life of the time. If
you took from a *gentilhomme* his graces and his dissolute gallantry, it would be difficult to grasp the
ghostly remnant of an individuality which remained.
To be perfect in the social art, to wear your *noblesse*
as your skin and not as your clothing, you could not
be trained too early. And therefore little boys
and girls in stiff court dress were occupied with
bows, curtsies, compliments, and phrases, while
English children were rolling hoop or playing ball.
Parents, absorbed in the *vie du salon*, could see little
of each other or of their children, for did not they
owe their time to society? It was *ridicule* to be affectionate, and *bourgeois* to be domestic. Mme. de
Staël expresses her great surprise that such a character
as that of Lafayette should have been developed in
the ranks of the French nobility. It was Lafayette's
vigorous individuality which saved him froni the dangers of his education.

His mother passed her widowhood at Chavaniac,
where a country life allowed of affectionate intercourse between parent and child. The game laws
of France permitted wild animals to roam everywhere
without interference, and Lafayette's earliest recollec-
tion, when about eight years old, was the hope of en-
countering in his walks a wolf which had committed
depredations in the neighborhood. In his twelfth
year he was sent to the Collége du Plessis at Paris,
and while there, the death of his mother and grand-

father placed him in possession of a large fortune. He learned little enough at this college, but still acquired what was necessary for every French nobleman, — a capacity for writing his own language well. It is characteristic of him, that when directed to compose an essay on the horse, he took care to insist on the disposition of that animal to throw a too exacting rider. A letter written by Lafayette when fourteen years of age to his cousin, Mlle. de Chavaniac, illustrates the social and worldly character of his education : " I have just received your letter, my dear cousin, and the good news of my grandmother's health. Next to that news, which concerned my heart, I was very particularly interested in the hunt in the forest of Lata. I would be very glad to know if those dogs which neither walk nor bark contributed to the capture. The details of this hunt would have amused me extremely ; if I had mentioned a new-fashioned bonnet to you, I should have considered it a duty to describe the outlines and bows with a compass in my hand. Our cousin's marriage is not to take place ; there is another match in contemplation, but he must lower his pretensions very much. Mademoiselle de Roncherolles, a place about the person of Madame de Bourbon, worth a thousand écus a year, and a paltry income of five thousand francs, — that's the whole story. You see it's a very small matter, after all that has passed. My uncle, who came to see me the other day, consents to the marriage, on condition that the Prince de Condé will promise one of his cavalry regiments to our cousin. Madame de Montboissier thinks ⁀ that this is asking too much, and said to M. le Marquis de Canillac, that if he was so hard to please, her husband would have nothing more to do with his affairs ; that nettled the marquis, and there was a very lively dispute. The nephew takes very little interest in the marriage. He said that he knew of much better matches which would not be refused him, and he named them, too." There follows other gossip of society and politics which would be expected from a man of the world rather than from a boy of fourteen. In so forced a maturity, the uncalculating happiness, and the gradual, solid development of boyhood seem to have no place.

Lafayette was soon transferred from the Collége du Plessis to the academy at Versailles, and made an officer in the Mousquetaires Noirs, the reviews of which took him from a school-boy's bench to command men ; and at sixteen a wife was provided for him.

The family of Noailles was of such rank and consequence at court, that when Marie Antoinette's intimacy with Mme. de Polignac raised the latter to the most prominent position, the Countess de Noailles found it necessary to resign her charge, as it was impossible for her to occupy any but the first place. Mlle. Marie Adrienne de Noailles, the granddaughter of the Duc de Noailles, daughter of the Duc d'Ayen, and sister of the Vicomtesse de Noailles, was married to Lafayette on the 11th of April, 1774, when fourteen years of

age.   Her mother, the Duchesse d'Ayen, was a woman
of extraordinary piety, and brought up her daughters
in an atmosphere of religious fervor and domestic virtue hardly conceivable in the society to which she
belonged.   Her husband was essentially a man of his
time and class, found his own house far too austere' for
his taste, and passed very little time in it.   He it was
who perceived in Lafayette's rank and fortune the
proper qualities for his son-in-law.   When he announced to his wife the selection that he had made,
she irritated him by seeing a danger in the independent
fortune possessed by so young a man.   The difference
of opinion between the Duc and the Duchesse d'Ayen
regarding this marriage was so strong that husband
and wife were for some time wholly estranged.   The
duchesse was finally compelled to yield to her husband's determination, but she was gratified to find in
her son-in-law qualities which set at rest her fears for
the future.

Mlle. Adrienne had seen nothing of life previous to
her marriage but the domestic quiet and religious
observances of her mother's household.   Yet she had
passed through one painful experience which is illustrative of her character.   She was to have taken her
first communion at the same time with her elder sister,
but her extreme conscientiousness instilled in her mind
such doubts of her faith and fitness for the sacrament,
that, to her own and her mother's sorrow, her first
communion was postponed for two years.   It took
place when she was sixteen, just before the birth of

her eldest child, Henriette. When she became the wife of Lafayette, she was a child in everything but the strength of her faith and her virtues. Her education had been purely religious.

"The idea of regulating life by the principles of virtue," she afterwards wrote, "the disregard of all interest of whatever nature, had become so habitual to us, not only by the lessons of my mother, but by her constant example, and by that of my father in the unhappily too rare occasions when we had the opportunity of observing him, that the first examples that we encountered of a contrary conduct in those that are vulgarly called good people, caused in us a surprise that many years of life passed in the world have been required to weaken." Hardly could a greater contrast be imagined than is given by this picture of the d'Ayen household and the moral corruption which pervaded the atmosphere of the old monarchy. Mme. de Lafayette had qualities of mind destined to give her a reputation distinct from her husband's. But in her youth her whole nature was concentrated in her affections. These were lavished upon her mother and her youthful husband. The time of the marriage coincided with the signing of the Boston Port Bill by George III., which made the American war inevitable.

Lafayette's marriage afforded him an intimate introduction at court, where the young bridegroom of sixteen had an opportunity of studying royalty in the person of Louis XV., and the social virtues in that of Mme. du Barry, whose amiable desire it was to

make every woman who hoped for a heaven here-
after to experience a hell on earth. Lafayette was
present at the Du Barry's when the king had the
fainting-fit which announced his fatal disease. With
the advent to the throne of Louis XVI. in 1774, the
court was disinfected, and its tone considerably raised.
But the general standard of morality among the aristocracy remained much the same ; and if Lafayette's
life showed an observance of domestic duties, it was,
like his other good qualities, in spite of his education
and early influences.

Marie Antoinette, in the zenith of her young
beauty and happiness, retained much simplicity of
character, and longed to withdraw from conventional
grandeur to taste the satisfactions of private life.
She gathered together a select party of young people
for the purpose of acting plays and dancing quadrilles in fancy costume. Among these were included
Lafayette and Ségur. The company chose dresses
imitated from those of feudal times, and sought to
invest themselves with the character of knights and
ladies of chivalry. The quadrilles and the rehearsals
necessary for them became the favorite amusement
of the queen's household, and excited untold jealousy
among the uninitiated. The older courtiers, anxious
to keep up ancient ceremonies in unimpaired rigidity,
and fearing the influence of this new intimacy, made
every effort to break up the quadrilles. Their anxiety
was greatly increased when the dancers induced the
king to publish an order compelling all persons who

attended the queen's ball to 'appear in similar costumes; for Ségur says, with a touch of malice, that,
although very becoming to youthful and slender figures, they were ridiculous for stout or elderly persons.
The contest between ceremony and pleasure resulted
finally in favor of the former; and the quadrilles with
their fancy costumes and cherished intimacy came to
an end. With them ceased Lafayette's frequent appearances at court. The inborn independence of his
nature stiffened the hinges of his knee. The serious
bent of his mind unfitted him for the endless flow of
frivolous small-talk which was necessary to popularity.
He has himself said that he was silent in company,
because the things he thought or heard did not seem
to him worth saying, and that he could neither unbend
sufficiently for the graces of the court, nor for the
liveliness of a supper in town. As time passed, he
grew more averse to Versailles and more fond of
being with his regiment. When the Noailles family
undertook to procure for him a place about the person of the Duc de Provence, he secretly resolved to
defeat the project. He seized the opportunity presented by a masked ball, accosted the duke, allowed
himself to be recognized, and expressed liberal sentiments highly repugnant to his hearer. When the
prince informed him sharply that he would remember
the interview, Lafayette replied that memory was the
wit of fools. This remark, of course, settled the
question of employment at court, and the Duc de
Provence, even when Louis XVIII., retained the ani-

mosity aroused by this scene. The family of Noailles, which Lafayette had adopted and loved as his own, could not understand the young man's character. His reserve and independence were the very opposite of the qualities which his courtly relatives wished to see in him. His young friend Ségur was much better informed, as the following extract will show : " At every period of his life, and above all in his youth, Lafayette displayed a _cold and grave exterior, which sometimes gave to his demeanor an air of timidity and embarrassment which did not really belong to him. His reserved manners and his silent disposition presented a singular contrast to the petulance, the levity, and the ostentatious loquacity of persons of his own age ; but under this exterior, to all appearance so phlegmatic, he concealed the most active mind, the most determined character, and the most enthusiastic spirit. Of this fact I was better enabled to judge than others. During the preceding winter he had become attached to a lady as amiable as she was beautiful, and, having erroneously conceived an idea that I was his rival, in a fit of jealousy he had put aside all consideration of our friendship, and had passed the greater part of the night with me, endeavoring to prevail on me to decide by the sword which of us should be the favored suitor of a lady to whom I made no pretensions. Some days after our quarrel and reconciliation, I could not refrain from laughing when I heard the Marshal de Noailles and other individuals of his family entreat me to use my influence

with him to animate his torpidity, to rouse him from
his inaction, and to communicate some animation to
his character. It is easy to conceive their astonishment when they learned suddenly that this young sage
of nineteen, so cool and so indifferent, had been so
far carried away by the love of glory and of danger as
to intend to cross the ocean and fight in the cause
of American freedom."

Lafayette lost no time in putting into execution
the resolution which he had taken at Metz. On his
arrival in Paris, he soon concluded, from various slight
indications, that nothing but opposition was to be
expected from his family, and that he must depend
entirely upon himself. To strengthen his purpose, to
provide an answer to his own misgivings and discouragements, he adopted the motto, *" Cur non ?"* The
first business was to form an acquaintance with the
American agents. Silas Deane was officially ignored
by the French government, which was endeavoring to
keep up appearances with England; but he was
secretly despatching arms and accoutrements to
America with the connivance of the ministers and
the help of the celebrated Beaumarchais, whose claims
for repayment were destined to cause a dispute with
the United States. Deane was so closely watched
by the spies of Lord Stormont, the English ambassador, that it was exceedingly difficult to see him
without exciting suspicion. Lafayette's first action,
therefore, was to make acquaintance with De Kalb,
an officer of German origin, whom Choiseul had sent

to America some years before to report on the prospects of profitable French interference. De Kalb
himself was arranging to go to the colonies; he introduced Lafayette to Deane, and interpreted the short
conversation which took place. Lafayette realized
that his boyish countenance and inexperience were
not strong recommendations; he therefore made a
great point of his zeal in the cause, and of the sensation that his departure would undoubtedly make.
Deane was glad enough to meet this new ally. He
drew up an agreement, by which he promised, on the
part of the United States, the rank of major-general to
Lafayette, carefully stating that he did so on account
of the zeal, the rank, influence, and many good qualities of the young man, and also because the great
family to which he belonged would never permit him
to join the cause without so high a commission.
Lafayette, on his part, signed a contract to proceed to
the United States whenever requested by Deane, and
there serve to the best of his ability, without pay or
remuneration of any kind. The contracts made by
Deane with other French officers contained express
stipulations as to the pay they should receive, and
frequently bear acknowledgments for money advanced.
Franklin and Lee soon after joined Deane as commissioners. They were all so closely watched that it was
only safe to communicate with them through Carmichael, an American then living in Paris.[1]

---

[1] The original contract between Deane and Lafayette is among the
Deane papers in the library of the Connecticut Historical Society at

Secrecy was so important for Lafayette that he hardly knew where to look for necessary assistance. An application to the Marshal de Broglie met with strenuous opposition. The old soldier could see nothing but danger in the project. In several interviews he urged that the cause itself was doubtful ; that the success of the colonies was very unlikely ; that Lafayette was risking his own life and fortune, the peace of his family and connections, without a prospect of reward. " I have seen your uncle die in the wars of Italy, I have witnessed your father's death at Minden, and I will not be accessory to the ruin of the last remaining branch of the family." But in response to the most urgent requests, he promised not to betray the plan he could not approve, and even indicated some officers who might be of service. Lafayette then confided his intentions to his brother-in-law, the Vicomte de Noailles, and to his uncle by marriage, the Vicomte de Ségur, son of the Ségur who soon afterwards became minister of war. To his great joy, they received his proposals with enthusiasm, and all three entered into an agreement of secrecy until the disposition of the government could be ascertained, and the arrangements for departure completed. But the secret was too glorious to be kept long. They endeavored to enlist the interest of some other young men, through whose indiscretion the affair came to the ears

---

Hartford. Other papers regarding the work of the American commissions are to be found there, and among the Franklin papers in the State Department at Washington.

of the court, and an explosion of astonishment and
disapprobation immediately followed. The . ministers
feared that the departure as volunteers of noblemen
of such rank would be interpreted by the English government as an open acknowledgment of the intention
of France to support the colonies. Formal orders
were at once issued to the young men to abandon
their enterprise, while their families warmly reproached
them for their folly and rashness. Ségur and Noailles,
being dependent on their parents, were compelled to
acquiesce. Lafayette, conscious of the independence
conferred by his private fortune, was only irritated by
opposition. He outwardly appeared to yield, but
secretly determined that nothing should keep him
from America. *Cur non ?*

At this juncture came another severe discouragement. News arrived that Washington had been defeated at Long Island, and was now retreating through
New Jersey with a ragged and suffering army of three
thousand men before Howe's victorious and well-
accoutred troops. The credit of the colonies immediately fell, the cause seemed to the French too
hopeless to be worth aiding, and it became impossible
to send the vessel. The American commissioners
honestly informed Lafayette of the state of affairs,
and discouraged his perseverance. But in this hour
of adversity, Lafayette's unselfish devotion to what he
believed a noble cause overcame every obstacle.
Thanking Deane for his frankness, he said, " Until
this moment, sir, you have seen only my zeal ; now,

perhaps, I may become really useful. I shall purchase a vessel myself to carry your officers. We
must show our confidence in the cause ; and it is in
the time of your danger that I wish to share your
fortunes." The old people were not unjustified in
their accusations of rashness and folly.

Franklin, through Carmichael, assented gladly to
this new proposal. But it was extremely difficult to
procure a vessel without discovery by Lord Stormont.
Fortunately, when the Comte de Broglie saw that
Lafayette's resolution was irrevocable, he lent a
surreptitious assistance. Lieutenant Dubois Martin,
the brother of De Broglie's secretary, was secretly
despatched to Bordeaux, which was considered the
port most free from suspicion, and there secured a
ship.[1] Repairs, however, were necessary, and some
time must elapse before departure could be thought
of.

Meanwhile the secret must be kept. It happened
opportunely that Lafayette had a long-standing engagement with his cousin, the Prince de Poix, to
take a journey to England. To fulfil this engagement was evidently the best way to disarm suspicion
and pass the time until the vessel could be made
ready. The two friends set out for London, where
Lafayette's uncle, the Marquis de Noailles, was

---

[1] This vessel, " La Victoire," was purchased from the firm of Recules
de Basmarins, Rainbaux, et Cie; the captain was Le Boursier, and
the price 112,000 francs, including the cargo. Lafayette paid a quarter
on delivery, and the balance in fifteen months.

ambassador, and on their arrival were treated with great distinction. It was the cue of the English government to keep up the appearance of undiminished friendship with France, and the arrival of the young strangers afforded a favorable opportunity for a demonstration of affection. Lafayette has recorded his feelings of amusement on being presented to His Britannic Majesty, against whom he was soon to be in arms ; how he enjoyed dancing at the house of Lord George Germain, the secretary for the colonies, in company with Lord Rawdon, lately arrived from New York. At the opera he met Clinton, whom he was next to encounter at the battle of Monmouth. His open expressions of sympathy with the rebels procured him an invitation to breakfast at Lord Shelburne's. He has been accused by English writers of making use of his visit to obtain information, but he declined an invitation given by King George himself to see the military preparations then making at Portsmouth, and avoided every action which could be construed into a breach of confidence. When three weeks had passed amidst the gayeties of London, Lafayette could endure the delay no longer, and resolved to return to France and to join his vessel. He told his uncle, the ambassador, that he had taken a fancy to cross the channel for a few days' visit at home. The latter opposed the idea strongly, on the ground that so abrupt a departure would be disrespectful to the English court. But as Lafayette persisted, the Marquis de Noailles offered to give out that his nephew was sick until his return. " I would not have proposed this stratagem," said Lafayette, " but I did not object to it."

After suffering severely from sea-sickness in the channel, Lafayette arrived at De Kalb's house in Paris, and proceeded thence to Chaillot, where he had his final interview with the American commissioners, and gave his directions to the officers who were to accompany him. So far no suspicions were entertained by his family or at court that the project was still on foot. On the morning of the 16th of March, about two months after the prohibition had been issued which discontinued the conferences of himself, Ségur, and Noailles, Lafayette entered Ségur's room in Paris, at seven o'clock, in haste, carefully closed the door behind him, seated himself at Ségur's bedside, and said, " I am going to America. No one knows it; but I love you too well to set off without intrusting you with the secret." — " And how have you been able," inquired Ségur, " to secure your passage ? " The story was soon told, and Ségur congratulated his friend on the success which he longed to share.

In company with De Kalb, Lafayette arrived at Bordeaux on the 19th of March. De Kalb, through the influence of the Comte de Broglie, had secured the connivance of the ministers at his departure. It has been said, that as he and Lafayette travelled together, what was true of one must be true of the other. But such a view could only arise from ignorance of the relative positions of the two men. De Kalb was an officer in the army, unconnected with the court, whose movements could be ignored and disavowed, who might go to America, as other officers had already gone, without attracting any special attention from the British. But the Marquis de Lafayette, so closely bound to the Noailles family and the court, was a person who could take no important step without raising the presumption that he had the king's permission. Individual officers might go without seriously compromising the government in the eyes of the British minister; but the departure of one so near the court was resented as an evidence that the cause of the rebellious colonies was favorably looked upon by those in authority. Moreover, it was at express request of the Duc d'Ayen that Lafayette had been forbidden to carry out his plans.

The French government made no effort to detain De Kalb and other officers, nor were any steps ever taken to call them to account afterwards. But the most decided steps were taken to prevent Lafayette from sailing; and after he had escaped, the government forced Deane to write a letter to Congress, requesting, on its part, that the young man should not be given employment. This letter is still to be seen. Lafayette had hardly set out for Bordeaux when the fact became known to Lord Stormont, who immediately informed the Noailles family, and sent a remonstrance to the ministers.

On arriving at the seaport, Lafayette found that the

vessel was not yet ready. Soon after, on receiving an intimation that the court was fully informed of his proceedings, he suspended the repairs, and set sail immediately for Passage, a neighboring port in Spain. There he was met by two officers, who had followed by land from Bordeaux, bearing a peremptory *lettre de cachet,* which forbade him, under the severest penalties, to go to America, and commanded him to repair at once to Marseilles and there await further orders. The messengers also brought family letters which Lafayette himself described as terrible. They pointed out the consequences of the anger of the government, which might punish with extreme severity the disobedience of a military officer. The Duc d'Ayen projected a tour in Italy, and insisted that Lafayette should join him and his family at Marseilles, and accompany them on the journey.

Lafayette was exceedingly troubled at the effect which his difficulties might have upon his wife. Moreover, he feared that direct disobedience to the *lettre de cachet* might involve others besides himself. In the hope of obtaining some modification of the interdict, he left the vessel at Passage, accompanied the king's officers back to Bordeaux, and reported to the commandant there. Then he despatched letters to Paris. To his family he urged the worthiness of the cause in which he was engaged, and begged their support. To the ministers he justified his position, mentioning as precedents an Irish officer in the French service who had lately joined the British forces in America, and the case of Duportail and two other French engineers who had obtained permission to enter the American army.   In one of his letters he let fall the characteristic remark that the ministers could talk with better grace of the sanctity of his oath of allegiance when they began to observe their own pledges, — a statement which was duly reported to the government, and was too true not to excite irritation.   A special courier was sent with a letter for an intimate friend of Lafayette, named De Coigny, who was requested to ascertain as soon as possible whether there was any chance that the government would yield, and to return the answer at once.   The reply from De Coigny, brought by the special courier, was to the effect that the court was much incensed, and there was not the remotest possibility that permission to sail would be granted.   From all the information he could obtain, Lafayette concluded that the most serious opposition resulted from the application of his father-in-law, and he became assured that disobedience on his part would compromise no one but himself.   His resolution, therefore, was soon taken.   Only one course remained, — to cross the Spanish border and embark before any further obstacle could be placed in his way.   To Maurepas, the old prime minister, he wrote, that receiving no reply to his letters, he took the government's silence to imply a tacit consent. Then, allowing the commandant at Bordeaux to suppose that he was about to obey orders by repairing to Marseilles, he set out on the route to that city in a post-chaise, accompanied by an officer named De Mauroy, who was anxious to go to America. As soon as the carriage reached the open country, Lafayette disguised himself as a courier, and in that capacity galloped on ahead and ordered the relays. Leaving the Marseilles road, the party arrived at Bayonne, where occurred a delay of three hours. During this time Lafayette lay on the straw in the stable in his disguise as courier. He was now pursuing the same route that he had lately passed over on his way from Passage to Bordeaux in company with the royal officers, and there was danger of recognition. At a little village, called St. Jean de Luz, this actually happened, and nearly proved fatal to the enterprise. As the pretended courier rode into the post-yard and called for horses, he was recognized by the innkeeper's daughter as a young gentleman whom she had seen driven by in a carriage but a few days before. Her surprise was evident; but a sign from Lafayette made her understand that secrecy was desired. She required no more to remain faithful to the stranger. Soon after, when the officers in pursuit rode up and inquired if such a carriage had passed, she replied that she had seen a carriage, but it contained no such persons as were described. The baffled pursuers returned, and Lafayette arrived at Passage without further accident. After six months of constant effort, discouragement, and anxiety, he stood at last on the deck of " La Victoire," and on the 20th of April gave the order to set sail.

The departure of Lafayette made a sensation which was of considerable political importance. At a time when substantial assistance from France was extremely doubtful, the incident afforded an opportunity for the expression of public opinion, which had a strong effect on the government. The news was received in Paris with enthusiasm. The coffee-houses echoed with the young lieutenant's name, and at the theatres no passage which could be made to apply to the favorite subject was allowed to go without applause. It was well known that no member of the Noailles family undertook anything of importance without the sanction of a family consultation; it was difficult to believe that Lafayette had acted independently, and his course was taken as a good augury. Walpole and Gibbon recorded the circumstances in their diaries, and took it for granted that the opposition of the French government was only feigned. The general desire that France should form an alliance with the colonies, and the popularity of such a policy, were no longer in doubt.

In the fashionable world opinions varied. "All Paris," wrote the Chevalier de Marais to his mother, "is discussing the adventure of a young courtier, the son-in-law of Noailles, who has a pretty wife, two children, fifty thousand crowns a year, — in fact, everything which can make life here agreeable and dear, but who deserted all that a week ago to join the insurgents. His name is M. de Lafayette." And the marquise replied from her château in the country,

"What new kind of folly is this, my dear child? What! the madness of knight-errantry still exists! It has disciples! Go to help the insurgents! I am delighted that you reassure me about yourself, for I should tremble for you; but since you see that M. de Lafayette is a madman, I am tranquil. How I pity his mother!" Mme. du Deffand wrote to Horace Walpole, "Of course it is a piece of folly, but it does him no discredit. He receives more praise than blame." There were few *salons* in which the young man's praises were not sung in unqualified terms. One *grande dame* went so far as to say that "if the Duc d'Ayen will thwart such a son-in-law in such a project, he cannot expect to marry his other daughters."

As "La Victoire" spread her sails to the wind, Franklin despatched the following communication to the American Congress: "The Marquis de Lafayette, a young nobleman of great family connections here and great wealth, is gone to America in a ship of his own, accompanied by some officers of distinction, in order to serve in our armies. He is exceedingly beloved, and everybody's good wishes attend him. We cannot but hope he may meet with such a reception as will make the country and his expedition agreeable to him. Those who censure it as imprudent in him, do, nevertheless, applaud his spirit; and we are satisfied that the civilities and respect that may be shown him will be serviceable to our affairs here, as pleasing not only to his powerful relations and the court, but to the whole French nation. He has left a beautiful young wife; and for her sake, particularly, we hope that his bravery and ardent desire to distinguish himself will be a little restrained by the General's prudence, so as not to permit his being hazarded much, except on some important occasion." [1]

---

[1] With Lafayette, on "La Victoire," were Baron de Kalb, Vicomte de Mauroy, Colonels Delesser and Valfort, Lieutenant-Colonels de Fayolles and Franval, Majors Dubuysson and de Gimat, Captains de Vrigny, de Bedaulx, and de la Colombe, Lieutenant Dubois Martin, and an American named Brice.

CHAPTER II.

Arrival in South Carolina. — Letters to his Wife. — Receives Commission as Major-General from Congress. — Meets Washington and becomes a Member of his Staff. — Is wounded at Brandywine. — The Fight at Gloucester. — Lafayette receives a Command.

THE family of Major Benjamin Huger of South Carolina was alarmed one night in the middle of June, 1777, by the violent barking of their dogs. The house lay close to the Pedee river, which communicated with the sea; and as English cruisers were constantly hovering about the coast, an attack of marauders from the enemy was feared. The inmates prepared for defence, and challenged the new-comers from the window. The answer was in the broken English of De Kalb, who told in a few words that M. de Lafayette and a party of officers had just arrived on the coast in a French vessel to fight for American independence, that they had come up the river in a small boat, and, guided by a light in this house, had sought the owner's hospitality.

When Lafayette awoke on his first morning in America, everything that he saw and heard seemed to gratify the sanguine anticipations which had cheered the long and dangerous voyage across the Atlantic. The mosquito-nettings which enclosed his bed, the black servant who came to attend to his wants, the luxuriance of the vegetation which spread out before his window, all was novel and delightful. His first impressions were conveyed in a hurried note to his wife, despatched by a vessel just leaving Georgetown : " The manners of the people here are simple, frank, and in every respect worthy of the land which resounds with the noble name of liberty."

The party only stayed long enough at Major Huger's to obtain a much-needed rest. · The voyage had lasted seven weeks, and had been dangerous as well as tedious. Papers had been taken out for the West Indies, as was usual with vessels bound for America. But Lafayette, fearing lest he might be stopped by government order, resolved to sail directly for the American coast. To this plan the captain of " La Victoire " opposed an obstinate resistance, which Lafayette could only overcome by threatening to displace him in favor of the mate. It soon leaked out that the captain's real reason for wishing to touch at the West Indies lay in his having embarked about eight thousand dollars' worth of merchandise, which he intended to sell for his own profit. Lafayette's habitual generosity led him to guarantee to the captain the reimbursement of any loss which he might suffer, — a promise which at once smoothed over the difficulty. " La Victoire," being exceedingly slow and miserably armed, could not have coped with the smallest privateer, and every sail descried gave rise to alarm. With a Dutch officer named Bedaulx, who had deserted from the royal army, and had only a gibbet to expect in case of capture, Lafayette agreed to blow up the vessel rather than surrender. On approaching the coast, no little alarm was caused by the sight of a ship advancing toward them. A show of defence was made, but it turned out to be an American privateer, which, on parting from " La Victoire," was itself taken by two British cruisers.

To Lafayette, the voyage was inexpressibly wearisome. During the first two or three weeks he suffered severely from sea-sickness; but when this difficulty had ceased, he applied himself vigorously to the study of the English language, and of military works. Time for reflection was not wanting. During the weary days which succeeded each other so monotonously at sea, his mind turned to the possible dangers which lay before him, and back again to France and the wife, child, and friends whom he had left there. He felt the full extent of the sacrifice he was making, but he never for an instant regretted it. To his wife he wrote : "I am writing to you from a great distance, my dear heart, and to this cruel separation I add the still more dreadful uncertainty regarding the time when I can have news of you. . . . How many fears, how much uneasiness I have to add to my great sorrow at being separated from all that is dearest to me ! How will you have taken my second departure? Will you have loved me less for it? Will you have forgiven me? . . . Will you have considered that in any event I must have been separated from you, wandering in Italy, and dragging out

a life without honor, among people in the highest degree opposed to my projects and to my way of thinking?   All these reflections did not prevent me from
experiencing a dreadful sensation in the terrible
moments which separated me from the shore.   Your
regrets, those of my friends, of Henriette,[1] all was
pictured to my soul in a heart-rending manner. Then,
indeed, I could no longer find an excuse for myself.
If you knew all that I have suffered, the sad days
that I have passed in fleeing from all that I love on
earth ! Shall I join to this misfortune that of learning
that you do not forgive me?   In truth, my heart, I
should be too much to be pitied. . . . Do not
believe that I am to run any real risk in the position
that I shall have.   The rank of general officer has
always been looked upon as a patent right to immor-
tality. . . .   Now let us speak of yourself, of dear
Henriette, of her brother, or of her sister.   Henriette is so lovely that she gives one a taste for girls.
Whichever our new child may be, I shall welcome it
with great joy.   Do not lose a moment in hastening
my happiness by informing me of its birth."

But the regret that Lafayette felt for what he had
left behind did not dampen his enthusiasm for what
lay before him. " Defender of that liberty which I
worship," he continues, " free myself, more than any
one, in coming as a friend to offer my services to this
so interesting republic, I bring nothing but my frankness and my good-will, — no ambition, no private

---

[1] His infant daughter, who died during his absence.

interest; in striving for my glory, I strive for their happiness. I hope that for my sake you will become a good American; it is a sentiment created for virtuous hearts. The happiness of America is intimately bound to the happiness of all humanity; she will become the worthy and safe asylum of virtue, of integrity, of tolerance, of equality, and of a peaceful liberty."

Among the family who welcomed Lafayette on his first arrival in America was Francis Kinloch Huger, then a little boy, to whom the general showed great kindness, and who acquired in this early acquaintance the enthusiastic admiration for his father's guest which afterwards led to his gallant attempt to rescue him from the prison of Olmutz.

Lafayette and his companions left Major Huger's hospitable house for Charleston, ordering " La Victoire " to proceed to the same place. On arriving at Charleston, information was given that the vessel would almost surely be taken by British frigates which were blockading the port. Lafayette sent word to the captain to burn the vessel in case of danger; but by a lucky accident, a storm drove the frigates to a distance, and in the mean time " La Victoire " came safely into port. She discharged her cargo and was loaded with rice, but was afterwards wrecked on the bar, and proved a total loss.

Lafayette's reception at Charleston was exceedingly flattering. He wrote that he was overwhelmed with politeness, " not the politeness of Europe." A dinner

was given, attended by Generals Gulden, Howe, Moultrie, and the French officers, where Lafayette had an
opportunity to practise his English. The interest
taken in the young stranger and his unselfish purpose
was extended to all his companions. They passed
some days in a pleasant intercourse with the inhabitants, and in visiting the fortifications in company with
American officers. The first impressions of the young
Frenchman on mingling with American society are
too illustrative of his character to be omitted. The
ideal of social conditions aimed at by the young
reformers of France seemed to find a realization in
America; and Lafayette, brought up in an atmosphere
of arbitrary government and social distinctions of an
often cruel severity, accustomed to moral obliquity
and corruption, took, in the political and social virtues of the new land, a delight which showed that
the ideas which inspired him concerned, not the
aggrandizement of any one nation, but the improvement and welfare of humanity. On the 19th of
June he wrote to his wife, "I shall now speak of
the country, my dear heart, and of its inhabitants.
They are as attractive as my enthusiasm could picture
them. Simplicity of manners, a desire to oblige, a
love of country and of liberty, a sweet equality, prevail
here universally. The richest man and the poorest
are on a level; and although there are immense fortunes in this country, I challenge any one to find the
least difference in the manners of men towards each
other, caused by dissimilarity of fortune. I began

with a country life at Major Huger's; now, I am in town. Everything is much after the English fashion, except that here is more simplicity. The city of Charleston is one of the prettiest and the best built that I have ever seen, and its inhabitants are most agreeable. The American women are very pretty, very unaffected, and exhibit a charming neatness,— a quality which is most studiously cultivated here, much more even than in England. What enchants me here is that all the citizens are brethren. There are no poor people in America, nor even what we call peasants. All the citizens have a moderate property, and all have the same rights as the most powerful proprietor. The inns are very different from those of Europe: the innkeeper and his wife sit at table with you, do the honors of a good repast, and on leaving, you pay without haggling. When you do not choose to go to an inn, you can find country houses where it is enough to be a good American to be received with such attentions as in Europe would be paid to friends. . . . Considering the agreeable existence that I lead in this country, the sympathy which puts me as much at my ease with the inhabitants as if I had known them for twenty years, the resemblance of their way of thinking to mine, my love for glory and for liberty, one might believe that I am very happy; but I miss you, my dear heart; I miss my friends; there is no happiness for me far from you and them. I ask you if you still love me, but I ask it much more often of myself, and my heart

always answers, yes. I hope it does not deceive
me. . . . It is late at night and terribly hot; I
am devoured by mosquitoes which cover one with
large blisters; but the best countries, as you see, have
their drawbacks."

Lafayette purchased horses and carriages to convey
himself and his companions to Philadelphia, a journey
of nine hundred miles, over bad roads, which soon
broke the carriages, and obliged him to continue on
horseback. But the time was agreeably occupied in
studying the language, in observing the character and
productions of the country, in admiring the vast forests and great rivers, which seemed to Lafayette to
endow nature with an air of youth and majesty. The
French officers, who, in their journeys in France, had
been accustomed to the sight of misery and starvation,
of a ragged and densely ignorant peasantry whose
countenances expressed only despair, were struck with
astonishment at the modest comfort, prosperity, and
contentment of the people among whom they passed.
The journey lasted a month, the party visiting Governor Caswell in North Carolina, and stopping for a
short time at Petersburg and Annapolis, where Lafayette met Major Brice, to whom he had a letter from
Carmichael, and who afterwards became his aide-de-
camp. At last, on the 27th of July, he arrived in
Philadelphia, in good health, his happiness in his new
experiences marred only by the pain of separation
from his wife.

The outlook for the Americans was gloomy when

Lafayette arrived in Philadelphia. Newport and New York were in the hands of the enemy. In the North, Burgoyne's army had taken Ticonderoga, and threatened to separate New England from the other States; at the South, Howe was arranging to attack Philadelphia with a much larger and better-equipped army than Washington could bring against him.

Although the superiority of the enemy in numbers and in arms, and their presence in so many quarters, were such as to make very welcome any help from abroad, the moment was unpropitious for Lafayette's application to Congress. Deane had been instructed to offer commissions to a few French officers, as the American army was in want of men experienced in military tactics. But, beset by requests for employment from idle Frenchmen whom he feared to offend, he had promised commissions far beyond his authority. These men, as a rule, were simply military adventurers, who cared little for the merits of either side, and sought only employment in their profession. They had come with extravagant expectations, founded on their own self-esteem and Deane's unwilling promises, and had already made the idea of foreign officers extremely unpopular. Duportail and three other French engineers had received employment, and were already useful in their department, as were also Kosciusko and Pulaski, the Polish patriots. The claim of Du Coudray, a French officer who had furnished supplies to Deane, to command the artillery with the rank of major-general, had aroused so well-founded an opposition that Generals Greene, Sullivan, and Knox threatened to resign if his demands were conceded. The drowning of Du Coudray in the Schuylkill set his claims at rest, but it was impossible to satisfy many of the foreigners without doing great injustice to American officers, and numbers of Frenchmen returned home to vent their disappointment in libels on the country.

Lafayette came for different reasons and with different expectations. Rank and pay he had in France, and had abandoned to fight for American liberty. At first, however, his motives were unknown, and he experienced a rebuff. On arriving in Philadelphia, he had placed his credentials in the hands of Mr. Lovell, the chairman of the Committee on Foreign Affairs, who laid them before Congress. But that body, weary of similar applications, slow to grant pay under any circumstances, and, practical men of business as they were, looking askance at the kind of enthusiasm which made men travel three thousand miles across the sea to fight other people's battles, paid no attention to Lafayette's communication. The next day, when he went up to the Hall of Congress, Lovell came out and said that the prospects of success in his case were bad. Suspecting that his papers had not even been read, Lafayette sat down and wrote a note which he requested Lovell to communicate to Congress, in which he claimed that, in consideration of the sacrifices he had made, he should be granted the favor of serving at his own expense and in the character of a volunteer.

This application contrasted so favorably with previous foreign demands, that the attention of Congress was won ; and after reading Lafayette's papers, they fulfilled Deane's promise of the rank of major-general, but without command and without pay. Congress, however, did not lose sight of the fact that the young foreigner whom they had just elevated to so high a position was not yet twenty years of age, and it was carefully stated that this action was based on the fact that Lafayette had quitted his family and country to expose his life without pay in the service of the United States, and *on account of his zeal, his illustrious family, and connections.*

The court of France had directed the American envoys to write home, requesting that Lafayette should not be employed. But the envoys took no pains to hasten the letter, and it arrived too late. Lafayette assisted Kalb in obtaining a commission similar to his own, and of the same date. Some of his other companions on " La Victoire " also obtained employment ; but most of them, ignorant of the English language, were of no use, and he could only soften their disappointment by gifts from his own purse.

The appearance of Howe's fleet off the mouth of the Delaware river seemed to threaten Philadelphia, and Washington left his camp in New Jersey to consult with Congress. At a dinner tendered to the commander-in-chief, the first meeting between him and Lafayette took place. Then began one of those tender and lasting friendships which exist between men who share great perils in defence of great principles. "Although surrounded by officers and citizens," wrote the young Frenchman, " Washington was to be recognized at once by the majesty of his countenance and of his figure." On the other hand, the commander-in-chief was so much pleased with the modesty and zeal which he perceived in the new recruit, that he honored him with a long interview, invited him to join a tour of inspection of the fortifications about Philadelphia, and finally adopted him as a member of his own military family.

Lafayette reached camp just as Washington, in company with Generals Stirling, Greene, and Knox, was about to review the army. The troops which marched past numbered about eleven thousand men, poorly armed and worse clad. Their ragged clothes were without any attempt at uniformity, and the men themselves were lacking in knowledge of the ordinary principles of military tactics. But courage took the place of science, and zeal inspired discipline. During the progress of the review, Washington observed, "We should feel some embarrassment in showing ourselves to an officer who has just left French troops." — "It is to learn, and not to teach, that I am here," answered Lafayette ; and he afterwards mentioned that this tone produced a good impression, as it was in pleasing contrast to that generally assumed by Europeans.

Howe had left New York with a large fleet of transports and men-of-war containing about sixteen thousand soldiers. A decoy letter had been allowed to fall into the hands of Washington, intended to persuade him that the destination of the fleet was Boston. But Washington suspected the ruse, and from his New Jersey camp awaited the appearance of the British in the South. On the 30th of July the fleet appeared off the Delaware, and Washington repaired to Philadelphia to consult with Congress, when all calculations were again unsettled by the disappearance of the fleet to the eastward. Howe had found the landing in the Delaware impracticable, and sought an entrance through Chesapeake bay. As soon as information of this movement arrived, Washington set out to meet the enemy. The army marched through Philadelphia to the sound of fife and drum, the soldiers' heads adorned with green branches, amidst the cheers of the inhabitants who filled the streets. Lafayette rode by the side of the commander-in-chief, proud and happy at the prospect of action. When the army arrived on the heights of Wilmington, Lafayette had his first opportunity to share danger with his beloved commander. Washington, in company with Lafayette and Greene, had made a long reconnaissance, and, overtaken by darkness and a storm, was obliged to pass the night so near to the British lines that any traitor might have betrayed him to the enemy.

A few days after the British landing a council of war was held, which determined Washington to take up a position on the Brandywine creek, and there await attack. The army was posted on high ground on the north bank of the river, opposite Chadd's Ford, by which it was supposed the enemy would attempt to cross. The ensuing battle showed the advantage which the British derived from their knowledge of the art of war, as well as from their superiority in numbers and equipment.

The effective force of the American army numbered about eleven thousand men, who were posted on the north bank of the stream, Washington commanding the centre opposite Chadd's Ford, with Armstrong's division on the left and Sullivan's on the right. Howe's army, about sixteen thousand strong, advanced in two columns. One of these, under Knyphausen, marched to Chadd's Ford, where it arrived early on the morning of the 11th of September, and drove a skirmishing force under Maxwell across the river to the American camp. The wooded character of the Brandywine's banks prevented Washington from knowing whether or not the whole force of the enemy was before him. Knyphausen acted as if he were attempting to force a passage, and a brisk though ineffective cannonade was kept up, when news reached the American commander which changed the whole face of events. Howe's second column, which he himself accompanied, and which was under the immediate command of Cornwallis, numbering about eight thousand men including the guards and grenadiers, had made a long *détour*, crossed the stream some miles above Chadd's Ford, and was now bearing down on the right and rear of the American

army, threatening its total destruction. Some information regarding this movement had reached Washington, but it was of so contradictory a character
that the certain news, when it came, was practically
a surprise. Washington at once detached Sullivan,
Stirling, and Stephen with five thousand men to meet
the force on the right. Lafayette's post was with the
commander-in-chief; but the left being quiet, and it
becoming evident that the real fighting was to be done
on the right, Lafayette asked and obtained permission
to join Sullivan. On arriving, he found Howe and
Cornwallis advancing in line of battle against Sullivan's troops, who had not had time to form properly.
The half-formed wings of the American army fell back
before the severe British fire, and the centre, where
eight hundred men were fighting bravely under Conway,
and where Lafayette stood with Stirling, then received
the concentrated British attack. Two of Sullivan's
aides were killed. The confusion soon became great,
and a disorderly retreat began. While vainly attempting to rally the men, Lafayette had dismounted, and,
as he stood sword in hand urging the soldiers to make
a stand, a musket-ball passed through the calf of his
leg. The wound was unnoticed until the blood was
seen running over his boot. As the rout was becoming general, he must have been left on the field, had
not his aide-de-camp, Gimat, assisted him to mount.
Washington was coming up with fresh troops, and
Lafayette attempted to join him; but the loss of blood
soon made itself felt, and he was obliged to stop to

have a temporary bandage applied. While the retreat of Sullivan's division was in progress, Knyphausen forced his way across the ford, driving before him the small number of American troops which had been left there, and the whole American force fell back in disorder on the road to Chester, pursued by both divisions of the British army. Washington could only impede the advance of the enemy with such troops as remained in order, and cover the retreat of the demoralized regiments. Night came on in the midst of the retreat, and darkness added to the confusion. Finally, at Chester, twelve miles from the battle-field, Lafayette found a bridge where he made a stand, placed a guard, and stopped the retreat until Washington and the other generals came up. Here his wound was dressed by a surgeon.

The battle-field of the Brandywine was about twenty-six miles from Philadelphia, and the cannonade could be distinctly heard in the city. Tories and patriots, separated into groups in houses and in the streets, anxiously awaited the result of the conflict. The arrival of the last courier filled the patriot party with consternation. The departure of Congress was at once resolved upon, and many of the inhabitants left their homes to seek refuge without the city. The morning after the battle, Lafayette was conveyed by water to Philadelphia, where he was kindly provided for, and transferred in a few days to Bristol. Here Congress was temporarily assembled, and President Laurens, being on his way to York, took Lafayette in his own carriage, and conveyed him to Bethlehem, the retreat of a peaceful community called Moravians, who cared for him during his six weeks' confinement with affectionate attention. When Henry Laurens became a prisoner in the Tower of London, Mme. de Lafayette acknowledged his kindness to her husband by seeking the aid of Vergennes and the French government in obtaining his release.

Lafayette's confinement at Bethlehem was irksome to his active nature. The Moravians discoursed to him of the follies of war, but to so little purpose that he occupied his forced idleness with projects of French and American invasion of English colonies, which he planned in detail, and communicated to Maurepas and to De Bouillé, governor of Martinique. The plans were not adopted, but Maurepas was favorably impressed by them.

Washington sent his physician with instructions to treat Lafayette as his own son, for he loved him as such. Pulaski and some other officers were able to visit him occasionally, but most of his time was occupied in thinking of his wife and in writing to her. " Now," he wrote, " that you are the wife of an American general officer, I must give you a lesson. People will say, 'They have been beaten.' You must answer, 'It is true, but with two armies equal in number, and on level ground, old soldiers always have an advantage over new ones; besides, the Americans inflicted a greater loss than they sustained.' Then, people will add, 'That's all very well; but Philadelphia, the capital of America, the high-road of liberty, is taken.' You will reply politely, 'You are fools ! Philadelphia is a poor city, open on every side, of which the port was already closed. The presence of Congress made it famous, I know not why; that's what this famous city amounts to, which, by the way, we shall re-take sooner or later.' If they continue to ply you with questions, send them about their business in terms that the Vicomte de Noailles will supply you with. . . . Consider, my dear heart, that the only news I have received from you.has been by the Count Pulaski. Think how terrible to be far from all that I love, in so hopeless an uncertainty. I cannot bear it; and yet I feel that I deserve no pity. Why was I crazy to come here? I am well punished. . . . My dear heart, if I have good news of you, of all that I love, if these charming letters arrive to-day, how happy I can be ! But, also, with what anxiety I shall open them ! . . . My poor little Henriette ; kiss her a thousand times, speak to her of me, but do not tell her all the evil things which I deserve. My punishment will be, not to be recognized by her on my return. That is the penalty which Henriette will impose upon me. Has she a sister or a brother? It is the same to me, so long as I have the . second time the pleasure of being a father, and that I soon know it. If I have a son, I will tell him to study his own heart; and if he have a tender heart, if he have a wife whom he loves as I love you, then I shall warn him not to give himself up to an enthusiasm which separates him from the object of his affection, because, afterwards, this affection will give him terrible anxiety."

It was early in November before Lafayette was permitted to rejoin the army, and his wound was not yet sufficiently healed to allow him to wear a boot. The battle of Germantown, by which Washington had hoped to dislodge the British from Philadelphia, had been fought, and the season's campaign was nearly concluded. Two defeats had been suffered in the South, but from the North had come the glorious news of Burgoyne's surrender. Washington's headquarters were now at Whitemarsh, and Lafayette had not been there long before he found an opportunity to do some active service. Cornwallis having entered New Jersey with five thousand men, Greene was sent to oppose him with an equal number. Lafayette joined him as a volunteer, and at Mount Holly was detached to reconnoitre. On the 25th of November he found the enemy at Gloucester, near Philadelphia. Their forage wagons were crossing the river, and to make a more thorough examination of their position, he advanced dangerously far on a tongue of land called Stony Point, which extended into the water. Here he might have been cut to pieces or taken prisoner, but he was quick enough to escape without injury. At four o'clock in the afternoon he found himself before a post of Hessians, numbering four hundred men with cannon. Lafayette had one hundred and fifty sharpshooters under

Colonel Butler, and about two hundred militia-men and light-horse under Colonels Hite, Ellis, and Lindsey. Four French officers also accompanied him. The strength of the enemy was at first unknown; but Lafayette attacked boldly, and drove them in with such impetuosity that Cornwallis, who supposed he had to do with Greene's whole force, and was not prepared for an engagement, allowed himself to be driven back to Gloucester with a loss of sixty men. Greene being informed of the action, arrived during the night, but did not think it best to attack. Cornwallis then crossed the river, and the American forces returned to Whitemarsh.

This unimportant, but well-conducted, engagement was highly favorable to Lafayette's military prospects. His personal popularity in the army was already great, and his conduct at Brandywine and Gloucester showed him to be a fighting man of coolness and judgment.

With the progress of events, the majority of foreign officers in the American army became more embarrassing to Washington, more detested by the troops, and more discontented themselves. The cause in which they had enlisted was essentially one of self-sacrifice; but their object in coming to the United States had been self-advancement. They asked for high commands which could not be given without great injustice to Americans, and they expected an amount of pay which was not forthcoming for any one. Ignorant of the language, more ignorant still of the character of the people, they were constantly

giving and receiving offence. Notable exceptions
there certainly were, like General de Kalb, Major de
Fleury, and some of Lafayette's companions. But in
the midst of this mutual distrust, Lafayette acquired
and retained the affection of the Americans to an extraordinary degree. He had come prepared for every
sacrifice, happy to serve at any cost a cause which he
considered his own and that of humanity. He threw
aside with pleasure the prejudices of his education,
entered sympathetically into the interests and feelings
of the people with whom he was to fight, and became,
indeed, an American. The cause of the colonies was
not to him a mere opportunity to injure the heredi-
tary enemy of France ; it was the sacred cause of
freedom now destined to receive a stunning blow or
to achieve a victory which would shake the power of
tyranny throughout the Christian world. As some
men feel drawn in their youth to consecrate their lives
to religion, Lafayette had now adopted the cause of
civil liberty. For that, he had already suffered in his
tenderest feelings, and had gladly exposed himself to
hardship and danger. No doubt the pure metal of
self-devotion was somewhat alloyed with a love of
fame and popular applause; but the young man
united modesty with his other merits, and the
advancement now to come met with universal approval.

When Washington first heard of the appointment
of Lafayette to the rank of major-general, he took
pains to assure himself that the action of Congress

meant no more than a compliment. But as time passed, the commander-in-chief acquired a high regard for his aide-de-camp, and gradually came to the opinion that his military capacity, energy, and fidelity to the cause would be of real use to the army. After the affair at Gloucester, therefore, he thought the moment opportune to suggest to Congress the assignment of Lafayette to the command of a division. Congress readily assented, and early in December Washington placed him at the head of the Virginia militia, formerly commanded by General Stephen. These troops were thin in numbers and ragged in appearance, but their condition afforded the better opportunity for their general's exertions. Thus, shortly after his twentieth birthday, and a year from the time when the Duke of Gloucester first let him know that there was a great cause to be defended across the Atlantic, Lafayette found himself considered worthy to command a division in the patriot army. From the position of aide-de-camp, granted in compliment to his birth and family influence, he had become a general officer by proof of fitness. The responsibility was great, and events were preparing which would severely test his ability to bear it.

CHAPTER III.

The Winter at Valley Forge. — The Conway Cabal. — Lafayette commands an Expedition against Canada. — Return to Valley Forge. — The French Alliance. — Death of his Daughter Henriette.

In December, the army went into winter quarters at Valley Forge. Then began a period of suffering and anxiety which called forth the highest qualities of moral courage and endurance on the part of all those who shared the fortunes of Washington.

During that winter Lafayette first acquired a definite knowledge of the various difficulties which the Americans had to surmount. Looking at the Revolution from a distance, he had fancied that the contest lay between British armies on the one side, and on the other, a united people determined to be free, and certain to become so if they could muster sufficient military strength. But Lafayette soon found that many obstacles quite as serious as British soldiery stood in the patriots' path. The people were not united. Throughout the Middle and Southern States Tories enlisted in the British army, supplied the invaders with provisions and information, thwarted and betrayed the American forces. The war had many of the features of a civil conflict. Patriot officers, travelling through the country, were in constant danger from secret enemies. Families were divided, and in communities where the British forces gave the Tories the ascendant, bands of robbers were encouraged to prey upon the property and lives of the Whigs. The stagnation of business created a great scarcity of clothing, shoes, and other necessaries for the army, while the · lack of power in Congress to impose and collect taxes made it almost impossible to raise money to carry on the war. The paper currency, issued for this purpose, depended for its value entirely on the ultimate success and credit of the States. Counterfeited by the enemy, distrusted by Americans, it depreciated with fatal rapidity. While the disaffected made fortunes by avoiding taxation, and supplying provisions to the enemy, want and privation fell to the lot of the patriot. In the Northern States, the great victory over Burgoyne had lulled the people into a feeling of security which blinded them to the constant needs of the army. In the South, the defeats of Brandywine and Germantown had discouraged the Whigs and emboldened their enemies.

While this unhappy state of American affairs disgusted many foreigners with the cause, and even created disaffection among Washington's chief officers and in Congress, Lafayette found in it only additional reason for the exercise of energy and fidelity. The temptation to return home for a visit was almost irresistible. Patrick Henry forwarded to Washington two letters for Lafayette. " One of them," he said, " is from his lady, I believe. I beg to be presented to him in the most acceptable manner. I greatly revere his person and amiable character." The few letters which the exile could receive from home, the approaching birth of his child, were powerful motives for departure ; but Lafayette, having once faced the prospect held out by Valley Forge, could not do otherwise than share its miseries with the men who he had now come to consider as compatriots, and who in their turn looked upon him as one of themselves.

Washington had chosen the position at Valley Forge because it enabled him to keep constant watch over the enemy, to confine the British occupation to its own picket lines, and to cut off supplies going into Philadelphia. But otherwise the position had nothing to recommend it. The few farm-houses in the vicinity could accommodate only a fraction of the two thousand men who were on the sick-list, whose shoeless feet had been torn and frozen on the march, whose illness was aggravated by exposure and hunger. The army had to construct its own shelter. Logs were cut and hauled from the woods, rudely covered with mud, and made into huts, each one of which had to protect fourteen men. A military village soon arose, accurately arranged in streets, where the American forces, in want of food and blankets, shivered around their camp-fires, while the British were playing cards in warm houses.

General Mifflin, by resigning his post of commissary-general at so critical a time, was chiefly responsible for the absence of supplies. The want was sometimes so severe that for two days at a time there was no meat in camp, and hardly one ration of flour. Some of the starved soldiers deserted; those who remained mutinied. Favorable opportunities to attack the enemy were lost, through the incapacity of the men to march. Washington's earnest remonstrances to Congress, his ceaseless personal endeavors, were long in bringing relief to the suffering army. On one occasion a party of members of Congress came down to the camp to make a personal examination. The Pennsylvania and New Jersey members reported that their own soldiers were even worse off than the others. Yet these same men soon after addressed a remonstrance to Washington against keeping the troops in a state of inactivity, and urged an attack on Philadelphia. "I can assure those gentlemen," replied Washington, "that it is a much easier and less distressing thing to draw remonstrances in a comfortable room, by a good fireside, than to occupy a cold, bleak hill, and sleep under frost and snow, without clothes or blankets. However, although they seem to have little feeling for the naked and distressed soldiers, I feel superabundantly for them ; and from my soul I pity those miseries, which it is neither in my power to relieve nor prevent." Lafayette shared all the hardships of Valley Forge with the troops, laboring hard with the commander-in-chief to alleviate where it was possible, and to encourage where only endurance could meet the situation. Then was firmly cemented the bond of friendship which united the two men, and which important events were soon to put to the test.

The conspiracy against Washington, known as Conway's Cabal, had been gradually progressing since November. The lack of success in the South contrasted so unfavorably with the great victory over Burgoyne in the North, that a party arose in Congress who were inclined to put all the blame for the loss of Philadelphia on the commander-in-chief, and who privately desired to . see another in his place. The results of this opposition to Washington soon appeared. General Gates, who had treated Washington with contemptuous neglect by omitting to send him the least report of Burgoyne's surrender, was appointed president of the Board of War. With him on the board was placed Mifflin, whose conduct in leaving the post of commissary-general had entailed so much suffering on the army. Conway, an Irishman in the service of France, against whose intrigues and bad conduct Washington had frequently warned Congress, was raised to the post of inspector-general, over the heads of several officers conspicuously better suited for the place. The proceedings of the disaffected party in Congress were a great encouragement to discontented and ambitious officers. Mifflin and Conway, who had their own projects to serve, easily persuaded Gates, whose head was turned with exaggerated ideas of his military capacity, that he was destined to become the guiding-star of the Revolution. Gates entered readily into the intrigue, which was to have the happy result of benefiting the conspirators and the country at the same time. The members of the Cabal occupied themselves with the dissemination of doubts regarding Washington's fitness for the command, and with demonstrations of Gates' extraordinary ability. They impeded Washington as much as they could through their control of the Board of War, and their partisans even descended to the writing of defamatory anonymous letters. Two of these, sent to President Laurens and Patrick Henry, were honorably enclosed to Washington, and disclosed to him the projects of the Cabal. While the machinations of his enemies imbittered the difficulties of Valley Forge, the commander-in-chief often turned with pleasure and confidence to the unselfish devotion of his young aide-de-camp.

And Lafayette himself soon became the object of intrigue. His influence in France and his military rank made him naturally a leader among the foreigners in America. He had also won the thorough confidence and esteem of the army. Hence it became exceedingly important to the Cabal to deprive Washington of his support. Moreover, Conway, whose standing in France would be much affected by Lafayette's opinion, and whose patron there, the Marquis de Castries, was a friend of Lafayette's, could not afford to offend him. Conway fawned upon him, called himself Lafayette's soldier, and repeated that he was entirely at his disposition. But the Cabal soon found that the young Frenchman's fidelity was unassailable, and in their comfortable quarters at York they concerted a plan which would satisfactorily disembarrass them of his presence and influence. A new command was instituted, called the Army of the North, with headquarters at Albany, and the duty of making a winter attack on Canada. By placing Lafayette at the head of this independent command, they expected to separate him from Washington; and by making Conway second in rank, they hoped that the latter would be able to control his youthful chief, and make himself the real head of the expedition. Lafayette's military ambition was well known, and the bait was believed, with reason, to be a tempting one.

Late in January, 1778, Lafayette was sitting with Washington in his headquarters at Valley Forge, when a package of papers arrived from York. A letter from Gates to Washington stated the establishment of the Army of the North, and the nomination of Lafayette to the command. Enclosed was Lafayette's official appointment, with instructions to repair at once to Albany, and there await orders. Washington handed him the papers in silence. Lafayette's first impression was one of pleasure at the prospect of active employment; but a careful perusal of the orders, and the realization that the command was independent of Washington, placed him on his guard. He immediately declared his intention to decline the appointment. To a committee of Congress, then visiting at headquarters, he stated that he would rather return to his position as aide-de-camp to the commander-in-chief, which he considered the most enviable in the army, and that he should never accept a command which placed him beyond the orders of Washington. The latter, however, urged him to accept, saying that as long as the position had been created, he preferred that he should hold it.

Lafayette then determined to accept the commission, but to obtain from Congress such conditions that the projects of the Cabal should be defeated. In this he was greatly assisted by the friendly offices of Henry Laurens, the president, who was not unacquainted with the circumstances of the case. "It is feared," John Laurens had just written to his father, "that the ambition and intriguing spirit of Conway will be subversive of the public good, while he will proceed securely behind the shield of his commanding officer, taking to himself the merit of everything praiseworthy, and attributing every misfortune to the ostensible head. The person who is appointed quartermaster for this expedition is said to be a man skilful in enriching himself at the public expense. Our friend, the marquis, knowing the existence of a certain faction, and penetrating the character of his second, has prudently resolved to wait upon Congress, and to find out the extent of their views in sending forces into Canada, that he may act correspondingly, and not have the secret of their intentions deposited in another man while he has the command."

Lafayette repaired to York, where Gates, Mifflin,

Conway, and their friends were living in a comfort which contrasted with the hardships of Valley Forge. Gates gave a dinner-party, at which he presided with the joviality natural to his character, and heightened by the flattery which surrounded him. Here the Army of the North was talked over, and its brilliant prospects foretold, for the edification of its youthful commander. But the party became less gay when Lafayette announced his intention to remain subordinate to Washington's orders, and demanded that De Kalb should be appointed his second in rank, leaving only the third place for Conway. The hilarity was altogether dispelled, when, at the end of dinner, Lafayette rose, and calling attention to the fact that the most important toast had been omitted, proposed the health of the commander-in-chief. As the conspirators silently honored the toast, their interest in the Army of the North came to an end.

Conway's Cabal, formed to convince the country of Washington's unfitness for his position, existed long enough to fully establish the contrary in the minds of contemporaries and of posterity. When we contrast the petty bickerings, ambitions, and discontents of the useless intriguers at York, with the steady, self-sacrificing labors of Valley Forge, the truly noble character of Washington is brought into strong relief. As the objects of the Cabal were mean, so was its end ridiculous.

In the beginning of the conspiracy, Conway had written a letter to Gates containing the following phrase, or words to the same effect: "Heaven has been determined to save your country, or a weak general and bad counsellors would have ruined it." Colonel Wilkinson, one of Gates' aides, became acquainted with the passage. On his way to Congress with the official report of Burgoyne's surrender, he met Lord Stirling at Reading, and stopping there, as he did everywhere, to do a little boasting and drinking, he communicated the phrase to Major McWilliams, Stirling's aide, who reported it to his chief. Stirling lost no time in conveying the information to Washington, with the remark, "Such wicked duplicity of conduct I shall always think it my duty to detect." Washington wrote to Conway, simply quoting the remark attributed to him. The news that a portion of their correspondence had reached Washington created the greatest consternation in the Cabal. Conway put on a bold front, and relied on his impudence to carry him through. Gates was in terrible uncertainty as to how much or what part of his correspondence was known. He sought the aid of Mifflin and Conway to discover "the villain that had played him this treacherous trick. There is scarcely a man living," he wrote in his distress, "who takes a greater care of his letters than I do. I never fail to lock them up, and keep the key in my pocket. . . . No punishment is too severe for the wretch who betrayed me; and I doubt not your friendship for me, as well as your zeal for our safety, will bring the name of this miscreant to light." Gates then wrote to Washington, taking a very high

tone, asking the commander-in-chief to do him and
the United States the important service of discovering
the wretch, a matter "which so deeply affects the
safety of the States." Washington was very sarcastic
in his reply: he did not see how the safety of the
States was concerned, and he informed Gates that it
was only the loquaciousness of his own aide, Wilkinson, that had exposed him. When Gates and his
companions found that no more than that one sentence had become known, they found it easy to discover that the words had not been exactly quoted;
and on this ground they asserted that the whole
phrase, the existence of which had been acknowledged
by their efforts to find the betrayer of it, was an impudent forgery, and had never been written. But
Washington's calling attention to their unwillingness to
produce the letter in verification of their statement
threw them again into confusion. Gates, in his anxiety to turn attention from himself by making the supposed violation of his correspondence a matter of
national concern, had committed the great error of
transmitting to Congress copies of his letters to Washington. Washington naturally sent his replies through
the same channel. The country and the army thus
became acquainted with the facts of the conspiracy,
and the burst of indignation which followed showed
how deeply rooted was the general respect for Washington, and made it necessary for his enemies to deny
their connection with the Cabal, which thus came to
an ignominious end.

While the events of this trying winter make it evident that Lafayette's presence was of real advantage to .the army, his letters to his wife show how great was the sacrifice he made by remaining. " What a season, my dear heart, and what a country to write from in the month of January! It is in a camp, it is in the midst of the woods, it is three thousand miles from you, that I see myself enchained in the midst of the winter. . . . The bearer of this letter will describe the agreeable residence that I prefer to the happiness of being with you, with all my friends, among all possible pleasures. Truly, my dear heart, do you not believe that strong reasons were necessary to determine me to make this sacrifice? Everything told me to depart; honor told me to remain; and, indeed, when you come to know in detail the circumstances in which I am, in which the army is, my friend who commands it, the whole American cause, you will forgive me, my dear heart, you will even excuse me, and I almost dare say that you will approve my course. What pleasure I shall have in telling you myself all my reasons — in begging, while I embrace you, a pardon which I shall then be sure to obtain! But do not condemn me without a hearing. Besides the reason I have given, I have still another that I would not like to tell to every one, because it would seem to be giving myself a ridiculous importance. At the present moment my presence is more important to the American cause than you can imagine. So many foreigners who have been refused employment, or whose ambition has not been satisfied, have made powerful cabals ; they have tried by every kind of device to disgust me with the Revolution and with its chief; they have reported as widely as they could that I was about to leave the continent. On the other hand, the English have asserted it positively. I cannot conscientiously give countenance to what those people say. If I go, many Frenchmen, useful here, will follow my example. General Washington would be truly unhappy if I spoke of departure. His confidence in me is greater than I dare admit, on account of my age. In the place that he occupies, a man may be surrounded with flatterers or with secret enemies ; he finds in me a sure friend, in whom he can confide the feelings of his heart, and who will always tell him the truth. . . . You will already have received letters that I sent you as soon as I heard of your confinement. How happy this occurrence has made me, my dear heart ! I love to speak of it in all my letters, because I love to think of it at all times. What pleasure I shall have in embracing my two poor little girls, and in making them ask for my pardon from their mother. . . . Adieu, adieu ! Love me always, and do not forget for a moment the unhappy exile who thinks of you with an ever-increasing tenderness."

Early in February, the commander of the Army of the North started out on the expedition which was destined to produce only fruitless expense to the country and mortification to himself. The Board of War had never taken a very serious view of the undertaking, and when they were disappointed in their real object, they still further neglected their half-concerted arrangements. Lafayette proceeded slowly over bad roads. The rain and snow, which alternately fell upon him, did not cheer the prospect, and his absence from Washington was a source of real sorrow. He had been instructed to meet Mr. Duer at Ringo's Tavern, in Flemingtown, and to confer with him. But Mr. Duer was not there, and Ringo had never heard of him. As Lafayette journeyed through the country, he was struck with the domestic virtues and thrift of the inhabitants, which contrasted so strongly with the laxity of Parisian morals, and the misery of 'the French peasantry. Everywhere his filial affection for Washington was gratified by the expressions of confidence which he heard. After an agreeable interview with Governor Clinton, he arrived at Albany on the 17th of February. Conway had preceded him by three days, and Lafayette wrote to Washington that he was bound to admit that that officer seemed active and well-intentioned, "although we know a great deal about him in this respect." Conway's first words were, that the expedition was impossible. But for a time the hopeful youth refused to believe it.

The object of the campaign was to ascend Lake Champlain on the ice, to burn the British shipping there, and then to attack Montreal. For this purpose Lafayette had been promised twenty-five hundred men at Albany, a considerable force of militia, two millions in paper, some hard money, and the means of crossing the ice. But as little care had been taken by the Board of War to fulfil these promises as to calculate the feasibility of the expedition. Conway had letters from Generals Schuyler, Lincoln, and Arnold, expressing in the strongest terms their disapproval of attacking Canada under existing circumstances. With their opinion every one agreed. A few Canadians under Colonel Hazen, who wished to return home, were the only men who entertained a hope of success. The available force did not exceed twelve hundred men, and these not clothed for even a summer campaign. At the dinner-party at York, Gates had cheerfully assured Lafayette that Stark and his militia would have burned the fleet before his arrival. But the first letter he received at Albany was from Stark himself, inquiring what number of men, in what place, for what time, he should recruit. In short, there being neither the men nor the money for the expedition, and no time to collect them, it was plain that nothing could be done.

The ardent young commander hesitated long before arriving at this conclusion, but he was too prudent to risk his handful of men in a foolhardy attempt. His mortification was extreme. His heart had been bent on making a glorious campaign. He had written to his friends in Europe about his new command, and in America the public eye was upon the Army of the North. Now, he was not only disappointed in the hope of distinguishing himself, but he feared that he

and his expedition were to become a general laugh-
ing-stock. Wounded alike in his pride as a soldier
and his vanity as a Frenchman, his letters to Washington were pathetic in their expressions of disappointment. "I have written lately to you my distressing,
ridiculous, and, indeed, nameless situation. I am
sent with a great noise, at the head of an army, to
do great things. The whole continent, France and
Europe, and what is worse, the British army, are in
great expectations. How far they will be deceived,
how much we shall be ridiculed, you may judge by
the candid account I have given of our affairs. . . .
I confess, my dear general, that I cannot control the
liveliness of my feelings when my reputation and my
glory are affected. . . . I am more unhappy
than I have ever been." Washington replied very
consolingly: "It will be no disadvantage to you to
have it known in Europe that you have received so
manifest a proof of the good opinion and confidence
of Congress as an important detached command;
and I am persuaded that every one will applaud your
prudence in renouncing a project, in pursuing which
you would vainly have attempted physical impossi-
bilities. . . . However sensibly your ardor for
glory may make you feel this disappointment, you may
be assured that your character stands as fair as ever
it did, and that no new enterprise is necessary to
wipe off this imaginary stain."

Congress, discovering the futility of the Canadian
expedition, recalled Lafayette in flattering terms.

His presence in Albany, however, had not been useless. He put the soldiers in better humor by paying them part of their long-delayed arrears, and passed his time in improving the forts and in pacifying the Indians. Accompanying Schuyler and Duane to a council at Johnstown on the Mohawk, he tried his eloquence with some effect on the Oneidas and Tuscaroras, from whom he received the appellation of Kayoula. Hearing of the arrival in America of General Steuben, he hastened to forestall possible misinformation by writing him a letter full of admiration and praise of Washington.

Early in April, Lafayette returned to Valley Forge, happy to share again the fortunes of the commander-in-chief. His first occupation was to aid in administering the oath of allegiance recently prescribed by Congress. The duty required delicacy and tact, as not a few military men who were perfectly loyal to the American cause hesitated to cut off themselves and their country from all future connection with the British crown. In this matter, as in many others, is evident the kind of service by which Lafayette won the regard and gratitude of his American contemporaries. It was not the greatness of any one act which distinguished him, but the energy and intelligence with which he followed up every duty, however small, with which he was intrusted.

On the 2d of May arrived at York the bearer of the great news, that France acknowledged the independence of the United States, and had concluded a treaty of alliance.

The ultimate results of this alliance, and the circumstances under which it occurred, combine to make it an extraordinarily interesting historical event. In America, it aided the establishment of a new nation, which was destined soon to rank among the greatest of the earth, and to demonstrate the practicability of a purely popular form of government. In France, it had much to do with kindling the long latent fires which were to destroy the traditions of the past, and to create in Europe a wholly new social organization. A sincere alliance between the French monarchy and the free people of America was naturally an unlooked-for event. But both the circumstances and the man to utilize them were happily present. When Franklin arrived at Paris in December, 1776, he found the ground well prepared for him.

The ministers, while ready to welcome any opportunity to injure England, were too well aware of their impoverished condition to venture lightly on a war. They cared nothing, of course, for the cause of the colonies, and would assist them only when assured that a blow could thus be dealt at British power. But the pressure upon the government of a growing public opinion had rapidly become too strong for resistance. From the countless minds to which the old order of things was hateful, and in which were fermenting new theories of government, the measured, conclusive words of the Declaration of Independence had met with an enthusiastic response. The nobility, penetrated with the new social doctrines which taught them to welcome whatever bore the name of liberty, and, moreover, weary of passing their lives in dancing · attendance at court, furnished many individuals who longed for a war to afford them occupation and an opportunity of gaining distinction. The great middle classes, — the merchants, lawyers, physicians, artists, authors, — who saw themselves despised as *roturiers,* their property arbitrarily taken from them, even their personal liberty subject to the caprice of the court, viewed with deep satisfaction a people in revolt against arbitrary power, and loudly called for military interference. All the memoirs of the time bear testimony to the almost universal enthusiasm with which were received the tidings of this youthful nation fighting for its political rights. The American envoys were besieged in their own apartments by military men who wished to serve the States: in the *salons* of Paris they were sought after as the lions of the day. Mme. Campan describes an entertainment given in compliment to Franklin, at which the handsomest woman was deputed to place a wreath on his head and a kiss on each cheek. No person of fashion was complete without a snuff-box or a ring bearing a medallion of the envoy. "These," wrote Franklin to his daughter, "with the pictures, busts, and prints (of which copies upon copies are spread everywhere), have made your father's face as well known as that of the moon, so that he durst not do anything that would oblige him to run away, as his phiz would discover him wherever he should venture to show it." A medal was struck off representing the head of Franklin, with the inscription, "*Eripuit cælo fulmen sceptrumque tyrannis;*" and this medal was freely sought for and exhibited, even in the presence of the king.

The American agents were invested, indeed, with a character more exalted than Congress had intended for them. The enthusiastic young reformers of the time, says Ségur, were struck with the contrast between the almost rustic apparel, the plain but proud bearing, the free and honest language, the powderless hair of the Americans, and the luxury of Paris, the magnificence of .Versailles, the remaining traces of. the monarchic pride of Louis XIV., the elegance of fashions, the polite but superb dignity of the nobility. It seemed as though the "antique simplicity of dress and appearance of the envoys had introduced within our walls, in the midst of the effeminate and servile refinement of the eighteenth century, some sages contemporary with Plato, or republicans of the age of Cato and of Fabius." To the numberless dreamers of France, who sought in the states of antiquity an example of the ideal government at which they aimed, "the old man with gray hair, appearing under a martin-fur cap amidst the powdered heads of Paris," was a practical illustration of their theories.

But among the sympathizers with the American cause, whether nobles or *roturiers*, existed a most complete misapprehension regarding the points at issue in the quarrel, — a misapprehension which only the failure and ruin to come could clear up. We are told that the most eager of those who flocked about Franklin were the philosophers and writers, who attributed to their own influence the progress of liberal opinions in the New World, and who secretly desired to see themselves legislators in Europe as their disciples were in America. Astonished, indeed, would have been the practical men of business in Boston to hear that their objections to the Port Bill were inspired by the visionary doctrines of Rousseau; or the pioneers of the frontier, who gathered together in the forest to resolve that they could not be taxed without representation, to be told that their knowledge óf their rights was derived from French philosophy. The French were striving to gain a freedom that they never had had. The Americans were striving to retain a freedom which had been inherited from remote ancestors. The French were seeking to destroy an arbitrary government in order to build up a Utopian democracy which was contrary to every national tradition. The Americans were only resisting encroachments on the rights of free citizens. One revolution, aiming at unlimited innovation, was to pass through anarchy to despotism; the other, resisting innovation, was to insure a familiar and rational liberty.

While the condition of France highly favored the alliance, that event was largely due to the diplomatic skill of Franklin himself. A plain, practical man, wholly unused to courts, but possessing the dignity of intellect and long-tried virtue, the resources of wit and tact, he moved amid the most polished and the

most corrupt society of Europe master of himself
and the situation. His eye always on the main
chance, he turned to good account the thoughtless
tendencies of fashion, the wild theories of philosophy,
directing all enthusiasm into the important channel of
French interference. Never did trained diplomatist
shape the circumstances of the time more surely to
the desired end. In all of Paris the wisest and most
astute mind belonged to him who walked through her
salons the picture of republican simplicity.

Although Vergennes and Maurepas had been inclined, in 1776, to substitute an open alliance for the
secret assistance which they then rendered the American cause, they were deterred by the prudence of
Turgot 'and Necker, who well knew the financial unfitness of France to enter upon a war. As we have
seen, the defeat of Washington on Long Island, at the
time Lafayette was preparing to leave Paris, determined the government against open interference.
But the surrender of Burgoyne changed the face of
events. It was evident that the colonies could help
themselves, and therefore it would pay to help them.
Gérard, the secretary of the French cabinet, personally requested Franklin to reopen the negotiations,
and on the 6th of February the treaties were signed.
A remarkable scene took place on the 20th of March,
when the American envoys were presented to the
king. Even the rigid etiquette of the French court
could not subdue the applause which greeted the
entrance of Franklin; and the vast crowds which

surrounded the palace significantly marked the popular interest which was beginning to make itself felt
in public affairs.

The joy was great at Valley Forge when the news
of the alliance was received. The 6th of May was
devoted to celebrating the event, when religious
services, a grand parade, salvos of artillery, and a
public dinner testified to the general satisfaction.
Lafayette took a prominent part in the proceedings;
but his happiness was clouded by the news of a severe
affliction, brought in the same letters which announced
the treaty. Many months had elapsed since he had
heard from home. " I am perfectly sure," he wrote
to his wife in April, " that you will miss no opportunity to write to me. I should be more so, if possible,
if I could hope that you knew how happy your letters
make me. I love you more than ever, my dear heart;
the assurances of your affection are absolutely necessary to my repose, and to that kind of felicity which
I can taste far from what I love, even if the word
felicity is applicable to my sad exile. Exert yourself,
at least, to console me, my heart; neglect no occasion
for sending me news of yourself. I have received
none from any one for millions of centuries. This terrible ignorance of the lot of all who are dear to me is
a cruel situation. However, I have reason to flatter
myself that it will soon cease; the scene will become
interesting; France will take some action, and then
there will be vessels to bring me news." The letters
came, but they contained the information that the little

Henriette, whom Lafayette had left behind, and to whom his letters always tenderly referred, had died some months before. "Several vessels have gone," he wrote in June, "all of which carried letters from me. These will have renewed your grief by the addition of mine. How terrible this separation is! I have never so cruelly felt the horror of this situation. My heart is afflicted with my own grief and with yours, which I have been unable to share. The event is made worse by the immensely long time which has passed before I could learn it. Consider, my heart, how painful it is, while weeping for what I have lost, still to tremble for what is left to me. The distance between Europe and America seems to me more immense than ever. The loss of our unhappy child is on my mind at almost every moment. This news reached me immediately after that of the treaty; and while my heart was devoured by grief, I had to take part in the demonstrations of public happiness."

When John Adams went to France in January, 1778, Lafayette had intrusted several letters to him, and had also requested his friends in Paris to pay him suitable attention. Adams' diary about this time affords a glimpse of Mme. de Lafayette and her family. "April 13, 1778. This morning the Duchesse d'Ayen and Mme. la Marquise de Lafayette came to visit me and inquire after the marquis. April 30, Jeudi. Dined with the Marshal de Mouchy, with the Duke and Duchess d'Ayen, their daughter, the Marquise de Lafayette, and a great deal of other great company.

He (the marshal) lives in all the splendor and magnificence of a viceroy, which is little inferior to that of a king." May 1, he dined with the Duc d'Ayen. "When I began to attempt a little conversation in French, I was very inquisitive concerning the great family of Noailles, and I was told by some of the most intelligent men in France, ecclesiastics as well as others, that there were no less than six marshals of France of this family; that they held so many offices under the king that they received eighteen million livres annually from the crown; that the family had been remarkable for ages for their harmony with one another, and for doing nothing of any consequence without a previous council and concert."

CHAPTER IV.

The Campaign of 1778. — Lafayette at Barren Hill. — The Battle of Monmouth. — The Expedition against Newport. — Quarrels between French and Americans. — Lafayette obtains Leave of Absence and sails for Europe. — His Popularity in America.

THE campaign of 1778 opened under encouraging circumstances. Although no immediate aid was to be expected from France, the moral effect of the alliance was excellent. Congress ordered a council of war at headquarters, which was held on the 8th of May, and attended by Generals Washington, Greene, Armstrong, Mifflin, Stirling, Gates, Lafayette, De Kalb, Steuben, Duportail, and Knox. It was agreed that the army should remain for a time on the defensive, awaiting the movements of the enemy. In Philadelphia, the British were busy with preparations for the Mischianza, the celebrated entertainment devised to soothe the ruffled feelings of Sir William Howe, now relieved of his command by Sir Henry Clinton. Major André, who figured in it as a knight of the Blended Rose, was working so hard over the costumes that he afterwards declared he had learned the trade of a milliner, and offered his services in that capacity to Benedict Arnold's wife.

At the Brandywine and at Gloucester, Lafayette had given evidence of courage and activity in the field. An event was now to take place which would call for very different, but not less important, military qualities. On the 18th of May he received instructions from Washington to take up a position near Philadelphia, whence he could observe the movements of the enemy, intercept their communications, and be prepared to fall upon their rear in case Philadelphia were evacuated.

Lafayette's force numbered about two thousand picked men, the flower of the army; and on this account Washington had warned him that any error or precipitation imperilling his force would be attended with the most disastrous consequences. With this responsible command, Lafayette posted himself on an elevation called Barren Hill, between the Schuylkill river and Philadelphia, about eleven miles from both the American and British forces. His position was well chosen, having the river on the right, a rocky ledge surmounted by cannon in front, a wood and some defensible stone houses on the left. He established his headquarters near a stone church surrounded by a wall; and while he was making his arrangements, spies carried to Philadelphia information of his position. There the Mischianza, with its fireworks, fancy costumes, dancing, and revelry was still in progress, and the British officers naturally considered that the capture of Lafayette and his detachment would be a triumphant climax to the festivities. Sir William Howe went so far as to invite a party to his house for the next evening to meet the marquis.

The British plans were well laid. At least nine thousand men were detached against Lafayette's two thousand, and advantage was taken of the darkness to surprise him. Generals Grant and Erskine, with five thousand men, proceeded very early on the morning of the 20th, with the object of surrounding Barren Hill, and cutting off Lafayette's retreat to Valley Forge by way of Swede's Ford. This operation was successfully and secretly performed. Two other divisions of about two thousand men each, one under General Grey and the other under Sir Henry Clinton himself, approached Barren Hill from different directions, completely surrounding the American position, except on the side of the river, by which escape was considered impossible.

Lafayette was conversing with a young woman who had agreed to go to Philadelphia to procure information, under the pretext of visiting her relations, when word was brought that red uniforms had been seen in the rear. He was expecting a small force of dragoons who wore scarlet, and his first impression was that these were arriving. But he prudently sent out scouts, who soon reported the presence of British soldiery. A change of front was immediately made, under cover of the stone houses and the wood. Then came news of the real state of affairs. Men cried out to him in the presence of the troops that he was surrounded, and, although fully alive to the danger, he had to keep on smiling, as he afterwards observed. The situation was extremely perilous, and a much older head might easily have become confused, with fatal result. But Lafayette had studied the ground thoroughly. His mind at once determined upon the proper course, and not a moment was lost in confusion or doubt. Behind the American force was a road, hidden from the British by trees, which led to Matson's Ford, a crossing little used, and unknown to the enemy, who were, however, much nearer to it than Lafayette was. The marquis immediately threw out "false heads of columns," designed to impress the British with the idea that he was preparing to fight. While these were occupying their attention, he sent all his other troops down the hidden road and across the ford, bringing up the rear himself with the men who had formed the false columns, and who withdrew gradually. The army was almost across the river before the enemy perceived that something was going on, and began their attack. As the three British columns, according to the plan, ascended the hill to crush the Americans at a blow, they met only each other. They had been fairly outwitted, and loud were the mutual recriminations indulged in by the exasperated commanders. A slight attack was made on Lafayette's rear, somewhat delayed by the guns; but all of these were got across safely, and the American forces at once assumed a position which the British dared not attack. All that Sir Henry Clinton could do was to march his nine thousand men back to Philadelphia with such explanations as invention could supply.

Washington had seen from Valley Forge the advance of the enemy, and had ordered signal guns to be fired to warn Lafayette; but the retreat had been performed almost as soon as the danger became known. The great anxiety felt at headquarters over the fate of the detachment was succeeded by the liveliest satisfaction when Lafayette led his troops back to camp. Washington's confidence in his young friend had been fully justified, and the personal affection he already felt for him was deepened by this display of prudence, skill, and presence of mind. Lafayette had a good story to tell on his return. A small body of Indian warriors had been posted in ambush to stop stray parties of the British. As they lay among the bushes by the roadside, they saw approaching a company of grenadiers in tall bear-skin hats and scarlet coats. Never having seen the human form under such circumstances, they were struck with terror; throwing down their arms, and uttering unearthly yells, they fled to the river and swam across. The grenadiers, on their part, took the Indians for so many painted devils, and galloped back to Philadelphia as fast as their horses could carry them.

The position of the British had become untenable. As Franklin said, instead of their having taken Philadelphia, Philadelphia had taken them. Unless they intended passing the summer in the same idleness which had wasted the winter, evacuation must soon occur. In expectation of this event, Washington called a council of war on the 17th of June. At this council Lee opposed any offensive measures with all his strength, asserting that the American forces stood no chance against the discipline and equipment of the British. As Lee had still great influence in the army, his opinion prevailed, although Generals Greene, Wayne, Cadwalader, and Lafayette expressed very opposite views. Washington ordered the officers to put their views in writing; but before this could be done, word was brought that the British were evacuating the city. They had made their preparations with great secrecy. The march began at three o'clock in the morning of the 18th, and before ten o'clock, the whole army had crossed the Delaware, bound for New York.

Washington at once prepared to follow. A division of militia, under General Maxwell, sent on in advance, impeded the enemy's progress by burning bridges and felling trees. Fearing an attack, General Clinton sent his baggage-train ahead in charge of Knyphausen, and brought up the rear himself with his best troops. When Washington, in pursuit, arrived near Princeton, he held another council of war, when Lee and his supporters again objected to active measures of attack, and recommended the annoyance of the enemy by small detachments only. This advice, Hamilton said, "would have done honor to the most honorable society of midwives." Greene, Wayne, and Lafayette agreed with Hamilton. They had condemned from the first, as utterly unworthy, the idea of allowing the British to march safely through New Jersey. They therefore submitted to Washington their written opinion, that a strong detachment should take the first favorable opportunity to attack, the main army being kept ready to give support. This was Washington's own view of the situation, and he at once gave orders to carry it out. Wayne was sent forward to join the advanced corps, which would now number four thousand men. As Lee had opposed the idea of attack so strenuously, it was supposed that he would not care to take the command of the advance, which rightfully belonged to him as senior major-general. Lafayette, therefore, eagerly applied for it, and received Washington's promise of the honor, in case Lee would agree. The latter consented, saying, with his customary cheerfulness, that he was glad to be freed from responsibility in executing plans which he was sure would fail.

Lafayette set out with Wayne's division of one thousand men to join the forces under Maxwell and Scott, and to assume command of the whole. His orders were to take such measures as would cause the most loss and injury to the enemy in his march. From Robin's Tavern and from Icetown he wrote to Washington in terms which showed his anxiety to strike an effective blow. But while thus occupied, an event occurred which put an end to his hopes, and no doubt proved of great injury to the American army. Lee no sooner saw Lafayette in command of the advanced corps, a position only second in importance to that of the commander-in-chief, than his jealousy was aroused, and he regretted his action in resigning his own claim to the post. He wrote to Washington that he had at first thought the command important enough only for a young volunteering general, but now he particularly wished it himself, because, as he said, " If this detachment, with Maxwell's corps, Scott's, Morgan's, and Jackson's, is to be considered as a separate, chosen, active corps, and put under the marquis' command until the enemy leave the Jerseys, both myself and Lord Stirling will be disgraced." Washington was thus placed under the embarrassing necessity of either refusing Lee's request or of disappointing and relieving Lafayette. But his duty was made easy by the tact, good-feeling, and disinterestedness of the marquis, — qualities which did more to win the affection of the Americans than any military services which he was able to perform. Knowing something of the state of affairs, he wrote to Washington from Icetown during the evening of the 26th, " I want to repeat to you in writing what I have told to you ; which is, that if you believe it, or if it is believed, necessary or useful to the good of the service and the honor of General Lee to send him down with a couple of thousand men or any greater force, I will cheerfully obey and serve him, not only out of duty, but out of what I owe to that gentleman's character." Washington, therefore, sent Lee, with Scott's and Varnum's brigades, to reënforce and take command of the advanced corps.

He arrived on the 27th, and met Lafayette, whose disappointment at the loss of command was manifest.

But Lee excused his vacillations by saying, "I place my fortune and my honor in your hands; you are too generous to deprive me of them." To this appeal Lafayette could make but one reply; and thus on the eve of the battle of Monmouth an officer, confident of success and longing for action, was replaced by one who had repeatedly foretold defeat, and opposed offensive measures. Young and comparatively inexperienced as Lafayette was, the fate of the advanced corps would have been safer in his hands.

Early the next morning, on receiving intelligence that the enemy was in motion, Washington sent orders to Lee to make an attack. The details of Lee's movement would require more space than we have at command. He assaulted what he thought a division of the enemy, but what turned out to be the main body; he was repulsed and attacked in his turn. He then ordered a retreat, which he allowed to become disorderly. Washington, coming up with the main body, met the fugitive soldiers, and was shocked at their demoralized condition. The officers whom he met and questioned could give no reason for the retreat; and by the time he found General Lee his anger and indignation were so roused that he took that officer to task in the severest terms. There was no time for discussion; the enemy was pressing on rapidly. Washington's presence and the orders instantly given stopped the retreat. A stand was made on the spot, and the British troops repulsed with considerable loss. Lafayette's part in the action calls for no special mention. A story is related to the effect that his aide-de-camp was killed by his side, and that he showed great coolness and courage in remaining under fire while he personally satisfied himself that his friend was beyond succor.

" In this affair, badly prepared but well concluded," he afterwards wrote, " Washington seemed by a glance to stop the course of fortune ; and his nobility, his grace, his presence of mind, were never displayed to greater advantage. Wayne distinguished himself, Greene and the brave Stirling did good service in front." Night coming on, the troops encamped where they stood. Washington lay on his cloak at the foot of a tree, with Lafayette by his side ; and before they slept, the two friends talked over the events of the day, and tried to determine Lee's part in it. When the drums beat at daybreak it was found that the British had disappeared, leaving their wounded behind them.

Sir Henry Clinton arrived near Sandy Hook on the 30th of June, having lost about two thousand men during his march by desertion and the action at Monmouth. He found the English fleet riding at anchor in the lower bay, having arrived the day before from the Delaware. Heavy storms had cut through the narrow strip of sand which connects the Hook with the mainland, and it was now divided by a deep channel. A bridge was made with the ships' boats, and the British army crossed over to the Hook, and were thence distributed to Long Island, Staten

Island, and New York. Washington moved from Monmouth to Paramus, and there rested his troops, exhausted by their long march and the excessive heat.

While the two hostile armies were marching through New Jersey, the French fleet, in command of Count d'Estaing, arrived at the mouth of the Delaware river. M. Gérard, the minister sent from the court of France, and Silas Deane, one of Franklin's coadjutors, were on board. Being informed of the departure of Lord Howe's squadron, d'Estaing sent Deane and Gérard up to Philadelphia in a frigate, and sailed up the coast to Sandy Hook, where he saw the English ships at anchor inside. D'Estaing had considerable advantage over Lord Howe in point of strength, and great hopes were entertained of his being able to destroy the English vessels. Preparations for the struggle were made on both sides; and in anticipation of this event, Washington crossed the Hudson at King's Ferry, and on the 20th of July took up a position at White Plains. But to the great disappointment of the American and French commanders, no pilots could be found willing to take the large French ships into New York harbor. All agreed that enough water was wanting, and d'Estaing's soundings verified their opinion.

A very friendly correspondence had been kept up between Washington and d'Estaing, and it was soon agreed upon between them that an expedition against Newport, Rhode Island, would present the best opportunity for the coöperation of the American forces and the French fleet. In accordance with this resolution, Washington sent orders to General Sullivan, at Providence, to request in his name, from the States of Massachusetts, Connecticut, and Rhode Island, sufficient forces of militia to make up his command to five thousand men. Sullivan was also ordered to establish a chain of expresses from a high point of land, which would give him the earliest information of d'Estaing's approach. The brave and useful Colonel Laurens was despatched soon after with further instructions.

A detachment from the main army, consisting of Glover's, Varnum's, and Jackson's troops, was then sent to Rhode Island in charge of Lafayette. His orders were to proceed to Providence as quickly as possible, and there to place himself under the command of General Sullivan. Washington ended his letter of instructions by declaring his most perfect reliance on Lafayette's activity and zeal, and by wishing him all the success, honor, and glory that his heart could desire. The marquis led his troops rapidly along the Sound, passing, as he significantly said, "through a smiling country, covered with villages, where the equality of the population indicated a perfect democracy; for by the prosperity of each colony one could judge of the degree of liberty which its constitution enjoyed."

The confidence and affection that Lafayette had won from the commander-in-chief were to be tested in the events now preparing. While his detachment

was on its way to Providence, Washington resolved
that the great abilities of General Greene, and the fact
that he was a native of Rhode Island, made it important that that officer should take part in the expedition. His position in the army was now that of
quartermaster-general, but Washington thought it only
proper that he should have a regular command. He
therefore sent orders to Sullivan to divide his whole
force into two equal parts, each equally composed of
continentals and militia, one to be commanded by
Lafayette, and the other by Greene. To Lafayette he
wrote, announcing the change, and the reasons for it.
This new arrangement would diminish Lafayette's
force very considerably, and to so ambitious an officer
it would be a great disappointment. "I willingly
part," he replied to Washington, "with half my detachment, since you find it for the good of the service,
though I had great dependence on them. Anything,
my dear general, which you shall order or can wish,
will always be infinitely agreeable to me ; and I shall
always be happy in doing anything that may please
you or forward the public good." In thus receiving
the orders of the commander-in-chief, Lafayette was
doing no more than his duty ; but any one who reads
the letters which Washington wrote about this time to
the President of Congress, will readily see the reason
why he distinguished Lafayette above all other foreigners by marks of favor.

Harassed daily by the applications of the foreign
officers for promotion and increase of pay, his patience

tried to the utmost limit by their dissensions and complaints, he had cause to welcome the evidence that Lafayette placed the public interest above his own. "Your favor of the 6th instant," he wrote to the marquis, "afforded a fresh proof of the noble principles on which you act, and has a just claim to my sincere and hearty thanks. . . . Your cheerful acquiescence obviated every difficulty, and gave me singular pleasure."

On the 29th of July, 1778, d'Estaing's fleet arrived off Point Judith, and came to anchor about five miles from Newport. Generals Sullivan, Lafayette, and other officers went aboard to concert arrangements for the attack. The British troops numbered about six thousand men, under the command of Sir Robert Pigott. The main body was strongly intrenched in the middle and on the east side of the island, their batteries commanding Seaconnet Channel. A smaller force was intrenched on the north end of the island, in the direction of Tiverton. To attack these forces the allies had about four thousand men on board the French ships, and between nine and ten thousand Americans at Providence, of whom the greater part were militia, assembled for the occasion only.

In concerting measures for the attack, a great deal of difficulty arose. It was generally doubted in Europe that two nations so opposed in character as the French and Americans could act together, and present events did much to strengthen that opinion. The French officers were imbued with the etiquette

and punctilio of their profession,—matters ignored
by the American commanders, and exciting only their
impatience. The chief obstacle encountered was
the question whether the . French troops should act
separately, or whether a force of Americans should
be added to them. According to Colonel Laurens,
Sullivan objected strongly to parting with any portion
of his command. On the other hand, d'Estaing insisted on the union of an American force with his,
for reasons of a military nature, and for the effect
that it would produce on the French government.
He furthermore desired that the French force and the
American detachment annexed to it should be under
the command of Lafayette, because the acquaintance
that officer had with the military service of both nations would facilitate the junction of the troops ; and
in case d'Estaing's presence were required on board
the fleet, Lafayette would be the most suitable person
to take his place. Colonel Laurens,[1] in a letter
to his father, the President of Congress, put
the blame for these differences on the national pride
of the French and the ambition of Lafayette. Writing in the bitter disappointment felt by every one
after the failure of the enterprise, he said that the
" Marquis de Lafayette aspired to the command of
the French troops in conjunction with the flower
of General Sullivan's army," and that " his private
views withdrew his attention wholly from the general
interest." Colonel Laurens was among the most

---

[1] John Laurens to Henry Laurens, 22 Aug., 1778.

intelligent and valuable officers in the American service, but it is evident that his view of Lafayette's
conduct was founded on a misapprehension of the
circumstances. The marquis wrote to Washington
on the 6th of August, " The admiral wants me to
join the French troops to those I command as soon
as possible. I confess I feel very happy to think of
my coöperating with them; and had I contrived in
my mind an agreeable dream, I could not have
wished a more pleasing event than my joining my
countrymen with my brothers of America, under my
command and the same standards. When I left
Europe, I was very far from hoping such an agreeable
turn of our business, in the American glorious revolution." To this Washington replied on August 10,
" I am very happy to find that the standards of
France and America are likely to be united under
your command at Rhode Island. I am persuaded
that the supporters of each will be emulous to acquire
honor and promote your glory upon this occasion."

It appears, therefore, that Lafayette's desire to
command a combined force of French and American
forces was in accordance with d'Estaing's particular
wishes, had the approval of Washington, and arose
solely from an honorable ambition to distinguish himself in the eyes of both nations.

The plan of operations finally decided upon provided that on the 10th of August the French troops
should land on the west side, at a point nearly opposite Byer's Island. At the same time, Sullivan's army

was to cross over from Tiverton, at Howland's Ferry, and move on the British intrenchments at the north end of the island. On the 8th, d'Estaing passed through the main channel, exchanging broadsides with the British batteries, and took up his position. The same night the English abandoned their northern intrenchments, and withdrew all their forces within their main line. On the morning of the 9th, Sullivan discovered this movement, and, without waiting for the moment agreed upon, crossed over and took possession of the evacuated works. This action gave great umbrage to the French officers, who considered that, as the evacuation had taken place in consequence of their demonstration, the honor of occupation should have been left to them. Colonel Laurens thought that they "talked like women disputing precedence in a country dance, instead of men engaged in pursuing the common interests of two great nations." The French officers, after all, were only jealous of their share of the honors of the expedition. D'Estaing himself proceeded to Sullivan's camp, and expressed his approval of the latter's course.

In this situation, the fleet of Lord Howe, somewhat reënforced, was seen approaching the entrance to the harbor. D'Estaing at once collected his vessels, which were scattered, and in danger of being attacked in detachments. Then, conceiving his chief object to be the destruction of the British-fleet, he stood out to sea with that purpose. While the two fleets were manœuvring for position, an extraordinarily violent

storm came up, which not only separated the comba-
tants, but did great damage to the vessels of both
squadrons. The same storm which prevented the
naval encounter raged furiously on shore for two days,
destroying the American encampment, and causing
such suffering among the men that several died. As
soon as they had recovered from this disaster, Sullivan
moved to within two miles of the English lines, and
intrenched himself on Honeyman's Hill. The discouragement caused by the long delay, and the great
anxiety felt for the safety of the French fleet, were relieved on the evening of the 19th, when d'Estaing
was seen approaching the harbor. All rejoiced at
the thought that the combined attack would now be
made, and all were confident of victory. But the
American hopes were bitterly disappointed when
d'Estaing declared that it was impossible for him to
carry out his part of the plan. His ships were so dis-
mantled, his men so demoralized, that he was in no
condition to act on the offensive. Moreover, his
orders compelled him to make the safety of the fleet
his first consideration, and he must repair at once to
Boston to refit. Despair was caused in the American
camp by this information. Greene and Lafayette
hastened on board to urge a reconsideration, and
d'Estaing would, no doubt, have yielded to their en-
treaties, had not his officers unanimously opposed it.
It is thought that they were jealous that the count,
whose regular position had been that of a land officer,
had been placed over them in the navy. It was in

vain that Greene and Lafayette represented the disastrous effects that this departure would cause, and
urged that two days more would be sufficient to crown
all their efforts with success.   They were obliged to
return disappointed to camp, with only d'Estaing's assurance to Lafayette that as soon as the repairs were
effected he would return to fight " for the glory of the
French name and the interests of America."

The American officers naturally felt themselves un-
necessarily deserted, and their indignation was boundless. A protest was hastily drawn up, declaring that
the departure of the fleet was contrary to the intentions of the French government, fatal to the American
cause, and injurious to the alliance between the two
nations.   Sail was already being made, when Colonel
Laurens arrived on board the admiral's ship with the
protest.   However just and natural were the feelings
which prompted the communication, the latter was not
couched in terms calculated to persuade the French
mind.   D'Estaing was offended, declared that the
message "imposed on the commander of the king's
squadron the painful, but necessary, law of profound
silence," and continued his voyage.

In the midst of these dissensions, and surrounded
by the evidences of general exasperation, Lafayette's
position was becoming more and more difficult.   Being firmly convinced of d'Estaing's honesty of purpose, feeling sure that the departure of the fleet was
caused by unfortunate necessity, he had refused to sign
the protest, but had written a letter to much the same

effect. A most patriotic Frenchman himself, he was extremely jealous of his country's honor. On the other hand, he had sincerely adopted the American cause, and loved to consider himself an American in heart as well as in military rank. To him the quarrel was doubly painful. He could not leave his tent without perceiving in the countenances and hearing in the words of those whom so lately he had regarded as friends the most bitter reproaches against his country. He wrote to Washington that he was afflicted and injured by the very men whom he had come so far to love and support ; that he was on a more warlike footing in the American camp than before the English lines.

It was not unnatural that the feelings of disappointment and grief at the action of the Count d'Estaing should extend beyond him to the whole French people, — a nation for whom the Americans, like the English, had never had any affection. By that action the present expedition was ruined, and even worse results might be expected.

Such was the discouragement in the camp, and so unlikely any success, that great numbers of the volunteers returned home, leaving the American forces unequal to the British. As the harbor was now open, and reënforcements in ships and men would certainly be sent to General Pigott, the American force was in danger of being cut off. General Sullivan withdrew his troops to the works at the north end of the island, where he made a resolute stand.

Lafayette set out for Boston to urge d'Estaing to return in time for another combined attack. He rode the seventy miles, at night, in seven hours, and with the assistance of General Hancock and Dr. Cooper succeeded in smoothing over the difficulties in the way of a good understanding between the French and the people of Boston. A public dinner was given to d'Estaing, at which the situation was thoroughly discussed, and the admiral expressed himself as ready to send his troops by land to Sullivan's assistance. But it was now too late. News was brought that Sir Henry Clinton had arrived at Newport with a light squadron and four thousand men, — a force sufficient to cut off Sullivan's army which was therefore withdrawing from the island.

Lafayette rode back faster than he came, and much disappointed at missing the fighting, took command of the rear and covered the retreat across Howland's Ferry. Sullivan retired with the greater part of his army to Providence, leaving Lafayette in command of a detachment at Bristol. At this time a serious disturbance arose at Boston between the French and Americans, in which an officer of the fleet was accidentally killed; and again Lafayette rode back to assist in establishing peace. The success which attended his efforts in this direction is sufficient testimony to the confidence that was universally felt in his fairness and fidelity to the service of both nations. The Tories were naturally elated at the differences between the allies, and one of their newpapers related that " the renowned Don Quixotto, Drawcansiro de Fayetto " rode post to Congress and delivered a challenge to each member of that august assembly. A difficulty arising as to the choice of weapon, it was left to the determination of the French ambassador. "Three members of Congress were immediately deputed to wait on Monsieur Gerard ; they approached his Excellency with three times three bows, to which his Excellency returned twelve ; the deputies, determined not to be outdone by French politeness, bowed thirteen times, the exact number of the United States, and then proceeded to business. Monsieur Gerard requested a moment for consideration ; the Marquis meanwhile amused himself before the glass, taking snuff and now and then cutting a little caper." The result being unsatisfactory, "the young Quixote swears, parbleu ! that Franklin, the Congress, their generals, etc., are all a pack of ———." [1]

The most acute grief was felt throughout the country at the failure of this expedition. It was not only that Newport remained in the hands of the British, but the French alliance, from which so much had been hoped, seemed likely to bring only disappointment.

Lafayette poured out his heart in his letters to Washington, but while deploring the unhappy series of events, he sought only to justify d'Estaing's honesty of purpose, and to allay the feeling of resentment which existed against the French. Never

---

[1] Rivington's Royal Gazette, Oct. 21, 1778.

during the whole war did Washington show himself greater than in this misfortune. The magnanimity, dignity, and patience with which he wrote to Sullivan, Green, Lafayette, and d'Estaing, reconciling differences, allaying discontent, and arousing new hopes, show how preëminently nature had fitted him for his work.

Lafayette had borne with patience and self-restraint the misunderstandings between his countrymen and his American friends, but when Lord Carlisle, in one of his proclamations, referred to the " perfidy " of the French nation, the young blood of the marquis boiled with indignation. Longing for an opportunity to fight an Englishman and uphold his country's honor at the same time, he disregarded the advice of Washington and sent his aide-de-camp, Gimat, to Carlisle with a challenge. The English commissioner naturally replied that he was responsible for his language only to his king, and that a public insult of this kind had better be left to d'Estaing and the English admiral.

The autumn was now far advanced, and it was evident that no further active operations would take place for the present in America. France and England being at war, an opportunity for service might occur in Europe. Thus the pleasing thought took possession of Lafayette's mind, that a favorable opportunity existed for a visit at home. Without neglecting his duty he might see his wife again, and become acquainted with the little Anastasie, who had taken the place of the lost Henriette. The hope was checked

for a time by the news of a projected expedition to
Canada, and his unwillingness to miss such an opportunity. But Washington assured him that the
chances of such an event were so unlikely that he
ought not to postpone his departure on that account.

In October Lafayette arrived in Philadelphia, and
enjoyed a short period of rest and social intercourse.
An anecdote is related of him which throws much
light on the cause of his popularity in America.
Hearing that the theatre was to be open, one night he
begged President Laurens to accompany him to the
play. The president excusing himself, the marquis
pressed him to go ; but Laurens explained that Congress, disapproving of theatrical amusements in a time
of public danger, had passed a resolution urging the
different States to suppress the theatre. " Ah," replied the marquis, " have Congress passed such a
resolution ? Then I will not go to the play."

In his request to Congress for a leave of absence,
Lafayette expressed his hope that he would be looked
upon as a soldier on furlough who heartily wished
soon again to rejoin his colors. The same Congress,
which sixteen months before had hesitated, and
wisely, to employ the youthful Frenchman, now
exerted itself to do him sufficient honor. Resolutions were adopted thanking him for his services and
disinterested zeal, and directing the American minister in Paris to present him with a valuable sword,
adorned with appropriate emblems. Henry Laurens,
the president, was also directed to write a letter to

Louis XVI., in which it was stated that Congress could not allow Lafayette to depart without testifying its appreciation of his courage, devotion, patience, and the uniform excellence of conduct which had won the confidence of the United States and the affection of its citizens. A good reception in France was further assured to him by the despatches of M. Gérard, the French minister at Philadelphia. "You know how little inclined I am to flattery," he wrote, "but I cannot resist saying that the prudent, courageous, and amiable conduct of the Marquis de Lafayette has made him the idol of the Congress, the army, and the people of America."

Happy at the success which had crowned his adventurous undertaking, but happier at the prospect of being again at home, Lafayette set out for Boston, whence he expected to set sail. But his constitution, already weakened by the exposures and anxieties of the campaign, was unequal to the long journey on horseback which lay before him. A ride of many hours through an autumn rain brought on a fever, which at Fishkill, seven miles from headquarters, prostrated him completely. For three weeks he lay dangerously ill, cared for by Dr. Cochrane, the surgeon-general, and the object of anxious solicitude throughout the country. Washington took care that no pains were spared on his behalf, and these efforts were finally rewarded by a return of sufficient strength to continue the journey. According to Lafayette's account, his cure was completed by the

Madeira wine with which the Boston people supplied him. On account of this and other delays, it was not till January, 1779, that the "Alliance" actually set sail on what was to prove a very stormy voyage in more senses than one.

In every position in which Lafayette had been placed during his service in America, he had acted with a courage and good sense which had won the approval of his superiors and fellow-soldiers. But the universal expressions of regard and affection, in the midst of which he left the American shores, had for their object his character rather than his abilities. Unselfish in the motives which had first brought him across the sea, he had maintained the same disinterestedness throughout his subsequent conduct. The fact that he was a foreigner was lost in genuine enthusiasm with which he adopted the American cause, and accepted the hardships of the patriot service. He had made himself an American, and was trusted as such. The other French officers, whatever their merits, came, and remained foreigners.

The efforts made by Lafayette to do justice to cases of individual merit was another cause of his personal popularity. Only praise of his fellow-officers are to be found in his letters. When Touzard lost his arm in a gallant attack at Newport, the circumstances were enthusiastically related to Washington, to the Duc d'Ayen, and to Mme. de Lafayette. Washington warned President Laurens against attaching too much importance to the marquis' letters of recommendation, "for his countrymen soon find access to his heart."

The difficulties arising out of the employment of French officers had been very vexatious. By far the greater number who worried Washington and Congress for promotion and increase of pay were merely military adventurers, with no interest but their own in view. Others, although of a high order of merit, could not adapt themselves to the privations and simplicity of the republican army. Their demands could only be gratified at the expense of native officers, whose rights were unjustly invaded. "I do most devoutly wish," wrote Washington to Gouverneur Morris, in the summer of 1778, "that we had not a single foreigner among us, except the Marquis de Lafayette, who acts upon very different principles from those which govern the rest."

The high military rank which Congress had conferred upon Lafayette at his arrival was not necessarily of advantage to him. It was no more than a compliment to his connections at home and his interest in America, and would not have carried any command or responsibility with it, had not he shown himself worthy. Indeed, if the title of Major-General, given to the youth of twenty, had not been backed by real services and capacity, it would only have cast ridicule on those who conferred and him who received it.

On the eve of his departure, Lafayette wrote to his friend, Colonel Hamilton, begging the latter to keep him fully informed of events in America; and down to the last moment he despatched letters to Washington, whose friendship he justly considered the most enviable result of his expedition, and which had lately been assured to him in the following words : " The sentiments of affection and attachment which breathe so conspicuously in all your letters to me, are at once pleasing and honorable, and afford me abundant cause to rejoice at the happiness of my acquaintance with you. Your love of liberty, the just sense you entertain of this valuable blessing, and your noble and disinterested exertions in the cause of it, added to the innate goodness of your heart, conspire to render you dear to me ; and I think myself happy in being linked with you in bonds of the strictest friendship." [1]

---

[1] Washington's Writings, Vol. 6, p. 70.

CHAPTER V.

Visit to France in 1779, and Enthusiastic Reception there. — Successful Exertions on Behalf of the United States. — Return to America in 1780. — Arrival of Rochambeau's Fleet. — The Treachery of Arnold. — The Winter at Philadelphia.

So much trouble had been experienced at Boston in completing the crew of the " Alliance," that a number of English prisoners had to be pressed into the service, and these considerably outnumbered the American and French sailors on board. A recent British law offered the full value of any American vessel which its crew would bring into an English port, and this incentive to mutiny came near ending the career of Lafayette. One afternoon as the " Alliance " was approaching the French coast, the officers were seated in the cabin, congratulating themselves on having escaped foundering in a recent storm, when an American sailor entered with a face of alarm. According to his story, hurriedly told, a mutiny had been planned. At the signal of " Sail ho ! " when the officers would naturally come on deck in a body, they were to be shot down by cannon loaded with grape-shot and the vessel headed for England. The mutineers, mistaking him for an Irishman, and one of themselves, had offered him the command in case of success. The signal would be given in an hour.

Seizing their swords, the officers and passengers rushed on deck, called the crew together, and with the aid of the loyal French and Americans, put in irons thirty of the mutineers. A week later, the "Alliance" came safely to anchor in the port of Brest.

Not having heard from his family for eight months, Lafayette thought only of reaching Paris in the shortest possible time, and the English sailors thus escaped the yard-arm. In passing through Versailles, he was presented to the ministers, interrogated, complimented, and ordered under arrest. But instead of the Bastille, his prison was appointed to be the Hôtel de Noailles, the home of his wife's family. The reception that awaited him there is nowhere described, but is easily imagined. He had the honor, he tells us, of being consulted by all the ministers, and, what was better, kissed by all the women. The kisses ceased the next day, but the confidence of the Cabinet lasted longer. From his father-in-law, the Duc d'Ayen, he had received a letter at Newport full of good-will and forgiveness, so that nothing remained but to make his peace at court. There the way had been made smooth by President Laurens' letter to the king, by the resolutions of Congress, and by the remarkable encomiums on Lafayette's conduct which Franklin had received from Samuel Cooper, Carmichael, and other individuals. Having written to the king to acknowledge his "happy fault," the latter allowed him to proceed to Versailles to receive a gentle reprimand, and to be set at liberty; but with a warning to avoid any places where the public might "consecrate his disobedience" by applause.[1]

The warning was not unnecessary, for the young general's popularity was boundless, and he could go nowhere without overwhelming praise and congratulation. The war and the alliance were in the highest favor with the people; Lafayette was regarded as the connecting link between the two nations, and the striking circumstances of his first departure, as well as the reputation he had won in America, combined to make him a public idol. He represented that "liberty" which was fast becoming the ruling thought in France. The audiences at the theatres needed only the remotest suggestion of his career to applaud vociferously. One passage in particular, describing a warrior who combined the prudence of age with the dash of youth, was considered particularly applicable, and could not be repeated too often. Mme. Campan relates that Marie Antoinette, who disliked the war and the principles involved in it, was yet so far carried away by the enthusiasm for Lafayette himself, that she copied these verses with her own hand. The copy, singularly enough, remained in Mme. Campan's possession until the sacking of her house on the infamous 10th of August, when the sceptre was so rudely torn from the hand which had written the lines. With

---

[1] "Mémoires de ma main, jusqu'en l'année 1780," end. This warning corroborates Lafayette's previous statements regarding the prohibition issued against his departure.

the confidence of the French and American governments, with the outspoken approval of two nations
ringing in his ears, it is not to be supposed that the
young man of twenty-one could resist an increase of
self-esteem. Indeed, the extraordinary reputation
acquired at this early period of his life may be counted
among his misfortunes. However, he showed no inclination to rest on his laurels, and in the midst of
what he called the whirlwinds of favor, he settled
down to work for the great cause.

The French cabinet, urged to active operations by
popular clamor, but dismayed by the hopeless insol-
vency of the public treasury, were anxious to strike a
decisive blow. A project which promised some success aimed at an attack on English ports by the celebrated Paul Jones and his no less famous vessel, the
"Bon Homme Richard." Another ship was to be
added, and the land forces placed under Lafayette ; but
this plan was laid aside in favor of one far more ex-
tensive. The Spanish government had at last shown
some signs of life, and agreed to a descent on England
by the combined forces of both nations. Great preparations were made in France for the event, but the
indecision and procrastination of Spain fatally delayed
the enterprise.

In this expedition, Lafayette held a high command,
and it was while waiting at Havre for the fleet to sail
that he received from the hands of Franklin's grandson
the sword which Congress had ordered to be presented
to him. Franklin had been at great pains to make

the gift worthy of the occasion, and it was a very beautiful object; the handle of gold, exquisitely wrought, and adorned, as well as the blade, with figures emblematical of Lafayette's career in America, his arms and his motto, *Cur non.*

Disappointed in his hope of fighting under the French flag, Lafayette had several schemes on foot to benefit the American cause. One of these was an invasion of Ireland with a view to establishing the independence of the island; another, the negotiation of a loan by Sweden to the United States, with his own private property as a guarantee. The letters of Franklin and Adams testify to his unceasing activity in their favor. His efforts to raise money for America made the finance minister fear him " like the devil." Maurepas said that he would sell out the furniture of Versailles to get money for the insurgents. His private resources were freely drawn upon, and to them were owing the new uniforms, cockades, and side-arms with which, in the next campaign, the men under his command were furnished. He lost no opportunity to win recruits, and Ségur says in his memoirs that his desire to serve the cause was increased by Lafayette's representations respecting the "manners, the enthusiasm, the heroic constancy and courage " of the Americans.

Lafayette kept up a constant correspondence with his friends across the Atlantic, upbraiding "that idle fellow, Hamilton," for not writing often enough. To President Laurens he declared that he would always consider the interests of America as his principal business while in Europe, and that he desired nothing so ardently as to return to that country of which he would always regard himself as a citizen. "However happy I find myself in France," he wrote to Washington, "however well treated by my country and my king, I am so accustomed to being near to you, I am bound to you, to America, to my companions in arms by such an affection, that the moment when I sail for your country will be among the happiest and most wished for of my life."

But Lafayette's great work during this year in Europe was his successful application for the coöperating French force, under Rochambeau, which was to contribute so much to the decisive victory at Yorktown. The fear of quarrels between French and American troops had caused Congress and even Washington to doubt the expediency of accepting any land auxiliaries. Indeed, Lafayette had left America with the distinct understanding that none but a naval force was desired. But his belief in the prospective utility of a French force, his ardent desire to see his countrymen fighting for America, and his own freedom from national jealousy gave him confidence in carrying out his own views. His efforts were rewarded by the promise of six thousand men, besides clothing and money for the Continental troops. When the question arose of his rank and command in the French army, he avoided exciting any jealousy on the part of his military seniors by deciding to act only under his American commission ; and it was in the uniform of a Continental major-general that he had his farewell audience at the court of Versailles. " His love of glory is not diminished," wrote John Adams to General Knox, " nor his affection for America, as you see by his return. He has been indefatigable in endeavors to promote the welfare and comfort of our army as well as to support their honor and character, and has had success in both."

At the end of April, 1780, Lafayette arrived at Boston on the French frigate " Hermione," and the whole population turned out to escort him from the wharf to General Hancock's house on Beacon Hill. Proceeding at once to Morristown, he was welcomed affectionately by Washington, and with enthusiasm by the army. His personal popularity was sufficient to insure a welcome ; but it was known, besides, that he had not come empty-handed. Retiring with Washington to his quarters, he anxiously inquired concerning the situation. Washington could only describe the hardships of the past winter,— not less severe than those of Valley Forge,— the fatal depreciation of the currency, the difficulty of recruiting the depleted army, the general discouragement of the country. It was with great satisfaction, therefore, that Lafayette communicated the results of his own efforts, the ready money brought with him, the troops and clothing on their way.

Lafayette knew that the necessary condition on

which help would be furnished from Europe, was that Americans should show by the vigor of their own efforts that their cause was worth helping. Fearing, therefore, the impression that would be made on the governments of France and Spain by the distressed condition of the Continental forces, he wrote a letter to the President of Congress which is worth reproduction. "Those people are coming, my good friend, full of ardor and of sanguine hopes, and may every day be expected. France and Spain are in high expectations. . . . It is from me, on the moment of their arrival, that the French generals expect intelligence; and you may guess that paquets will be by them immediately despatched to Europe. An army that is reduced to nothing, that wants provisions, that has not one of the necessary means to make war, — such is the situation wherein I found our troops; and however prepared I might have been to this unhappy sight by our past distresses, I confess I had no idea of such an extremity. Shall I be obliged to confess our inability? and what shall be my feelings on the occasion, not only as an American and American soldier, but also as one that has highly boasted in Europe of the spirit, the virtue, the resources of America? Though I had been directed to furnish the French court and the French generals with early and minute intelligence, I confess pride has stopped my pen, and, notwithstanding past promises, have avoided entering into any details, till our army is put in a better and more decent situation. We have

men, my dear sir, we have provisions, we have everything that is wanted, provided the country is awakened and its resources are brought forth. That, you
know, can't be done by Congress; and unless the
States take the whole matter on themselves, we are
lost."

Repairing to Philadelphia, Lafayette received the
thanks of Congress for his services in Europe, and
busied himself with the equipment of the army until
the arrival of Rochambeau in July. At Newport,
where the French fleet had come to anchor, he was
occupied for a long time in discussing plans. The
hands of the French officers were tied, as usual, by
their instructions, and the consultations did not proceed without some heat on Lafayette's part. His extreme anxiety that his countrymen should render a
great service led him to urge immediate action with
an impetuosity which called forth a good-natured re-
proof from Rochambeau. His confidence that no
difficulties need result from the presence of French
troops on American soil was fully justified. Rochambeau was able to write to President Huntington that
not a complaint had been made, and that the French
felt and meant to act as the brothers of their allies.
In the original copy of this letter, among the Rochambeau papers at Washington, is the following curious confirmation of the happy state of affairs : " The
hens with their chicks, all the animals with their
young, come to eat in the tents of our soldiers."
But this strong testimony to French self-restraint was

omitted from the copy actually sent. The number of men brought over by Rochambeau did not exceed four thousand, while the promised supplies of arms and clothing had been left behind, and did not arrive till much later. No disappointment, however, was felt, because Lafayette had been prudent enough to communicate the promises of the French government to Washington alone.

Lafayette soon rejoined the army, then encamped on the Hudson, and a pleasing description of his appearance there is given in the memoirs of the Marquis de Chastellux. " We profited by a cessation of the rain to accompany His Excellency to the camp of the marquis : we found all his troops drawn up on a height to the left, and himself at their head, expressing by his bearing and his face that he preferred to receive me there than on his lands in Auvergne. The confidence and attachment of his troops are precious possessions to him, — riches well gained that no one can take away ; but what I find most flattering for a young man of his age, is the influence, the consideration, that he has acquired in political as well as in military affairs. . . . Happy his country if she employs his services ; happier still if she has no use for them ! "

In September a conference was held at Hartford between the French and American commanders. The very day that Washington and Rochambeau were in consultation, Arnold and André were completing their plot on the banks of the Hudson. On his return from Hartford, Washington, in company with Generals Knox and Lafayette, took a somewhat circuitous route in order to show the marquis the works which had been constructed at West Point during his absence. On the morning of September 24, after a pleasant ride of eighteen miles, the party arrived within a mile of the Robinson house, where Mrs. Arnold was expecting them at breakfast. Washington, always absorbed in his work, turned his horse's head toward a side road, when he was stopped by Lafayette, who called his attention to the fact that breakfast and Mrs. Arnold were waiting. " Ah, marquis," laughed Washington, " you young men are all in love with Mrs. Arnold. I see you are eager to be with her as soon as possible. Go you and breakfast with her, and tell her not to wait for me. I must ride down and examine the redoubts on this side of the river, but will be with her shortly." Lafayette and Knox, however, preferred to accompany the general to the river, and the message was carried to the Robinson house by Colonel Hamilton and Major McHenry.

Mrs. Arnold, lately arrived with her baby, did the honors of the repast with her usual happy grace. Arnold's gloomy countenance gave but a slight indication of his state of mind. This very day was the one designated for the arrival of the British ships and the consummation of his treachery. The unexpected return of the commander-in-chief opened the door to endless apprehensions. But none of the guilty man's fears foretold so terrible a catastrophe as that which actually impended. A messenger galloped up to the door with a letter for Arnold. He opened it over his breakfast, and read that André had been captured, and the papers found upon him forwarded to Washington. Rising from the table, he made a sign to his wife to follow, led her up to her room, closed the door, and hurriedly exclaimed that he was a ruined man, and must flee for his life. Leaving her insensible on the floor, he left the house, mounted the messenger's horse, and galloped down to the river through a ravine still known as Arnold's path. There he entered his barge, and was rowed rapidly down the river to the British ship "The Vulture."

Washington, Lafayette, and Knox reached the Robinson house almost immediately after Arnold's departure. Supposing that Arnold had gone to West Point to prepare for his reception, Washington took a hasty breakfast, and crossed the river with the other generals. No salute was fired at their approach, nor was there any evidence that the party was expected. Colonel Lamb, the officer in command, came down to the shore and apologized, saying that he had received no information of the visit. " Is not General Arnold here? " inquired Washington. " No, sir ; he has not been here for two days, nor have I heard from him in that time." Surprised, but unsuspicious, Washington and his companions passed the morning in examining the works.

About mid-day, as they were returning to the Robinson house, they were met by Hamilton, who took

Washington aside, and handed him the papers found on André, together with an explanatory letter from André himself which had arrived while the commander-in-chief was at West Point. The whole plot was clear. Hamilton was despatched instantly to arrest Arnold, but it was too late. To Lafayette and Knox only Washington communicated the terrible news, asking in his grief, " Whom can we trust now ? "

Lafayette was one of the board of general officers who examined André's case. The board could render but one verdict. By his own evidence, — and no other was taken, — André was a spy, found within the American lines in disguise, with his fatal papers upon him. He was further engaged in conducting a scheme of treachery hateful to every man of honor. The pass which he held from his accomplice had no validity. On account of the attractions of his personal character, his fate has naturally met with much commiseration ; but Nathan Hale, the accomplished American officer executed at New York, was equally attractive in character, equally dear to his family, and equally sensitive to the manner of his death. But the British had shown no compunction in hanging him with all haste. The only difference between the cases of Hale and André was, that Hale died amidst brutal jeers, while André received every consolation which a generous enemy could give.

Lafayette was destined to see no active service during the year 1780. The autumn was passed in camp

on the Hudson or in New Jersey, and part of the winter in Philadelphia. There a number of French
officers had gathered, prominent among whom were
the Marquis de Chastellux, Vicomte de Noailles,
MM. de Montesquieu, de Damas, and Duplessis-Man-
duit. The presence of these accomplished visitors
added much to the social gayeties of the town, and
the Marquis de Chastellux recorded his impressions
of what he saw with his usual sympathetic penetra-
tion. One afternoon he and Lafayette went to take
tea at Mrs. Shippen's. "This is the first time since
my arrival in America that I have seen music appear
in society and mingle with amusements. Miss Rut-
ledge played on the harpsichord, and played very
well. Miss Shippen sang timidly, but had an attractive voice. M. Ottaw, secretary to the Chevalier de
la Luzerne, had his harp brought, accompanied Miss
Shippen, and also played some pieces. Music leads
naturally to dancing : the Vicomte de Noailles strung
some harp-strings on a violin, and then played for the
young people to dance, while the mothers and other
grave persons conversed in another room. If music
and the fine arts prosper in Philadelphia, if society
there becomes easy and gay, and if people learn to
receive pleasure when it comes without being formally invited, then Americans can enjoy all their
social and political advantages without having anything to envy in Europe." Such was the very just
reflection of a cultivated man of leisure on a society which was necessarily too much absorbed in its

work of building up a great nation in the wilderness
to enjoy the ornaments of life. The self-denying
seriousness which formed so important an element of
the national strength was a source of constant wonder
to the volatile and pleasure-loving Frenchman. An
instance of it which particularly amused Chastellux
is told in his "Travels." It was customary at the
social entertainments at Philadelphia to give the position of master of ceremonies to a Continental officer
of merit. At one ball the position was occupied by
a Colonel Mitchell, who showed that he carried into
private life the devotion to duty which had distinguished him in the field. Perceiving that one young
girl in a quadrille was too much occupied in conversation to pay proper attention to the figures of the
dance, he sternly addressed her, "Take care what
you are doing; do you suppose you are there for
your pleasure?"

Lafayette, with his friends, Chastellux, Noailles,
and Montesquieu, made a number of excursions in
the country about Philadelphia, visiting the Brandywine, Whitemarsh, and Barren Hill. Lafayette served
as guide, and explained the military operations which
had occurred at the different places. Chastellux describes these journeys with great interest, and men-
tions that sometimes he, Lafayette, and Noailles,
falling into conversation, as they rode along, about
their friends at home, would for a moment fancy
themselves again in Paris.

These pleasures, together with a lengthy correspond-

ence on military matters, filled up the time till Lafayette's return to headquarters and the preparations
for the great campaign of 1781. Opportunities for
communicating with his wife had been extremely rare
during this year, but a favorable one was offered by
the mission of Colonel Laurens to the court of France.
A son, named George Washington, had now taken the
place of the lost Henriette. " Embrace our children," wrote the young general from his winter camp,
" thousands of times for me. Although a vagabond,
their father is none the less tender, less constantly
thoughtful of them, less happy to hear from them.
My heart perceives, as in a delicious perspective, the
moment when my dear children will be presented to
me by you, and when we can kiss and caress them
together. Do you think that Anastasie will recognize
me?" Lafayette could never write without a good
word for the army. "Only *citizens* could support
the nakedness, the hunger, the labors, and the absolute lack of pay which constitute the conditions of our
soldiers, the most enduring and the most patient, I
believe, of any in the world."

CHAPTER VI.

Lafayette is sent to Virginia to fight Arnold. — His Campaign
against Cornwallis. — Washington and Rochambeau arrive at
Yorktown. — Surrender of Cornwallis.

In January, 1781, the news reached headquarters
in the Highlands of New York that General Arnold
had landed in Virginia with a considerable force, was
laying waste the country, and had already destroyed
the valuable stores collected at Richmond; opposed
to him were only the small commands of Steuben and
Muhlenberg. The situation was very alarming, and
threatened to place all the Southern States in the
hands of the British. If Arnold succeeded in destroying the few American troops in Virginia, he could
then march to the assistance of Cornwallis, who, with a
superior force, was pressing General Greene very hard
in the Carolinas.

To defeat or capture Arnold before he could
further prosecute his designs was, therefore, of the
utmost importance. For this purpose it was necessary to send a detachment from the main army
against Arnold by land, and a naval force to Chesapeake Bay to prevent his escape by sea. Washington
at once communicated the state of affairs to Rochambeau, who, with the French fleet, had long been block-
aded at Newport. Taking advantage of the serious

injuries lately suffered by the blockading English fleet
in consequence of a storm, Admiral Destouches despatched M. de Tilly to the Chesapeake with a ship-
of-the-line and two frigates. To coöperate with
these French vessels, Washington detached twelve
hundred light infantry from the main army, and placed
them under the command of Lafayette. That officer
was particularly chosen for this important trust, because the confidence reposed in him by both the
American and French troops made him, in Washington's opinion, the fittest person to conduct a combined
expedition.[1] Thus opened the only campaign in
America which afforded Lafayette an opportunity to
show what abilities he possessed as an independent
commander, and on this campaign his military reputation must chiefly rest.

Lafayette moved rapidly southward, reaching Philadelphia on the 2d of March, and the Head of
Elk on the 3d, three days earlier than had been expected. In order to be within communication with
the French vessels, he embarked the troops on small
boats and descended to Annapolis, about sixty miles
down the bay. Here he was surprised to see no signs
of De Tilly's squadron, which had left Newport early
in February; but he concluded that the vessels were
only delayed by adverse winds. Leaving the troops
at Annapolis, he set out with a few officers to seek
reënforcements and to consult with Baron Steuben.
That officer was now subordinate to Lafayette, but

---

[1] Washington's Writings, vol. viii., p. 1S.

the latter, "out of delicacy," declined to take the command from him.[1] Some companies of militia were secured at Williamsburg, near the York river, and then Lafayette proceeded to General Muhlenberg's camp near Suffolk to examine Benedict Arnold's defences at Portsmouth.

While thus occupied, on the 20th of March a large fleet appeared in the bay. Lafayette believed it to be the expected French squadron, and his opinion was shared by Arnold, whose camp gave evidence of the alarm excited there. But the American commander soon received information from Major McPherson at Hampton that the vessels were English. As it afterwards appeared, M. de Tilly had reached the Chesapeake in good season, but finding that his ship-of-the-line drew too much water to follow Arnold's small vessels up the bay, he had returned to Newport, capturing several prizes on the way. On Washington's solicitation, Admiral Destouches, now commanding at Newport, himself proceeded to Chesapeake Bay with eight ships-of-the-line and four frigates. But this fleet was pursued by Admiral Arbuthnot, lately stationed in Gardiner's Bay, overtaken, and forced to an action before it reached the Chesapeake. Both fleets were considerably injured, and Admiral Destouches returned to Newport to refit. The substantial victory, therefore, remained with the British, who had now cast anchor in the bay, not only relieving Arnold from danger,

---

[1] Washington's Writings, vol. viii., p. 511.

but bringing also a reënforcement of two new regiments under General Philips who now took command of all the English forces in Virginia.

Lafayette's orders from Washington were, that he should always bear in mind that the force under his command belonged to the main army in the North, and was detached only for the purpose of capturing Arnold; that, in case this object were defeated by the loss of naval superiority in the bay, he was to march his men back to headquarters without taking any further risk. He accordingly sent his militia back to Williamsburg, and despatched orders to Annapolis to have the troops prepared for immediate departure. To the same place he proceeded himself; but he could not resist the temptation of going some miles out of his way to pay a visit to Washington's mother, then at Fredericksburg, and he made up for lost time by hard riding at night.

Considerable difficulties opposed the transportation of the troops from Annapolis back to Elk. The scarcity of horses, wagons, and small boats for crossing ferries made the journey by land almost impossible. On the other hand, the port of Annapolis was blocked by the " Hope " of twenty guns and the " Monk " of eighteen guns, two English vessels stationed there expressly to oppose any movements. In this predicament, Lafayette had recourse to a stratagem which proved perfectly successful. On the 6th of April, he had two eighteen-pounders placed on a small sloop, which, with another vessel under Commodore Nicholson, sailed out toward the British vessels, firing their guns, and making a great show of attack. The " Hope " and the " Monk," probably through fear of being boarded, withdrew to a considerable distance down the bay, and the moment was seized by Lafayette to get his own boats laden with troops out of the harbor and on their way to Elk. There they arrived safely during the night, Lafayette and Nicholson bringing up the rear with the sloop.

When the arrival of General Philips in Virginia became known at headquarters, Washington's anxiety was naturally great. The situation of the Southern States had become extremely perilous. General Greene had all he could do to fight Lord Cornwallis' superior force in North Carolina. Unless a vigorous opposition could be made to Philips, he would have no difficulty in dispersing the militia of Virginia, and in effecting a junction with Cornwallis. With their forces so combined, the British would be masters in the South.

Washington at once determined to place the defence of Virginia in Lafayette's hands. The latter's presence in the South with a good force was an advantage to be considered. But in addition to this reason, Washington was confident of the young general's ability to bear this new responsibility. When objections were raised to Lafayette's youth, — and he was not yet twenty-four, — they were thus answered by the commander-in-chief: " It is my opinion that the command of the troops in that State cannot be in

better hands than the marquis's. He possesses uncommon military talents; is of a quick and sound
judgment; persevering and enterprising, without rashness; and besides these, he is of a very conciliating
temper and perfectly sober, — which are qualities that
rarely combine in the same person. And were I to
add that some men will gain as much experience in
the course of three or four years as some others will
in ten or a dozen, you cannot deny the fact and
attack me upon that ground."[1]

Lafayette was informed of his new expedition immediately on his arrival at Elk. Washington had
sent the orders on the 6th of April, and on the
11th he wrote to Colonel Laurens stating the instructions he had given to Lafayette, and adding,
" But how he can march without money or credit is
more than I can tell." The difficulty was indeed
great. The inability of Congress to raise money had
made the sufferings of the whole army during the
past year almost unbearable. The men under Lafayette had received no pay for many months, their
shoes were worn out, and what remained of their
winter clothing was unfit for the warm season now
approaching. Moreover, they were all from the
North, and extremely unwilling to serve so far from
home. No sooner was the new Southern expedition
announced than the utmost discontent was manifested,
and desertions took place with alarming frequency.

---

[1] MS. letter, Washington to Hon. Joseph Jones, delegate of Virginia
in Congress, 10 July, 1781.

As Lafayette was crossing the Susquehanna he was told that it would be difficult to keep six hundred men together as far as Baltimore. He first endeavored to cast a stigma on desertion by hanging a worthless soldier who was caught, and by dismissing from the ranks another who had previously borne a good character. But in his own words, his " feelings for the sufferings of the soldiers, and the peculiarity of their circumstances " prompted him to find other means to insure their fidelity. Borrowing ten thousand dollars from the merchants of Baltimore on his personal security, he expended the sum in equipping the men. He enlisted the sympathy of the ladies of Baltimore, who provided a large number of shirts. He then announced in general orders that the detachment was intended to fight an enemy far superior in numbers, under difficulties of every sort, and that any soldier who was unwilling to accompany his general might avoid the penalties of desertion by applying for a pass to the North. Placed on their mettle by this appeal, and relieved of their most urgent wants, the troops then followed cheerfully. A sick sergeant hired a conveyance at his own expense, that he might not be left behind.

Lafayette marched with such rapidity from Baltimore, that he reached Richmond, where there were valuable stores to be protected, a day in advance of General Philips. From his post on the heights of the town he saw the British set fire to the tobacco warehouses at Manchester, just across the river, but there were neither men nor boats enough to make an attack possible. Philips, on his part, was too much impressed with the show of strength made by the Americans to prosecute his plans on Richmond, and retreating down the James river, burning and laying waste as he went, he camped at Hog Island. Lafayette followed, harassing the enemy's rear, as far as the Chickahominy.

Here the situation underwent a considerable change. Lord Cornwallis, after his long and unsuccessful campaign against Greene in North Carolina, made up his mind that his exhausting labors there would prove unprofitable until Virginia should be subjugated. His men were worn out with incessant marching and fighting, while no substantial advantage had been gained. Hearing that General Greene had marched to attack Lord Rawdon at Camden in South Carolina, he determined to join Philips. That officer, accordingly, received orders while at Hog Island to take possession of Petersburg and there await Cornwallis's arrival. When Lafayette saw Philips returning up the James river, he concluded that another attack on Richmond was meditated, and he hastened to take possession of that place. But at Richmond, hearing that Cornwallis was moving northward and Philips landing his men below at Brandon, he divined the intended junction and hastened toward Petersburg to prevent it. Philips, however, being much nearer, arrived first, and Lafayette fell back on Richmond and busied himself with removing the stores to safer places. Sending

Colonel Gimat, with artillery, to occupy the enemy's attention, he safely despatched a quantity of ammunition, under the escort of Muhlenberg, to General Greene.

On the 13th of May, General Philips died at Petersburg of a fever. Twenty-four years before, Lafayette's father had fallen before his guns at Minden. On taking command in Philips' place, Arnold wrote a letter to Lafayette, which he sent under a flag. Lafayette no sooner learned the name of the writer than he informed the bearers that while glad to communicate with any other British officer, he could not even read a message from Arnold. This course placed the traitor in an awkward position with his own command, and was resented by a threat to send all American prisoners to the West Indies. But the country was pleased at Lafayette's action, and Washington wrote : —

"Your conduct upon every occasion meets my approbation, but in none more than in your refusing to hold a correspondence with Arnold."

Cornwallis arrived at Petersburg on the 20th of May. His forces now amounted to over five thousand men, which number was soon increased to eight thousand. Among these were about one thousand cavalry mounted on fast horses taken from the stables of Virginia planters. The men were all veterans, and the cavalry, from the suddenness and rapidity of their movements, were particularly formidable to the American militia. In addition to his greatly superior force,

Cornwallis controlled the numerous water-courses of the State, in itself a great advantage. To place the entire South under British control, he had now only to disperse the small army, chiefly militia, which lay before him, and to destroy the stores on which Greene and the Virginia forces depended for existence. The prospect was so bright that he forgot the hardships of his North Carolina campaign, and, as Tarleton says, conceived " brilliant hopes of a glorious campaign in those parts of America where he commanded."

Between Cornwallis and the realization of his hopes stood Lafayette, with Generals Steuben and Muhlenberg and about three thousand men. Of these only one-third were regulars ; the rest were inexperienced militia, and the cavalry consisted of a small body of Southern gentlemen mounted on their own horses. In the course of the campaign Lafayette succeeded in raising the number under his command by the enlistment of young men along the line of march ; but his force always remained much inferior to the enemy in numbers as well as in equipment. Up to the time of General Philips's death, Lafayette had been nominally under the orders of Greene, making his reports to that officer and sending copies to headquarters. But it was impossible for Greene, fighting Rawdon in South Carolina, to direct the movements in Virginia, and Lafayette had necessarily acted for himself. On the 18th of May he received orders from Greene to take entire command of the army in Virginia and to report directly to headquarters. Thus the responsibility for defeating the plans of Cornwallis was placed on his shoulders. The seriousness of his position was fully appreciated. " Independence," he wrote to Hamilton, " has made me the more cautious, as I know my own warmth." He declared that he feared himself more than the enemy, and resolved that he would not risk a battle unless with such reënforcements that he could " be beat with some decency." The business in hand was to prevent Cornwallis from taking possession of Virginia, and to save the stores collected in that State from destruction. For these objects Lafayette stationed himself between Wilton and Richmond, on the north side of the James river, and there awaited the movements of the enemy.

On the 24th of May, Cornwallis, having rested his troops, marched from Petersburg, and endeavored to engage the American forces. But Lafayette, having removed the military stores from Richmond, retreated across the Chickahominy to Fredericksburg, where he expected to meet General Wayne and a battalion of Pennsylvania troops, without whose assistance he could not venture any fighting. The British followed in pursuit, but were unable to come up with the Americans. Failing in this attempt, Cornwallis sent Colonel Simcoe to Point of Fork, where he destroyed some stores, and Colonel Tarleton to Charlottesville, where the State Legislature was frightened into a hasty adjournment, but only seven members were captured. These expeditions were conducted with great rapidity by the well-mounted British cavalry, and no opposition could be made to them. Cornwallis then moved between Lafayette and the town of Albemarle, where had been placed a great part of the military stores from Richmond, which now seemed doomed to destruction.

But on the 10th of June Lafayette had received his expected reënforcement of Wayne's Pennsylvanians, and thus strengthened felt able to assume the offensive. Rapidly crossing the Rapidan he approached close to the British army, which blocked the road to Albemarle. Nothing could have better suited Cornwallis, who prepared for a conflict in which he felt sure of a decisive victory. Lafayette, however, had not lost sight of the vital feature of his campaign, — to protect the property of the State without losing his army. Through his scouts he discovered an old unused road to Albemarle, unknown to the enemy. While Cornwallis was preparing for battle, he had the road cleared, and under cover of the night marched his men through it and took up a strong position before the town. There he was joined by militia from the neighboring mountains, and he showed so strong a front that the British commander did not venture an attack. Soon after leaving Petersburg, Cornwallis had written a letter, which was intercepted, containing his assurance of success and the phrase, " the boy cannot escape me." The boy had now shown himself a much more formidable adversary than was expected ; the British commander, so far foiled in his objects, had to march back to Richmond and thence to Williamsburg, near the coast, thus practically abandoning control over any part of Virginia except where naval forces gave possession.

Lafayette effected a junction with Baron Steuben on the 18th of June, and thus increased his force to about four thousand men. The Americans had now become the pursuers instead of the pursued, and followed the British, harassing their rear and flanks. Colonel Tarleton, the celebrated cavalry officer serving under Cornwallis, thus describes these movements : " The Marquis de Lafayette, who had previously practised defensive manœuvres with skill and security, being now reënforced by General Wayne and about eight hundred Continentals and some detachments of militia, followed the British as they proceeded down James river. This design, being judiciously arranged and executed with extreme caution, allowed opportunity for the junction of Baron Steuben, confined the small detachments of the king's troops, and both saved the property and animated the drooping spirits of the Virginians." Thus Lafayette, according to the testimony of his enemy, was attaining the objects of his campaign.

Near Williamsburg, a spirited action took place between the Queen's Rangers under Colonel Simcoe, who had been sent out to forage, and a detachment of cavalry and riflemen under Colonel Butler. Although neither party could boast a victory, the advantage lay with the Americans, whose skilful riflemen did great

execution among the British cavalry. At Williamsburg, Lord Cornwallis received important advices from
General Clinton at New York, according to which a
portion of the British troops in Virginia were ordered
to the North. In order to embark these men, Cornwallis set out for Portsmouth on the 4th of July.

As the British army would be obliged to cross the
James river at James Island, Lafayette determined to
attack their rear as soon as a considerable portion
should have passed the ford. He followed accordingly, and camped the next day at Green Spring,
about nine miles from the river. But Cornwallis,
always on the alert, divined his intention, and took
excellent measures to defeat it. All the baggage-
wagons and pack-horses were sent across the ford
under the escort of the Queen's Rangers with as much
display as possible. The main body of the troops
was distributed along the bank under cover of the
trees. On the British right was a pond ; in the centre
and on left a stretch of marshy ground which
could only be crossed by narrow causeways made of
logs. The outposts were instructed to resist any
attack, as if to allow the escape of the force behind
them. Thus skilfully disposed in a situation of the
greatest security, the British waited with well-founded
confidence.

On the 6th of July, Lafayette left his camp at
Green Spring at three o'clock in the afternoon, and
arrived near the ford at about five. The crossing of
the baggage and some troops had been reported to

him by the skirmishing parties which he had sent out to
annoy the enemy; and on the march from camp a
negro and a dragoon were picked up who asserted that
the British army had crossed with the exception of
the rear-guard.   These men, as it afterwards appeared, had been employed by Colonel Tarleton to
feign desertion in order to deceive the Americans,
but as their account agreed with previous information,
Lafayette accepted it as true.

Toward sunset, the American troops having crossed
the narrow causeways leading to the enemy's position,
the pickets were driven in and the action began.
General Wayne, whose spirit and valor had long made
him known as " Mad Anthony", led the advance with
a thousand riflemen, dragoons, and two pieces of artillery.   Lafayette, with twelve hundred infantry, stood
ready to give support.   Wayne easily drove in the
outposts and was soon upon the enemy.   But at the
first discharge of his artillery, the British formed on
the open ground, facing and outflanking the Americans.   Wayne saw at once that the whole British army
was before him; but thinking the boldest course the
safest, he sounded a charge and attacked with great
vigor.   The action, while it lasted, was extremely
warm.   But Lafayette, judging that the fire was too
heavy for a rear-guard only, galloped off to find a
spot from which he could gain a view of the enemy.
Fortunately a tongue of land was found commanding
a view of the river bank.   From this point he perceived the real state of affairs, spurred back to Wayne,

and ordered an immediate retreat to General Muhlenberg's station about half a mile in the rear. The troops fell back to Muhlenberg's brigade in good order, leaving two cannon on the field which could not be moved as the horses had been killed. Their losses were about one hundred and fifty in killed and wounded; the enemy's, half that number. After uniting wtth Muhlenberg, the American troops recrossed the causeways and returned to Green Spring. Had the enemy pursued, a substantial victory must have been theirs, for the retreat across the log bridges was necessarily slow and difficult. But Cornwallis, puzzled by the boldness of Wayne's attack, followed by the sudden retreat, feared that an ambuscade was being prepared for himself, and preferred to run no further risk. The advantages of the action belonged to the British, who could now cross the river without opposition and proceed to Portsmouth.

Lafayette distinguished himself during the action by his personal courage. " I will not condole with the marquis," wrote Wayne, "for the loss of two of his horses, as he was frequently requested to keep at a greater distance; his native bravery rendered him deaf to the admonition." The British Colonel Tarleton, who had sent the pretended deserters to deceive the Americans, expressed his opinion that Lafayette made his attack in consequence of " false intelligence, rather than through too great ardor; for it is the only instance of this officer's committing himself during a very difficult campaign." During the re-

mainder of July, while Cornwallis was occupied with
the embarkation of troops at Portsmouth, Lafayette
kept a close watch on the enemy, reporting to Washington every detail which might be of service in
future plans, and he attended to the wants of his men
with a personal interest which met with their frequently
expressed gratitude.

While the British and American forces in Virginia
were contending for the possession of that State, all
the operations in the North tended toward an attack
on New York by the combined armies of Washington
and Rochambeau. On the 21st of May, a conference
was held at Weathersfield in Connecticut between the
French and American commanders, and in pursuance
of the plan of campaign there agreed upon, the French
troops at Newport marched to the Hudson river and
joined forces with the American army. On the 11th
of June, Clinton wrote to Cornwallis that he was
threatened with an attack by a superior force, and
directed him to send a considerable portion of his
army to New York. It was in consequence of this
order and to embark the desired troops that Cornwallis had left Williamsburg and marched to Portsmouth, on which journey the James-river fight had
taken place. On the 12th of July, soon after his
arrival at Portsmouth, Cornwallis received another
and more urgent demand for assistance, in consequence of which he sent the troops on board as
fast as possible. The transports were loaded with
men, when, on the 20th of July, Clinton sent word

that he had received reënforcements from Europe, that he now felt able to hold his own, and that Cornwallis should retain his troops. On the 26th, Lafayette describing · the situation to Washington, wrote that there were in Hampton Roads forty vessels full of red-coats and cavalry ; supposing them to be destined for New York, he was surprised that they did not sail ; and he added in his usual sanguine spirit, " Should a French fleet now come into Hampton Roads, the British army would, I think, be ours."

The event here wished for by Lafayette was actually about to take place. His letter was hardly in Washington's hands when a French vessel arrived at Newport with the news that Count de Grasse's fleet had left the West Indies bound for Chesapeake Bay. This happy intelligence changed the whole face of affairs. Washington saw that his meditated blow should be struck, not at Clinton in New York, but at Cornwallis in Virginia.

Cornwallis, supposing Lafayette's army to be the only force against which he need provide, and desiring to establish himself in a strong post having easy communication with the sea, began to move his men to Yorktown on the 1st of August. The troops which Lafayette had seen on the transports were conveyed by water, the rest went by land. A detachment was left at Portsmouth to destroy the works, which, being threatened by Lafayette, soon rejoined the main army. By the end of August, all the British forces were concentrated at Yorktown, a small place on Chesapeake Bay at the mouth of the York river, and at Gloucester Point, directly opposite. The river, which separated the two divisions, was a mile wide, and deep enough to float large vessels of war. Access to Yorktown was made difficult by the creeks and swamps which marked the surrounded country, and Cornwallis's position was further strengthened by the works which he immediately began to construct. The British, confident of their ability to withstand any attack by land, worked at their fortifications with a feeling of perfect security. From the sea no danger was feared; it afforded communication with Clinton, and the means of obtaining any required assistance.

But the position which the British thought so advantageous was exactly that into which Lafayette wished to force them, and that which most favored the plans of Washington. Lafayette had posted himself by the 13th of August at the junction of the Pamunky and Mattaponey rivers, to the west of Yorktown. He knew nothing yet of the coming of the French fleet under De Grasse, but he hoped for such an event; and to provide for it he sent a detachment of light troops to the rear of Gloucester to prevent the enemy from marching northward, and instructed General Wayne to cross the James river and be ready to oppose Cornwallis in case he attempted to escape southward into North Carolina. These measures had already been taken by Lafayette when he received a letter from Washington, dated the 15th of August, containing instructions to the same effect, and the certain news of De Grasse's destination. Lafayette's arrangements to keep the British in their position were made with the utmost care. " His lordship plays so well," he wrote to Washington, " that no blunder can be hoped from him to recover a bad step of ours." Washington expressed great satisfaction with every thing that had been done : " By your military disposi-tions and prudent measures you have anticipated all my wishes."

For some months past, while the important event of the year's campaign had seemed to be the pro-jected attack on New York, Lafayette had shown a strong desire to rejoin the commander-in-chief and to share his fortunes in that attempt. But Washington had always replied, that being useful in Virginia, he had better remain there. Now the young general hastened to express his gratitude. " It is to your goodness that I am indebted for the most beautiful prospect my eyes may ever behold."

On the 30th of August the anxiously expected French fleet came to anchor before Yorktown. The Count de Grasse had been met at Cape Henry by Colonel Gimat, Lafayette's aide-de-camp, who ap-prised him of the situation of the opposing forces. Three days later the Count de St. Simon landed at James Island with over three thousand men and joined Lafayette at Green Spring. The allies immediately occupied Williamsburg, fifteen miles from Yorktown, and their ships-of-war controlled the James and York rivers. Cornwallis awoke too late from his dream of security. Completely blocked by land and sea, he could only write to Clinton for help, and strengthen his works with all possible haste.

Count de Grasse, having only a limited period of time at his disposal, and being anxious to return to the West Indies, now did his best to persuade Lafayette to attack Cornwallis at once without waiting for Washington and Rochambeau. St. Simon added his own urgent request to the same effect, even offering to waive his superiority of rank and serve under Lafayette's orders if he would comply. The French officers argued that the British works at Gloucester and Yorktown were still incomplete, and could be carried by storm. Moreover, Lafayette having driven Cornwallis into his present position, they represented that to him belonged the glory of completing the capture. No portion of Lafayette's conduct during his American campaigns was more creditable than his resolute resistance to this great temptation and his successful opposition to the wishes of the French. He replied that immediate attack must result in great loss of life, — a calamity which would be averted by awaiting the arrival of the Northern army, and maintained that the honor of giving Cornwallis his *coup de grace* belonged only to Washington.

At this juncture a British fleet under Admiral Graves appeared off the capes. A French squadron under De Barras, loaded with men and artillery for the siege of Yorktown, was expected from Newport, and it was evident that Admiral Graves was waiting to intercept it. De Grasse hastily put out to sea, manœuvred for some days before the British fleet without coming to a decisive action, and managed so well that De Barras slipped securely into the bay. His object attained, De Grasse returned, and the two French fleets took undisputed possession of the waters about Yorktown. Nothing was now wanting but the arrival of Washington.

In August, while Lafayette was watching Cornwallis, Washington perfected his plans. During the preparations for the Southern expedition, ingenious and completely successful efforts were made to deceive Clinton as to the real objective point. The troops were posted and moved as though an attack on New York were imminent. The secret was kept even from the American officers. A curious incident aided the effort at concealment. As soon as Lafayette realized the opportunity presented by Cornwallis's movements, he had written to Washington, pointing out that the British troops in Virginia might now be captured, and begging him to move southward for the purpose. At the same time, Washington wrote to Lafayette in a familiar vein, giving him positive information of his intended attack on New York. The letters crossed each other. Lafayette's reached its destination and accomplished its purpose. But the mail-bag containing Washington's letter was captured by one James Moody, who rendered his cause a poor service by sending it to Clinton, thus confirming the supposed safety of both Yorktown and New York.

The military display which Washington made before New York was such that the besieged thought
only of their own safety. " Humiliating as it may be
and is to confess," wrote Hon. G. Damer, from the
British camp, to Lord George Germain, "yet it is
most true that the apparent force which made us
tremble within our lines and behind our works did not
exceed our own numbers." Even when Washington's
army began to move southward, the British could not
realize what was impending. " Happy that this army
was gone, yet ignorant where it was going," wrote
Damer, "something offensive at length was to be
undertaken on our side, and Rhode Island to be the
object." It was only when they found that Newport
was evacuated, De Barras's fleet gone to join De Grasse
in the Chesapeake, Washington and Rochambeau
half-way through the Jerseys, that they awoke from
what Damer calls their "infatuations" and realized
the danger of their fellow-countrymen in Virginia.
Their mortification was without a remedy. Clinton
could find no way of helping Cornwallis but by sending Benedict Arnold on a ravaging expedition to Connecticut, in the vain hope of diverting Washington's
attention.

Meanwhile all was joyful anticipation in the American army on their southward march. At last Washington was to reap the reward of his tireless exertions,
and to find a solid compensation for the long series of
past discouragements. The Continental troops passed
through Philadelphia on the 2d of September. Many

were ragged ; all were covered thickly with the dust of the march. But their hats were adorned with sprigs of green, and they were greeted with boundless enthusiasm. The French, who followed a day later, halted before entering the city to brush the dust from their brilliant uniforms, and marched through with the military pomp and martial music of Europe.

On the 12th of September, Washington arrived at Mt. Vernon, which he had not seen for six years, and there entertained Rochambeau and other French generals. Two days later he took command of the combined forces at Williamsburg, and on the 17th visited De Grasse on board his ship, where the plans for the siege were concluded. Hardly had he returned to camp when an incident occurred which threatened the success now so confidently anticipated. De Grasse, hearing of the naval reënforcements recently received by the British at New York, thought it his duty to leave the Chesapeake with the greater part of his fleet, and either blockade the enemy or give them battle if they had left port. Washington was alarmed at a proceeding which might imperil the success of all the efforts made for the capture of Cornwallis, and sent Lafayette on board the count's ship with an urgent request that the fleet should remain until the operations at Yorktown were concluded. To the infinite satisfaction of the commander-in-chief, Lafayette succeeded in his mission. The combined armies advanced to within two miles of the British works on the 28th of September, and the siege began.

It was not until the 14th of October that Lafayette had an opportunity for active work. Two redoubts projecting beyond the British lines enfiladed the American intrenchments, and it was determined to take them by storm. One redoubt was confided to Lafayette and his American light infantry, the other to Baron de Viomenil with two French regiments. Before the attack, a lively dispute arose between Lafayette and Viomenil. The latter asserted that his grenadiers were the troops best adapted for the work in hand. Lafayette, who took great pride in regarding himself as an American officer, stoutly maintained the superiority of his men. Thus, when the rockets gave the signal for advance, great emulation prevailed in the two divisions. The American van, gallantly led by Colonel Hamilton, pressed forward over the parapet without waiting for sappers to clear the way, and carried their redoubt in a few minutes at the point of the bayonet. The French troops waited until the sappers had removed the abatis according to rule before they advanced, and thus lost a number of men by the British fire. They were still engaged with their task when a messenger arrived from Lafayette, stating that he was in his redoubt, and would be happy to lend the baron any assistance that he might require. Washington watched the operations with anxiety, and at their conclusion observed to General Knox, "The work is done, and well done."

The two redoubts having been included in the American works, the position of Cornwallis became untenable, and on the 17th of October he opened the negotiations for the surrender. On the 19th the British army marched out as prisoners of war, their colors cased, and drums beating the significant English air, "The world turned topsy-turvy." The French troops were ranged in a line about a mile long on one side of the road, the Americans on the other. Rochambeau and Washington stood at the head of their respective armies. Between these lines the British passed without meeting with one jeering word or look. Cornwallis, worn out with his long-protracted labors, sent his sword by General O'Hara.

The news of the surrender of Yorktown was received throughout the American States with every demonstration of joy. At last the long and distressing war seemed near its close. A swift ship carried the information to France, where it met with enthusiastic delight. Lord George Germain, in whose hands had been chiefly confided the conduct of the American war, received the despatch announcing the capitulation at his house in London. Jumping into his carriage with his secretary, he drove hastily to Lord Stormont's, thence to the chancellor's, and all proceeded together to Lord North's. "The first minister's firmness and even his presence of mind," wrote Wraxall, "gave way for a short time under this awful disaster. I asked Lord George afterwards how he took the communication when made to him. 'As he would have taken a ball in the breast,' replied Lord George, 'for he opened his arms, exclaiming wildly, as he paced up and down the apartment during a few minutes, "O God, it is all over!" words which he repeated many times under emotions of the greatest agitation and distress.' "

Cornwallis invited Lafayette to visit him at his camp after the surrender, and the two generals talked over the incidents of their late campaign. Cornwallis had shown himself an excellent soldier throughout the American war, and he lost no honor in the disaster which finally overtook him. In the siege of Yorktown, Lafayette had naturally played no important part; but in the Virginia campaign, which led up to that decisive event, he had acquitted himself with a credit acknowledged by both friends and enemies. He had entered so unreservedly into the American cause that his foreign birth was forgotten. His kindness and generosity to his men had won their devoted attachment. He had shown the prudence, steadiness, and conciliating temper which Washington had expected of him; and although no great military achievement is due to him, his record is that of an officer who had failed in no duty, and who had accomplished exactly what he had been ordered to perform. That Cornwallis was forced into his position at Yorktown, and that Rochambeau had an army in America ready to coöperate in taking the place are events largely due to the efforts of Lafayette. The 6th of September, when he commanded the allied troops before Yorktown, was his birthday, and it was under such circumstances that he completed his twenty-fourth year.

CHAPTER VII.

Lafayette sails for Europe. — Rejoicings of the French over the Yorktown Victory, and great Popularity of Lafayette. — He assists Franklin and Jefferson at Paris, and Carmichael at Madrid. — Visits America in 1784 and Germany in 1785. — His efforts on behalf of French Protestants, and his Plan to abolish Slavery.

NEARLY two years had passed since Lafayette's last departure from France, and his desire was great to return home for what he supposed would be a brief period. Arriving at Philadelphia from Yorktown in November, he received an unlimited leave of absence. Congress at the same time directed the American ministers in Europe to consult with him on national affairs, and warmly recommended him to the favor of Louis XVI. The people were still rejoicing over the Southern victory, and paid him every attention on his journey to Boston. There the French frigate "l'Alliance" was again placed at his service, and he arrived in France on the 17th of January, 1782.

The triumphant satisfaction felt by the French at the success of their arms in America raised Lafayette's popularity to an extraordinary pitch. His friend Ségur gives a graphic account of the enthusiasm aroused by his return, — a feeling shared even by those who disapproved of the war. The queen was fully alive to the dangers incurred by an arbitrary monarchy in supporting a people rebelling against its king, but even she was carried away by the pride of national success. When Lafayette alighted at the house of the Duke de Noailles, his wife was attending a grand *fête* given at the Hôtel de Ville in honor of the birth of the Dauphin. No sooner had his arrival become known than the queen took Mme. de Lafayette in her own carriage and accompanied her home. From the Minister of War Lafayette received a flattering letter, informing him that he was appointed field-marshal from the date of Cornwallis's surrender. He was soon invited to dine by the Marshal de Richelieu with all the marshals of France, on which occasion the health of Washington was drunk with every honor, as Lafayette proudly wrote to his beloved commander-in-chief. Presented at court by the American Minister, he received the strongest marks of favor. His reception from friends and the public was enough to turn any man's head.

The French, in their joy at their success, were naturally inclined to exaggerate Lafayette's part in procuring it, and in several memoirs of the time we find him mentioned as the " conquerer of Cornwallis," the " saviour of America with Washington," and under other equally absurd names. It is due to Lafayette to say that in his letters and memoirs, as well as in interviews recorded with him, he never lent countenance to such exaggerations. His services had been earnest and fruitful, but he knew that they had been far from indispensable, as French vanity liked to imagine them. The praise and popularity

which he now enjoyed was a distinct misfortune to
him, for it was inevitable that so much flattery should
give him a false idea of his abilities, and should ac-
custom him to looking without instead of within for
approbation.

He enjoyed with all the strength of his affectionate
nature the reunion with his " dear heart" and the
children, whom he found so much grown as to make
him feel quite old.

But his characteristic energy and the foreign affairs
of the colonies soon gave him plenty of business in
the midst of the rest he had earned. It is a testimony to the depth of his interest in America that he
served her as gladly in the obscure work of procuring money and commercial advantages, as he had in
the field where glory was to be won. In March, 1782,
Franklin wrote to Robert R. Livingston : " The Marquis de Lafayette was, at his return hither, received by
all ranks with all possible distinction. He daily gains
in the general esteem and affection, and promises to
be a great man here. He is extremely attached to
our cause ; we are on the most friendly and confiden-
tial footing with each other, and he is really very
serviceable to me in my applications for additional
assistance." Through this year the journals of Franklin and Adams contain constant references to the
labors which Lafayette was sharing with them. There
were long negotiations over the proposed terms of
peace with Messrs. Oswald and Grenville and the
Comte de Vergennes. The discharge of Lord Corn-

wallis from his parole was particularly referred to him, on which occasion Franklin observed, " He appears very prudently cautious of doing anything that may seem assuming a power he is not vested with."

During the summer, Lafayette was in constant expectation of rejoining the army in America. " In spite of all my happiness here," he wrote to Washington, " I cannot help wishing, ten times a day, to be on the other side of the Atlantic." But as the campaign in America promised no activity, Franklin prevailed upon him to remain in Europe where he was of " great use."

The cordiality of Lafayette's relations with the American representatives seems to have been interrupted only on one occasion. Adams records the circumstances in his diary, Nov. 23, 1782 : " Mr. Jay called at ten and went out with me to Passy to meet the Marquis de Lafayette at the invitation of Dr. Franklin. The marquis's business was to show us a letter he had written to the Count de Vergennes on the subject of money. This, I saw, nettled Franklin, as it seemed an attempt to take to himself the merit of obtaining the loan, if one should be procured. He gave us also a letter to us three, for our approbation of his going out with the Count d'Estaing. He recites in it that he had remained here by our advice as necessary to the negotiations. This nettled both Franklin and Jay. I knew nothing of it, not having been there, and they both denied it. This unlimited ambition will obstruct his rise ; he grasps at all, civil, political, and military, and would be thought the *unum necessarium* in everything; he has so much real merit, such family supports, and so much favor at court that he need not recur to artifice." The facts upon which Adams founded this severe arraignment hardly justified so extreme a conclusion, for Adams adds, "He said that Count de Vergennes told him, as the Chevalier de la Luzerne's despatches were not arrived, the count could do nothing in the affair of money without *something French to go upon;* his letter therefore was to supply the something French." Adams's supposition that Franklin denied that Lafayette had remained in France that summer at his request must be mistaken, as we find Franklin writing to Robert R. Livingston on the 25th of June, just the time in question, "The Marquis de Lafayette is of great use in our affairs here, and as the campaign is not likely to be very active in North America, I wish I may be able to prevail with him to stay a few weeks longer." Lafayette's desire to be considered an American officer, subject to the orders of the American government, was undoubtedly the cause of his having mentioned the fact that he had remained at Franklin's request, as it was also the cause of his application to the American representatives for their permission to join the expedition of d'Estaing, then preparing. But, although it is evident that Adams was unjust in the conclusions which he drew in this instance, it is certain that there must have been some justification for his feelings of irritation. Vanity is the Frenchman's weakness, and Lafayette was a thorough Frenchman. The praises of the world, which had been sounding so long and loudly in his ears, were no doubt producing their unhappy· effect and magnifying his importance in his own eyes. This weakness does not seem to have interfered with his usefulness, for a few days after the events recorded by Adams, Franklin wrote to Livingston, "I have been constant in my solicitations (for money) both directly and through the Marquis de Lafayette, who has employed himself diligently and warmly in the business."

As the negotiations for peace were endlessly protracted by the British ministry, the governments of France and Spain agreed upon a combined expedition against the English colonies in America sufficiently powerful to bring the war to a decisive issue. Sixty ships-of-the-line and twenty-four thousand men, under the command of the Count d'Estaing, were to attack Jamaica and then proceed against New York and Canada. Lafayette was appointed chief of staff of the combined army, and embarked at Brest early in December for Cadiz, whence the expedition was to start. He wrote to Washington that he intended to keep his American uniform and the exterior as well as the interior of an American soldier, and that he would watch for the happy moment when he might rejoin "our dear colors."

The great fleet was ready to set sail, when a courier arrived at Cadiz with the news that a general treaty of peace had just been signed at Paris. Lafayette immediately begged a vessel from the Count d'Estaing, which he despatched to America with the happy news. The vessel was appropriately selected because of its name, the "Triumph"; it reached Philadelphia at the end of March, bearing the first information of the treaty.

By the "Triumph," Lafayette wrote to Washington in terms of the warmest congratulation. " As for you, my dear general, who can truly say that all this is your work, what must be the feelings of your good and virtuous heart in this happy moment ! The eternal honor in which my descendants will glory," he continued, " will be to have had an ancestor among your soldiers, to know that he had the good fortune of being a friend of your heart; and I bequeath to the eldest among them, as long as my posterity shall endure, the favor that you have conferred upon my son George, by allowing him to bear your name."

Lafayette was well satisfied with such a termination to the great expedition, for, as he wrote to Vergennes, " My great affair is settled; America is sure of her independence; humanity has gained its cause, and liberty will never be without a refuge." Leaving Cadiz for Madrid, he found American affairs there in a very discouraging condition. Disgusted with Spanish procrastination and jealousy, Jay had left the country. His secretary, Carmichael, remained as *chargé d'affaires*, but had been unable to obtain any official recognition. Lafayette's pride as an American officer was wounded at the marked neglect of Carmichael, and he took steps in his energetic way to place matters on a better footing. As a prominent officer in the late expedition, he was well received by the king; and subsequently, in an interview with the minister, Florida-Blanca, he took a very high tone on the subject of America, declaring finally that if, on the next Saturday, ambassadors' day at court, Carmichael were not officially presented as the *chargé d'affaires* of the United States, he would take him out of the country, and it would be long before Madrid would see another American envoy. After some parleying, the minister yielded, and Lafayette himself accompanied Carmichael to court, and saw him properly presented.

The year 1783 was passed chiefly at Paris, with occasional visits to his estates in Auvergne. American affairs were not neglected, as is shown by his voluminous correspondence with Vergennes, with Washington and other friends in America. Among these was the duty of caring for the foreign interests of the Society of Cincinnatus. Horace Walpole gives an amusing account of the reception of the new order in Paris. *Diable St. Sénatus, voilà un plaisant saint! Qui est-ce qui en a jamais entendu parler?* With such questions the name was greeted, and the *dévotes*, says Walpole, finding no such apostle in their books, were very angry with Washington for encroaching on the pope's prerogative of creating peers of the upper house. The strong opposition made to the society at home was supported by many Americans in Paris. Lafayette says that Jay, Adams, and others blamed the army severely. Franklin, as might have been expected, said little. Lafayette's special business was to determine the claims of the French officers to membership, and to distribute the crosses among those who had a right to them. As these were ardently desired and persistently applied for, he found his duties far from easy.

On his return to France after the surrender of Yorktown, Lafayette had expected his absence to be very short, and, as we have seen, he had watched for the moment when he might rejoin "his dear colors." The general peace gave him an opportunity to revisit the country under very different circumstances. Washington had sent a pressing invitation to Mme. de Lafayette to accompany her husband and "taste the simplicity of rural life." The marquise found this impossible, but sent a letter from herself, and one from her little daughter, born while her husband was sharing the hardships of Valley Forge. The visit to America in 1784 is the first of those remarkable passages in Lafayette's life in which he marched through applauding crowds as a standard-bearer of civil liberty.

Leaving Havre the 1st of July, he arrived in New York, which he had never yet seen, on the 4th of August. His course lay through Philadelphia to Mt. Vernon, where he passed two weeks of great happiness with Washington. Thence, proceeding northward, he visited the principal cities as far as Albany, where he attended a conference with the Indians.

From Albany he travelled through New England as far as Portsmouth, New Hampshire. Returning to Boston, he embarked for Chesapeake Bay, and stopped at Yorktown, Williamsburg, and Richmond. At the latter city he met Washington again by appointment, and in his company revisited some of the scenes of the war. Thence he proceeded to Trenton, New Jersey, where he resigned his commission and took his leave of Congress. He sailed from New York for France on the "Nymphe" frigate, Christmas-day, 1784.

Throughout this long journey, his reception was a continual ovation. In every city, dinners, balls, and public gatherings in his honor took place, with the usual accompaniments of complimentary addresses and responses. The honors paid to him were justified on the one side and deserved on the other. The people of the United States celebrated their own hard-earned success in the attentions they paid to one who had worked so disinterestedly for their cause. On the other hand, Lafayette deserved the gratitude of which he was receiving such extraordinary testimony. In a dark hour of the American cause, he, a foreigner, had left wife, friends, fortune, and all the luxuries of aristocratic existence, to fight for the people among whom he now stood. He had risked his life and reputation in their struggle; he had cheerfully spent his energies and money in it; he had adopted their interests as his own, sharing their hardships with perfect patience, and thinking no sacrifice of consequence which could diminish them. He had indentified himself so thoroughly with the American people that in the operations of the war calling for the combined action of native and French troops, he had spared no excrtion to advance the honor of American soldiers. In Europe he had proudly borne testimony to American character and institutions, resenting any aspersions as a personal affront. In his military campaigns he had been a faithful and meritorious officer, doing his duty with bravery and discretion wherever placed by the orders of his superiors. His services in procuring money and troops from France are not to be exaggerated, and these are the most material advantages due to his efforts. But the presence of Lafayette in America in 1784, and the memory of his name since that time, have awakened feelings of enthusiasm and gratitude which are due to other sources than calculations of value received. The noble enthusiasm with which he first espoused their cause, and the unselfish devotion which he brought to it, will always meet with responsive affection in the hearts of Americans.

The newspapers of the time are filled with accounts of the festivities enjoyed and the speeches made during this journey, but only a few incidents can be alluded to here. An impressive scene occurred at Trenton, when Lafayette resigned his commission in the army, and Congress sent a committee composed of one representative from each State to express their thanks.

The visit to the Indian council at Fort Schuyler, in company with James Madison, Oliver Wolcott, and others was extremely interesting to Lafayette, and he often recurred to it with pleasure in after years. The Indian chiefs made long speeches in their peculiar vein to their "father Kayoula," and Kayoula made appropriate remarks in return, beseeching his "children" to live in peace with his good American allies. After parting with Lafayette, Madison wrote an account of this Indian visit to Jefferson. "The time I have passed with the marquis," he says, "has given me a pretty thorough insight into his character. With great natural frankness of temper, he unites much address and very considerable talents. In his politics, he says his three hobby-horses are the alliance between France and the United States, the union of the latter, and the manumission of slaves." In a later letter, Madison says that he had still further opportunities of penetrating the marquis's character. "Though his foibles did not disappear, all the favorable traits presented themselves in a stronger light on closer inspection. He certainly possesses talents which might figure in any line. If he is ambitious, it is rather of the praise which virtue dedicates to merit, than of the homage which fear renders to power. His disposition is naturally warm and affectionate, and his attachment to the United States unquestionable. Unless I am grossly deceived, you will find his zeal sincere and useful whenever it can be employed on behalf of the

United States without opposition to the essential interests of France."

The sincere cordiality and friendship which had
existed between Lafayette and his American fellow-
officers during the war were strengthened by this visit,
and should be mentioned to his credit. The arrival
of so many foreigners expecting appointments in the
army had naturally awakened great jealousy among
the native officers. Lafayette's disinterestedness had
been such as to awaken no animosities against himself.
It had been much more difficult for him to remain on
good terms with his fellow-countrymen in America.
They all came with extravagant expectations, and the
difficulty of satisfying even the most deserving among
them was a constant trial to Washington, who, as we
have seen, devoutly wished that no foreigners at all
had come except the Marquis de Lafayette.

Baron de Kalb complained constantly in his correspondence of the petty bickerings and mutual
jealousies of the French officers. "The people think
of nothing but their incessant intrigues and back-
bitings. They hate each other like the bitterest enemies, and endeavor to injure each other whenever an
opportunity offers. I have given up their society, and
very seldom see them. Lafayette is the sole exception ; I always meet him with the same cordiality and
the same pleasure." These remarks apply, of course,
to the officers who came out early in the war to enlist
in the American service, and not at all to those who
came with Rochambeau at a later time. From all

these troubles, Lafayette had succeeded in keeping himself free. His conduct toward Kalb had been such that when the two friends parted forever in 1779, on the marquis's return to France, the older officer wrote to his wife to " receive him kindly and courteously, and thank him for the numerous proofs of regard he has extended to me since the beginning of our friendship. I shall thank him as long as I live, and value and esteem him most highly."

It is not to be supposed that much sympathy could have existed between the adventurous young Frenchman and Baron Steuben, the methodical old German soldier. Steuben naturally felt aggrieved that the command of the army in Virginia in 1781 should have been given to Lafayette rather than to himself. But he could not say that his successful rival had not treated him with every consideration at that time. Steuben's stern military discipline and somewhat domineering ways acquired in European armies made him unpopular with the hot-headed Virginia gentlemen, and Washington considered that the country's interests could be more safely confided to Lafayette's " conciliating temper." Lafayette preserved no feeling but kindness for his old fellow-officer, as is shown by a letter to General Knox written in 1786, after his return from the visit in Germany. " Baron de Steuben was often mentioned to me, and while I had the opportunity to do justice to his services among us, I was happy to know he was esteemed in his own country as he deserves. His family made inquiries about him to me, and I felt a sincere pleasure in letting them know that he was well and much respected in America."

The success with which Lafayette acquired the friendship of both American and foreign officers was due to the unselfish devotion which animated him, and which made personal sacrifices for the cause seem easy. Kalb was an excellent officer, but even he found it difficult to bear the hardships of the war with patience. Writing from Valley Forge to the Comte de Broglie, he gave a sad picture of the poverty and sufferings of the army. " Everything here," he said, " combines to inspire disgust. At the smallest sign from you I shall return home." But the misery of Valley Forge never abated one jot of Lafayette's enthusiasm. The privations which he saw and shared only made him put his hand the more often into his own pocket, and redouble his efforts to obtain aid from the treasury of France.

To Lafayette, the happiest portion of this voyage to America was the time passed in the company of Washington. Hastening from New York immediately on his arrival, he allowed himself to be delayed only at Philadelphia. " There is no rest for me," he wrote thence to Washington, " until I go to Mt. Vernon. I long for the pleasure to embrace you, my dear general ; in a few days I shall be at Mt. Vernon, and I do already feel delighted with so charming a prospect." Two weeks of a proud pleasure were then passed in the society of the man who was always to remain his beau ideal. To walk about the beautiful grounds of Mt. Vernon with its honored master, discussing his agricultural plans; to sit with him in his library, and listen to his hopes regarding the new nation for which he had done so much, were honors which Lafayette fully appreciated. He has left on record the feelings of admiration with which he saw the man who had so long led a great people in a great struggle retire to private life, with no thought other than satisfaction at duty performed. And it was a legitimate source of pride to himself that he had enlisted under his standard before fortune had smiled upon it, and had worked with all his heart to crown it with victory. The two men thoroughly knew each other. That Lafayette's admiration was founded on no blind enthusiasm, that he appreciated the sterling character and perfect mental balance where lay Washington's greatness, is apparent everywhere in the records he has left, and notably in these few words: "As a private soldier, he would have been the bravest; as an obscure citizen, all his neighbors would have respected him. With a heart as just as his mind, he always judged himself as he judged circumstances. In creating him expressly for this revolution, Nature did honor to herself; and to show the perfection of her work, she placed him in such a position that each quality must have failed, had it not been sustained by all the others."

On his part, Washington had penetrated from the first the character of the young man who had brought his enthusiasm and his sword across the Atlantic to fight at his side. He had pointed out to him the dangers of enthusiasm indulged without a calm consideration of the worth and practicability of its object. " Look before you leap " had been, and was to be, the burden of his wise counsel. But the noble spirit of philanthropy, of unselfishness, which animated his young *protég* , his unassailable purity of character, had from the first pointed him out to Washington as the foreigner most worthy of his confidence and best adapted to aid him in his work. He responded to Lafayette's demonstrative regard by a sincere paternal affection.

Later in the summer, Lafayette met Washington again, and visited in his company some of the scenes of the late war. When the time for parting had come, Washington accompanied his guest as far as Annapolis in his carriage. There the two friends separated, not to meet again. On his return to Mt. Vernon, Washington added to his words of farewell a letter in which occur the following passages : " In the moment of our separation, upon the road as I travelled, and every hour since, I have felt all that love, respect, and attachment for you, with which length of years, close connection, and your merits have inspired me. I often asked myself, as our carriages separated, whether that was the last sight I ever should have of you. And though I wished to say no, my fears answered yes. I called to mind the days of my youth, and found they had long since fled, to return no more ; that I was now descending the hill I had been fifty-two years climbing, and that, though I was blest with a good constitution, I was of a short-lived family, and might soon expect to be entombed in the mansion of my fathers. These thoughts darkened the shades and gave a gloom to the picture, and consequently to my prospect of seeing you again. But I will not repine ; I have had my day. . . . It is unnecessary, I persuade myself, to repeat to you, my dear marquis, the sincerity of my regards and friendship ; nor have I words which could express my affection for you, were I to attempt it. My fervent prayers are offered for your safe and pleasant passage, happy meeting with Madame de Lafayette and family, and the completion of every wish of your heart." To these words Lafayette replied from on board the "Nymphe," on the eve of his departure for France : "Adieu, adieu, my dear general. It is with inexpressible pain that I feel I am going to be severed from you by the Atlantic. Everything that admiration, respect, gratitude, friendship, and filial love can inspire is combined in my affectionate heart to devote me most tenderly to you. In your friendship I find a delight which words cannot express. Adieu, my dear general. It is not without emotion that I write this word, although I know I shall soon visit you again. Be attentive to your health. Let me hear from you every month. Adieu, adieu."

The visit of Lafayette to America was supplemented in the following summer of 1785 by a journey through

Germany and Austria, an experience which could not fail to add much to his knowledge of the world and to deepen the convictions which were to control his after-life. He travelled under great advantages : on the one hand as a French field-marshal, with powerful connections at court; on the other as a sort of representative of America, the friend of Washington, who could answer the questions about the unknown country which all the world was eager to ask.

At Cassel he met the Hessian officers who had served in America, among them " Old Knyp," and the reminiscences exchanged were very agreeable, particularly so, Lafayette thought, to the successful side. At Brunswick he passed some time with the great military duke who was destined to lead the German forces against revolutionary France in 1792, and to issue the famous manifesto of that time. He went to Potsdam to pay his court to Frederick the Great, of whom he wrote an interesting description to Washington : " In spite of all that I had heard of him, I could not help being struck by a costume and figure which suggested an old, decrepit, and dirty corporal, covered with Spanish tobacco, his head almost resting on one shoulder and his fingers almost disjointed by the gout. But what surprised me much more was the fire, and sometimes the softness, of the most beautiful eyes that I have ever seen, which gives to his face an expression as charming as it can be harsh and threatening at the head of an army. During eight days, I passed three hours every day at his dinner-table; the conversation was chiefly between the Duke of York, the king, and myself, sometimes two or three others, which gave me an opportunity to hear him at my ease, and to admire the vivacity of his mind, the winning charm of his grace and kindness; so that I understood how people can, in his presence, forget his despotic, selfish, and harsh character."

Visiting at Potsdam, at the same time, were the Duke of York and Lord Cornwallis. The king placed Lafayette between them at table, and chose this curious opportunity to put to him many questions about America. Cornwallis wrote to a friend in England, " Lafayette and I were the best friends possible in Silesia ; " and again, " My reception in Silesia was not flattering ; there was a most marked preference for Lafayette ; whether it proceeded from the king's knowing more of France and liking better to talk about it, I know not." [2]

Lafayette wrote to Washington of the pleasure he experienced in seeing the reviews of the Prussian armies, and expressed the greatest admiration for the discipline, perfect training and equipment, which he sadly contrasted with the condition of the French service. German armies, as he saw them then, seem to have had the same characteristics which mark them at present ; but at the death of Frederick, a lack of great leaders made

---

[1] Translated from the letter to Washington given in French in the Memoirs.

[2] Cornwallis to Ross, Sept. 9 and Oct. 5, 1785.

their natural military qualities ineffectual. To General Knox, Lafayette wrote of the Prussian military establishment in the same strain of admiration, but he added, "The mode of recruiting is despotic; there is hardly any provision for old soldiers, and although I found much to admire, I had rather be the last farmer in America than the first general in Berlin." From Prussia, Lafayette went to Vienna, where he had a long interview with the emperor on the subject of America. In the course of his travels he examined a number of battle-fields with a view to adding to his military education. Many distinguished officers were met. At one camp, as he wrote to Washington, he found Lord Cornwallis, Colonels England, Abercrombie, and Musgrave; "on our side," Colonel Smith, Generals Duportail and Gouvion; "and we often remarked, Smith and I, that if we had been unfortunate in our struggle, we would have cut a poor figure there."

The most interesting feature of these travels relates to the constant conversations on the subject of America, — conversations in which Lafayette needed all his enthusiastic admiration for the country. Everywhere he heard nothing but compliments for the abilities and character of Washington, and the subject of America was generally introduced by praise of him. Lafayette says that all "who counted the rights of man for something" were enthusiastic for American principles. But these must have been very few, and his endless, indeed bootless, task was the attempt to explain the real character of the people, and to refute

the universal belief that they must soon return to the
good old system of government by kings and nobles.
The United States at this time were united little more
than in name; they did not yet present a solid front
to the world; their Congress had no power; public
debts remained unpaid, and evidences of national
weakness were everywhere apparent. These circumstances, placed in the worst light by English journals
and ambassadors, created a general disbelief in the
stability of the Union and in the continuance of a
republican form of government, not to be wondered at
among men who had no confidence in republican institutions under any circumstances, and no knowledge
of the peculiar conditions of American life which
made such a government the only one possible.

To his own mortification, Lafayette was unable to
deny the want of union and the incapacity of a Congress without adequate powers, which lent color to
foreign aspersions. These subjects had often been
matter of conversation with Washington, and Lafayette
frequently called the attention of his American corre-
spondents to them. We, who can look back on the
events of that time with the advantage of perspective,
can realize that circumstances that then seemed deplorable contained a hidden virtue. Internal differences, vexatious delays, gave time for mature reflection
and general agreement. No step was taken in haste,
none was taken backward. Where a people is to
decide its own future, it can hardly proceed too
slowly. Patient and laborious deliberation placed

American liberties on a sure foundation of law. Hasty enthusiasm was to substitute for French despotism a bloody anarchy. The efforts of Lafayette, during these travels, to place the United States in the best light are to be counted among his services. But the benefit which he himself derived cannot be said to have been equal to his opportunities. The reputation for republicanism which he had already was much increased by the freedom with which he praised America, and this reputation was far from turning to his advantage. Civil liberty was becoming with every year more and more his ruling thought, — the passion of his life. But did he sufficiently appreciate the real nature of civil liberty, its dependence for good on the character of the people destined to enjoy it? In reply, it must be said that nowhere in the records of his voyages in Europe do we find any observations on the people at large, showing that the question of their *fitness* for liberty had arisen in his mind.

Lafayette returned to Paris in the autumn of 1785. He had now no public duties, but his characteristic energy and philanthropy soon opened new avenues for employment. Two years before, he had written to Washington of his desire to find some means of procuring the emancipation of slaves. Then and afterwards Washington had expressed his sympathy with the project, together with his despair at seeing any change. In 1786, Lafayette wrote to Adams, " Whatever be the complexion of the enslaved, it does not, in my opinion, alter the complexion of the crime the enslaver commits, — a crime much blacker than any African face. It is to me a matter of great anxiety and concern to find that this trade is sometimes perpetrated under the flag of liberty, our dear and noble stripes to which virtue and glory have been constant standard-bearers." He now purchased a plantation in Cayenne, well stocked with negroes, for whom he provided suitable means of instruction. When sufficiently educated, and competent to care for themselves, they were to receive their freedom. A large sum of money was spent on this scheme, intended to be an example on a small scale of what governments might do on a large one. But the Revolution put an end to that, as to so much else.

At the same time, Lafayette was occupied with efforts to improve the miserable condition of the French Protestants. Unable to contract a marriage or make a will valid before the law, persecuted at the whim of the Church, a large number of the best subjects of the French crown were forced to choose between exile and intolerable suffering. Lafayette visited surreptitiously the cities of France where the Protestants chiefly lived, consulted with some of the principal preachers, and afterwards pleaded their unpopular cause at Versailles.

Meanwhile, he was not idle in American affairs. Jefferson was now the minister representing the United States. "The Marquis de Lafayette is a most valuable auxiliary to me," he wrote to Washington. "His zeal is unbounded, and his weight with

those in power great. His education having been
merely military, commerce was an unknown field to
him. But his good sense enabling him to compre-
hend perfectly whatever is explained to him, his
agency has been very efficacious. He has a great
deal of sound genius, is well remarked by the king,
and rising in popularity. He has nothing against
him but the suspicion of republican principles. I
think he will one day be of the ministry. His foible
is a canine appetite for popularity and fame ; but he
will get above this." The business in which Lafayette was now assisting Jefferson concerned the pro-
saic subjects of oil and tobacco. But they were very
important to America. The inhabitants of Nantucket,
" penetrated with gratitude " at the privileges he had
obtained for their whaling industry, assembled in
town-meeting and voted that each man should contribute the milk afforded by his cow during the period
of twenty-four hours ; that the whole quantity thus
obtained should be made into a cheese weighing five
hundred pounds, and " should be transmitted to the
Marquis de Lafayette, as a feeble, but not less sincere,
testimonial of their affection and gratitude." The
State of Virginia chose a more artistic method of
testifying her appreciation. Two busts of the marquis were executed by Houdon, one of which was
placed in the State Capitol and the other presented
to the city of Paris. The latter received a prominent
position in the Hotel de Ville, which it was not
destined to occupy long.

Events were now preparing in France which necessarily confined Lafayette's attention to his own country. But the cause of America never ceased to be his. " He combats for us," wrote Jefferson to Adams in 1788, " with the zeal of a native." When the national bankruptcy of France called angry attention to the non-payment of the interest on the sums loaned to the United States, he wrote to John Jay in terms which may be allowed to close that part of his biography which deals with the American Revolution. " I cannot express to you, my dear sir, the nature of my feelings, when, in the examination of the public accounts, the non-payment of the interest on the American debt has been discussed. May the convention be the happy period of energetic and patriotic Federal measures ! May the friends of America rejoice ! May her enemies be humiliated and her traducers reduced to silence by the news of her noble efforts to persevere in those principles which have placed her so high in the annals of history and among the nations of the earth ! "

CHAPTER VIII.

State of France before the Revolution. — Character of Lafayette. — The Assembly of the Notables. — Lafayette demands the Convocation of the States-General.

THE greatest convulsion of modern times was now preparing in France. To understand the leading part that Lafayette was destined to perform, it will be necessary to consider briefly the condition of the country and the influences which had been at work on Lafayette's mind.

France was still governed in accordance with ancient forms, which had been appropriate enough in the Middle Ages, but which every other country had modified to meet the necessities of advancing civilization. Now, the people of Europe, which boasted itself the most intelligent and polite, were groaning under a system of government no less than barbarous. The common people were reduced to the lowest ebb of misery, the treasury had reached the verge of bankruptcy. Starvation and ignorance pervaded the agricultural districts. The professional and trading classes were hampered by unjust laws and-prejudices. The nobility were idle, useless, and extravagant. The Church had almost lost her influence for good. The crown, in theory absolute, was practically powerless.

Only the most salient causes of this demoralization

can be touched upon here. In the French Revolution there were arrayed against each other the privileged and the unprivileged. The distinction between these two classes had been recognized in France since the Middle Ages, and for a long period had been a useful element in local government. The feudal rights and privileges of the nobility, which had come to weigh so intolerably on the people in the eighteenth century, had once their justification. The armed noble in his stone castle protected his poorer neighbors from foreign incursions and from the ravages of wild animals. In return, he exacted services and payments of various kinds which represented rent and taxes. Under such circumstances the noble was a useful member of his community, performing his well-defined duties and receiving his remuneration. In the history of England the noble played a similar part. But then came a divergence in the conduct of the English and the French nobility which permanently affected the history of their respective countries. In both England and France the crown ceaselessly endeavored to increase its power and to centre all government in itself. To this effort on the part of their sovereigns the English nobility opposed a steady and obstinate resistance. For centuries they repelled successive attacks on their rights, and in preserving their own liberties they preserved also those of the people at large. They continued to live on their estates in the midst of their tenants and less powerful neighbors, dispensing justice and charity; the natural leaders of their own communities, they were useful as a class, and therefore as a class excited no hatred.

But in France the victory had lain with the crown. Gradually the French nobility suffered their rights to be taken from them, till all power became centred in the sovereign, and Louis XIV. could sum up the constitution of France in his famous phrase, " *L'État c'est moi.*" With the progress of time, the crown took upon itself the duties hitherto performed by the nobility. It assumed the administration of local affairs, and levied taxes accordingly. But to allay the discontent of the noble at the loss of his influence, it allowed him to retain his emoluments. He no longer protected his neighbors, but still exacted the payments which formerly had been cheerfully granted in consideration of such protection. The peasant was then taxed twice over. As government became more and more centralized, the noble found himself idle on his estates. While the English landowner, honorably occupied with local affairs, lived by preference in the country, the Frenchman found himself without influence or occupation. Taking up his residence in Paris, he left his tenants to all the evils of absenteeism. The duty of keeping his neighborhood free from wild animals became an exclusive right to enjoy the pleasures of the chase, and game-laws of extreme severity were enacted. The peasant could not weed his garden during the most important part of the year lest the game-birds be disturbed. He saw his crops eaten by deer, but the sternest penalties forbade him to drive them away.

The crown not only took from the noble the occupations which make a country life desirable, but tempted him in other ways to live in Paris. He was taught that his first duty was personal attendance on his sovereign ; that to be near him, a constant member of the court, was his appropriate occupation and pleasure. Promotions, offices, and favors were given only to the regular attendant at court. The *gentil-homme* who lived on his estates, caring for his own interests and those of his tenants, was soon made to understand that such conduct indicated only disrespect for his sovereign. For him there was no favor ; for his son no commission in the army, no dignity in the Church. The system was carried out until the ordinary punishment of an offending nobleman was to be banished to his estates. If Louis XIV. or Louis XV. noticed the absence of a courtier, he was greeted on his return with, "Where have you been?" The offence of absence from the fountain of favor and pleasure could only be excused when caused by necessity, and treated as a misfortune. A misfortune it soon became in reality, for the *gentilhomme* found himself alone in the country, without companionship of his class, — a stranger on his own land.

This centralizing system had its inevitably evil result. At Versailles and Paris were concentrated all the wealth, intelligence, and activity of the nation. There were expended by king and court nearly all the taxes raised from the people at large. There the nobles and Church dignitaries lavished in luxurious living their rents and pensions. The whole of France was exhausted to support the splendor of Paris and Versailles. Almost nothing returned to the country in wages or improvements. Thus, as Paris grew in magnificence, the provinces fell into decay. As there arose at the centre the most splendid and numerous court, surrounded by the most polished and cultivated society of Europe, the traveller who journeyed through the rural districts saw all the signs of retro-gression, starvation, misery, — a constantly decreasing population buried in the deepest ignorance, and grow-ing with every year more like the beasts of the field. The rents and dues which the peasant owed his lord were collected by an agent who had only his employer to satisfy, and who showed no mercy to the unfortu-nate. Many a nobleman in Paris was cursed in his province for deeds done in his name which he him-self would have regarded with horror.

Hated, therefore, in the country for his exactions and neglect, the noble passed his time in seeking favor at court or in the pleasures of the town. Many years before the Revolution he had become a purely ornamental person, justly boasting himself more pol-ished in manners, more splendid in dress, and more cultivated in mind than any of his class in Europe. The social life which he created and brought to per-fection remains the most polite and agreeable which the world has ever seen. To that end all his abilities

and efforts were directed.   In man or woman, statesman or soldier, amiability was considered the first of
qualities.   The aristocratic writers of memoirs of
these times, in their judgments of individuals, almost
invariably apply the test of personal amiability.   Be-
senval had met Calonne at a supper-party, and found
it very difficult to believe that a gentleman of such
agreeable manners and conversation could make a
bad minister of finance.   The habitual silence and
gravity of the young Lafayette were considered radical faults of character by his family.   A serious cast
of mind, a desire to be usefully occupied, were inap-
propriate to a nobleman.   Lafayette's income was
derived from estates in the country; but he was
taught that to occupy an idle place at court was to
be the business of his life; that the charge of his
property was the affair of a hired plebeian.

With the pleasure-seeking and luxurious habits of
life came the usual vices.   Extravagance in dress and
household pomp grew enormously, necessitating ever-
increasing drains on the rent and tax paying public.
The marriage tie became so loose that conjugal fidelity
was only a subject for ridicule.   Personal effort of
every kind diminished, all advance in fortune being
sought from the favor of the sovereign or his mistress.
By this life of pleasure, of inactivity in either politics
or business, the French nobleman had become the
most amiable and the most helpless of men.   Blind
to the coming revolt, powerless to combine with his
fellows against it, he could find safety only in flight.

The higher ranks of the clergy were nobles by birth, and shared the habits of their class. They absorbed in their enormous incomes the greater part of the revenues of the Church. Despising the ordinary priests, they were hated in return. The country priest lived as miserably as the peasant in his charge, and like him, could not always avoid starvation. The bishop, in his palace, led a purely secular life. He differed from the lay noble in no respect save that of marriage. His expenditure was not less lavish nor his morals less loose. He, too, was paid great sums for services which he did not perform, and the sight of his idle luxury and open profligacy did more to bring about the destruction of religion than any atheistical writings. The *salons* of Paris were filled with dissolute *abbés*, who made no pretence of any religious belief, and never thought of their position in the Church except as a source of income.

Thus, neither the secular nor the religious nobility was in a position to control the convulsions in preparation. Although they apparently profited by the prevalent abuses, they were far from being satisfied with their position of political subordination. Indeed, it was in the higher ranks of society that the Revolution began. There the new and startling doctrines put forward by Voltaire and Rousseau found enthusiastic disciples. The *salons* of Paris had echoed for many years with words which were meaningless if not revolutionary. The flattering reception of Franklin and the adoption of the American cause showed how great had been the advance of liberal ideas. The reports brought home by French officers concerning the free institutions of America seemed a realization of the theories which occupied every active mind. Ségur speaks of his astonishment at hearing, in the theatre of the palace at Versailles, the whole court applauding Voltaire's tragedy of Brutus, and especially the lines, —

> Je suis fils de Brutus, et je porte en mon cœur
> La liberté gravée et les rois en horreur.

While the most despotic sovereign in Europe was lending aid to the rebellious subjects of a brother monarch, his own courtiers were making liberty and free institutions their favorite topics of conversation. The fashionable society of Paris and Versailles were only partly in earnest. The feeling was almost universal that a change must come, that the old order was outgrown ; but what particular reforms were desirable, who should make the necessary sacrifices, were questions left undecided. Among the higher ranks the new speculations were philanthropic theories, — general propositions relating to the good of man in the abstract, a pleasant occupation for idle minds. But meanwhile the people were reaching a point of suffering beyond which they would not be forced, and the new ideas which were sifting down to them were in their minds continually taking a more terribly practical form.

At the head of the privileged classes of France stood the king, whose privileges transcended all others. He was not only an absolute ruler, at once the maker and administrator of laws, — France was his ; the property of its inhabitants was his ; the movements, occupations, and speech of all Frenchmen were subject to his control. If he wasted the revenues, he was no more to blame than any other spendthrift. There was no distinction between the sums collected for his private expenditure and those intended for public objects. It was all his individual income. Part he was pleased to expend for the government of his kingdom, and part for the maintenance of his household. If he chose to lavish great sums, needed for public objects, on favorites, festivals, and palaces, it was solely his affair. France was his estate, and he could do what he willed with his own.

Louis XIV. had completed the centralization of power in the crown. He had reduced the nobility to idleness, and had handed over their duties to royal officers called intendants. But the administration of the great French monarchy was manifestly beyond the ability of any individual, and was necessarily shifted upon the shoulders of others than the king. Louis XIV., indeed, took a part upon himself. But his chief business, and the only one of Louis XV. and Louis XVI., was to be the centre and chief ornament of the most brilliant court in Europe. When the extent, the splendor, and the formalities of this court are considered, it is evident that he who presided over it could know little, and accomplish little, beyond its limits. Frederick the Great was an absolute sovereign, but he worked from daybreak till night, attending personally to all public affairs, from a new law to the petition of a peasant. His court was regulated with strict economy, and the public revenues were devoted to public uses. But the king of France had no time for such occupations. The levee, the reception, the dinner in public, the infinite number of court cere- monies, left him only time for hunting. When the king did not hunt, it was said at court, "*Le roi ne fait rien.*" As the public revenues were his own, he gave away vast sums without compunction to his courtiers. With the resources of France to draw upon, no object was too trivial, no caprice too temporary, for the most lavish expense. A favorite courtier would ask for a few thousand livres to pay his most urgent debts. What is such a paltry sum to the king? The minister of finance might observe that it was the tax of three villages already groaning under excessive exactions. But the courtier would get his money; for it was easy to sign an order on the treasury, and the king knew nothing about the three villages. At the end of the long and shameful reign of Louis XV. the kingdom was practically bankrupt.

Louis XVI. brought to the throne a sincere sense of duty and the warmest wishes for the happiness of his subjects; but he was incapable of doing any substantial good. The traditions among which he grew up designated as the proper occupations of the

king of France the maintenance of his court and
the amusements of the chase. He had received no
political education ; he had only a vague idea of how
affairs were carried on, and he was entirely ignorant
of the real condition of his subjects. Every reform
proposed met with his ready acceptance. He was
always willing to sacrifice his own privileges for the
benefit of the country. But surrounding influences,
as well as his own weak character, prevented the actual accomplishment of reforms. When Turgot and
Malesherbes, his two best ministers, were instituting
changes of incalculable value, he was too weak, politi-
cally as well as personally, to support them against the
selfish opposition of the privileged classes.

France was governed by the king's ministers, and
the most powerful influences were against a wise
selection of these. There was no legislative body in
which men could be trained to government, or in
which they could show a natural aptitude for it.
Louis XV. allowed his mistress to choose for him.
Louis XVI. was obliged to make his choice among
the nobles who were most assiduous at court, or their
friends. When such statesmen as Turgot, Malesherbes, or Vergennes were appointed, there was no
support strong enough to keep them in office against
the influence of those whose abuses they attempted
to reform. The king was usually obliged to name the
man most urged upon him, and that man was the one
who would gratify most shamelessly the demands of
his supporters at the expense of the nation.

The ministers were often unaccustomed to business, and were obliged in their turn to act by proxy. Thus, the most important function of government, the collection of the taxes, was farmed out to private individuals, who, on condition of turning into the treasury a fixed sum yearly, were permitted to pocket the balance of what they collected. This system, while yielding to the government a comparatively small portion of the total amount taken from the people, encouraged the farmers of the taxes to use the most cruel means to extort as much as possible from the miserable inhabitants. The tax-payers were robbed, while the treasury continued empty. The taxes were of so vexatious and short-sighted a character, and were levied with such remorseless severity, that in whole provinces the inhabitants were reduced to the verge of starvation, and no man would exert himself to accumulate property which could only escape confiscation by being buried in the ground.

During the reign of Louis XIV., a strong feeling of loyalty pervaded the people ; and although great suffering existed, the fault was laid upon the monarchical system. The habit of loyalty and submission carried France through the ignoble reign of Louis XV. without open revolt. But the long-accumulated series of abuses, the antiquated forms of tyranny, the excessive load of unfair taxation, could not be borne by a people who had become so advanced in intelligence and so conscious of their wrongs as the French under Louis XVI. The rottenness of the old system was sufficiently shown by the total collapse which followed the first attacks of the Revolution.

The unprivileged classes included all persons not noble. As the nobles were supposed to represent the ancient conquerors of France, and to stand as a superior race, they habitually looked upon the unprivileged as the descendants of the conquered, having no inherent rights, and existing only on sufferance. But in the eighteenth century had grown up a class of men unthought of in the formation of the old monarchy, and who could not rest under their humiliating inferiority. Wealthy merchants, physicians, lawyers, men of letters, — among them many of the most distinguished of Frenchmen, — found themselves without the smallest political right, treated with haughty contempt or kind condescension by the nobles, and without a voice in the ruinous taxes levied upon them. The despotic authority of the crown was felt in their depleted incomes and in their lack of personal liberty. Their vanity was perpetually wounded by their hopeless social inferiority. They rebelled against a system which forbade the entrance of their carefully educated sons into the army except as privates or into the Church except as curates, condemned in both professions to lifelong drudgery, while the nobles were made officers and bishops in their childhood. In the minds of these wealthy and intelligent men rankled a bitter sense of injustice, which allowed them to be almost willing spectators of the destruction of the throne and the aristocracy.

The shopkeepers in the cities and the small land-owners in the country had grievances quite as serious. The unlimited taxation to which they were subject and the restrictions placed upon their industry heaped wrong upon wrong, until the government became detested and the dangers of revolution less feared than actual sufferings. Descending the social scale, a yet worse condition was to be seen. Such descriptions as we occasionally receive of the Irish peasantry in times of famine may truly represent the chronic state of the laboring classes in many provinces of France as well as in the cities. On account of the exemption from taxation enjoyed by privileged persons, the burden fell chiefly on the peasant and the workman. The wretched peasant might sow his crop, but if game-birds made his field their nesting-place, he could not weed it lest they be disturbed. Deer who came there to feed were protected in their depredations by some of the sternest laws of the kingdom. When the crop, such as it was, had been harvested, a portion belonged to the Church, another to the noble, another went to pay direct taxes to the king, still another in indirect taxes to the king. The peasant was fortunate if one-quarter of his produce were left for the sustenance of his family; in many cases but one-fifth remained. Hence it frequently happened that starvation did its work before the next harvest. Nothing remained to improve the land, which became poorer with every year. Whenever an unusually bad season occurred, famine was universal in the country. In 1739, 1740, 1750, 1751, the deaths from starvation exceeded those in the wars of Louis XIV. In a single month in 1753, thousands died of want in Paris. In the Assembly of the Notables, Lafayette declared that further taxation was impossible; that in his own province of Auvergne the peasantry were abandoning their ploughs, the workmen their shops; that the most industrious citizens, despoiled of their gains, had no choice but beggary or emigration, and that the burdens of the people could not be increased without reducing them to the extremity of misery and despair. Great numbers of peasants, too strong to succumb to want, spread over the country begging and robbing. Many thousands fled every year across the frontier. Marriages in many provinces became of rare occurrence, and the population steadily fell off.

In the cities no individual was wretched enough to escape the tax-gatherer. The scavenger in the streets was hunted down, whipped, and imprisoned to force from him a sum which weeks of labor could hardly earn. These starving multitudes were reasoning beings. Their sufferings were imposed upon them in the name of the king, in the name of the nobles, in the name of the Church. Thus were these three names from generation to generation familiar in their ears as the causes of their endless misery. From father to son they had been starved, beaten, and despised, receiving less attention from the laws than is now accorded to domestic animals. They had been reduced to the level of savage beasts, and as savage beasts they were to turn on their oppressors.

Many of the prevailing causes of discontent had ex-isted in France for a hundred years, but the natural loyalty and submissiveness of the people had carried them through the ruinous wars of Louis XIV. and the scandalous misgovernment of the succeeding reign. But in the time of Louis XVI. the nation had undergone great changes. A weak king occupied the throne. The accumulated abuses and miseries had reached their point of culmination. At the same time the old spirit of passive submission had become supplanted by a sense of injury and the new belief that the governed had intrinsic rights of their own.

Voltaire among the upper classes and Rousseau among the lower were but two of many great writers who taught ideas of government incompatible with the old monarchic principle. That France belonged to the king to do therewith what he pleased was the foun-dation of the old *régime*. The new belief, that France belonged to Frenchmen and should be governed in their interests, penetrated every rank. Liberal ideas, which in France were revolutionary ideas, first found acceptance among the highest classes. The servant who waited at the noble's table overheard that free-dom was the birthright of man, and that all should be equal before the law. In the *salon*, these ideas were discussed as abstract truths, without much thought of their practical consequences. But the same truths, spread among the down-trodden classes and eagerly adopted by them, awaited only an opportunity to become facts. We have seen how widespread the yearning for liberty had become, how intense was the hatred of tyranny, when the American colonies applied to France for assistance and found her people ready to take up enthusiastically a cause of which they knew nothing except that liberty was its object. In the luxury of the court as well as in the misery of the hovel this new word meant emancipation from evils which pressed upon all. How little the word was understood, the events of the Revolution were to show. But now it meant to the nobleman that court favor was not to be the only source of honor, and that the *lettre de cachet* was not to control his movements. It meant to the soldier, that merit would be rewarded by promotion; to the author, that he might write his thoughts without molestation; to the lawyer, that he might practise his profession without fear; to the merchant and shopkeeper, that he would no longer be hampered by a thousand ruinous restrictions; to the peasant, that his family would no longer starve; to the curate, that eloquence and piety might raise him above contempt; to the great body of the unprivileged, relief from the overwhelming burden of taxation, and a recognized political position in their country.

Notwithstanding the growth of intelligence which had made known to the people their wrongs and their rights, such was their habit of submission that the old system might have gone on much longer, or have been gradually modified, had not national bankruptcy brought France face to face with her position. The king could not continue to govern without money, and now there was no money. The history of its finances is the most severe arraignment of the old *régime*. The enormous debts piled up by the waste of his predecessors had left to Louis XVI. an extremely embarrassed treasury. Yet the old extravagance went on. The court continued to be almost equally costly, and the nobility resented, as a national disgrace, that the king's state should be diminished. Turgot warned Louis that the American war would bring bankruptcy. The expense of that war added enough to the debt to make it impossible to pay the interest and to find means to carry on the government. Thus it became necessary to diminish expenses or to levy new taxes. The attempts to do the first was furiously resisted by the privileged classes; the resort to the other alternative brought on the Revolution.

At the end of the year 1786, Calonne, the minister of finance, was obliged to acknowledge the national bankruptcy, and advised the king to call an Assembly of the Notables, which, it was hoped, would find some way of relieving the embarrassment. The Assembly was composed almost exclusively of men belonging to the highest ranks, who felt in the least degree the distresses of the country. It was divided into eight *bureaux*, each one presided over by a prince of the blood, and was purely advisory in character.

Lafayette's republican principles had hitherto been looked upon as youthful vagaries; but as the situation became threatening, a more serious view was taken of them. A portion of the court opposed his membership in the Assembly, but unsuccessfully, as he finally took his seat in the division of the Comte d'Artois. As regards popularity, he had described his position very well in a letter to Washington. "The pit is unanimously in my favor; the boxes are divided." The Empress of Austria was at this time about to make a journey to the Crimea, and invited Lafayette to accompany her, but the importance of the events at home now claimed all his attention.

The meeting of the Notables marks the beginning of the Revolution, and the part that Lafayette took in their deliberations shows the spirit in which he entered on the great struggle. In September, 1787, he became thirty years of age. For so young a man, he had had a great deal of experience. Introduced on the most favorable footing, when only sixteen years old, at the licentious court of Louis XV., he was free to choose his own manner of life. His rank and wealth enabled him to shine at court, or to exhaust the pleasures of Paris. But the serious, ambitious, and elevated bent of his character controlled his actions from the first. The license of the old court was distasteful to one who had just started on a happy married life. The amusements and ceremonies of Marie Antoinette's gay company were much more attractive. But even there he found himself awkward in the minuet, and uninterested in the subjects of conversation. A serious object and an active life were necessary to him. Military matters at first absorbed his attention ; but he soon became deeply imbued with the liberal spirit which was then in the air. He accepted eagerly, and with little reflection, the principles of political freedom which were everywhere discussed. He longed for some philanthropic mission to which he might devote his life. In the Middle Ages he would have been an enthusiastic crusader. But religion, as then practised in France, could only repel an ardent, unselfish nature. It could hardly be said to have existed in Lafayette's environment as a serious subject. Its place was taken by a silly superstition which made a favorite object of social pleasantry.

But Lafayette's mind was naturally adapted to religious feeling. In place of Christianity, he substituted philanthropy. Political freedom, which seemed the greatest blessing which man could enjoy, became with him an article of faith which remained unshaken through all the vicissitudes of his later life. The news of the American war found him ready. To fight for this noble end he gladly left wife, child, and the advantages of rank and wealth. He served the cause with unselfish devotion, and in its success found his chief happiness. In his career, up to the French Revolution, the qualities of the heart more than of the head had been prominent. His natural enthusiasm, generosity, fidelity, and patience had been increased by his experience in America. Leaving a luxurious monarchy, he had been brought into intimate contact with a hard-working, simple people, whose intelligence and perseverance had enabled them to build up a self-governing nation in the wilderness. His admiration had been greatly excited by the results of the free institutions which he had seen. When he contrasted the extremes of luxury and misery which he knew at home with the even distribution of comfort which he saw in America, liberty seemed to him the key to national happiness. Thenceforth liberty became his religion, to be fought for with all the crusader's enthusiasm and a great deal of the crusader's blindness.

To understand the liberty which he had seen practised in Anglo-Saxon countries, Lafayette was too much of a Frenchman, too much of an enthusiast, and too little of a statesman. He failed to see that a great many national characteristics besides freedom made up American prosperity. Liberty can only exist among a self-controlling, conservative people; and to enjoy it, a nation must be gradually educated. Lafayette thought that to give his countrymen liberty was to give them happiness. Their entire unfitness for self-government, so evident to Adams, Morris, and other Americans in France, received little consideration from him. His philanthropy was great, but his judgment untrained. He was fitted to be a popular leader, but not to be a statesman in difficult times. The sufferings of his countrymen enlisted his deepest sympathies, and he longed to assist in alleviating them.

But he lacked the knowledge of human nature, which would have taught him that reforms must be gradual; that nations, like children, should not suddenly be given entire freedom of action.

Personally, Lafayette was well fitted for the part he was to play. Tall and commanding, though somewhat awkward, his dignified bearing and genial manner presented a good appearance in public. His natural good spirits were sustained by an extremely happy domestic life. He had the full sympathy of his beautiful and intelligent wife in all his undertakings. Two daughters and a son were destined to afford him unmingled satisfaction. Among his countrymen he was considered a particularly promising young man, although his political views were already raising up many enemies for him. Morris said that he found him " too republican for the genius of his country." Jefferson thought that it would need all of Lafayette's prudence and that of his friends to make France a safe residence for him. Weaknesses had already shown themselves in his character which were to diminish his usefulness. He attached undue importance to outward honors and public favor. A victory did not seem complete to him unless followed by sufficient applause. That he was inclined to mistake prominence for greatness and praise for fame was largely due to the unfortunately early age at which he had become accustomed to extraordinary popularity. The generosity and enthusiasm of his character blinded him to realities which even a less intelligent man would have perceived. He who had been able to appreciate the characters of Washington and Frederick the Great was easily deceived by shallow or insincere men who approached him with the words "liberty" and "patriotism" on their lips. Only the anarchy and the atrocity of the Revolution could teach him that all men were not kind-hearted patriots like himself.

The Notables had not been called together since the reign of Louis XIII., and in the disquieted state of public feeling their proceedings were watched with intense interest. They formed neither a representative nor a legislative body, and could do little except to agree to reforms proposed by the king. Their intentions were good, and some grievous abuses were corrected with their consent. The *corvée*, or forced labor, was abolished, and the restrictions on commerce in corn were removed. But the great issue before the country they failed to meet, partly through selfishness and partly through incapacity. They investigated the acts of Calonne, exposed his abuses, and drove him from office. But they would not agree to the measures of equal taxation proposed by his successor, Loménie de Brienne. The nation was bankrupt, and only one course could relieve it, — to place on the privileged classes their fair proportion of taxation. The Notables had no authority to do this themselves, but by recommending it they would have done much to strengthen the hands of the government in the only remedial measure possible. They failed to rise to

the importance of the situation, and were soon dis-
solved.

In the deliberations of the Assembly Lafayette took
a prominent part, and placed himself unequivocally
on the side of the people. Some remarks of his
having been reported by the Comte d'Artois to the
king, the latter declared that any one making statements so grave should sign them. Lafayette then
read several addresses to the Assembly which, with his
signature, were sent to the king. In the first of these
he enumerated many instances of waste on the part
of the court in the purchase of useless estates and in
gifts to courtiers, exposing the consequences of such
extravagance in forcible terms. "The millions that
are dissipated are raised by taxation, and taxation can
only be justified by the real needs of the State. All
the millions which are given up to depredation or to
cupidity are the fruit of the sweat, of the tears, and
even of the blood of the people; and a calculation of
the amount of misery caused by the collection of sums
so lightly wasted would seem terrible to the justice
and goodness which we know to be His Majesty's natural sentiments."

After showing the taxable resources of the State to
be exhausted, he enumerated various methods of reducing the expenditure, — methods simple in themselves,
but the neglect of which had ruined the country. He
begged the king to name some fixed sum for his private and military establishment, for the support of the
royal family, and for gifts.

To do away with costly ceremonies no longer valued, and only derived from tradition.

To give to each office a fixed salary, instead of allowing officials certain perquisites which enabled them to extend indefinitely the amount of their remuneration.

To insist on the keeping of regular accounts.

To give pensions and extraordinary gifts only as a recompense for public services.

To abolish the custom of anticipating the revenue.

The reduction of expenses, Lafayette declared, should precede the increase of taxation. The latter course should only be resorted to when all the opportunities for retrenchment had been exhausted. These reductions, he said, might not seem great in comparison to the luxury of the court and the highest classes of society ; "but follow these millions as they are dispersed among the cottages of the country, and we shall see among them the farthing of the widow and the orphan, the last exaction which forces the peasant to quit his plough and a family of honest mechanics to give themselves up to beggary."

"The moment has come, monseigneur," continued Lafayette in words which his feelings made eloquent, " in which each one of us sees with dread the menacing machinery of taxation, which seems only awaiting the signal to strike a terrified people. You have often repeated to us the necessity of taxation, but I appeal to your heart, to-day, when, being no longer able to slacken our march nor to turn away our eyes, we are obliged to confront these immense preparations of public calamity which are about to invade our unhappy country. May so disastrous an epoch, ceaselessly contrasted, as it is, to the devouring luxury and mechanical extravagance of the court, make as durable an impression upon those who can prevent the evil as upon those who are its innocent victims." He denounced the " taille " which weighed so heavily and exclusively upon the poorest classes, and exclaimed that if " the country-people claim no representative in this Assembly, we should prove to them that they do not lack friends and defenders."

But the Assembly of the Notables, and, soon after, all France, was startled when Lafayette concluded his speech by begging the king to convoke a NATIONAL ASSEMBLY.

" What, sir ! " exclaimed the Comte d'Artois, " you ask the convocation of the States-General ? "

" Yes, monseigneur, and even more than that."

" You wish that I write, and that I carry to the king, ' M. de Lafayette moves to convoke the States-General ' ? "

" Yes, monseigneur."

The States-General had not been summoned for one hundred and seventy-three years, and almost all memory of it was lost. The proposal to assemble it was a step which no one but Lafayette dared to take. His was the only name attached to the demand. The expression, " even more than that," was regarded at the time as a thoughtless phrase ; but it contained his ruling thought, destined to be realized, — a representative body in France, such as existed in England and America. The suggestion, received by the Notables with astonishment, was rapidly taken up by the people, and soon became a fixed thought in the public mind.

Two subjects of great importance were brought to the notice of the Notables by Lafayette before their dissolution : the reform of the criminal law, and the granting of civil rights to the Protestants, — objects for which he had long struggled, and which he lived to see attained. The position assumed by Lafayette that the deficit should be met by economies in expenditure instead of by new taxes placed him in direct opposition to the court, an attitude intensified by his proposition to summon the States-General. But although the queen and courtiers disliked him, the feelings of the king were still friendly. The latter remembered with satisfaction the part that the young general had played in the last war, in which so much lost lustre had been restored to French arms, and he well knew that Lafayette had no favors to ask.

The attempt to diminish public expenditure having totally failed through the opposition of the court and the extravagant habits of every one connected with the government, the ministers had no resource but to increase taxation. With the proposal of this measure, the Revolution practically began. The only bodies of men by whom the power of the king was in any way limited were the Parliaments of the pro-

vinces and of Paris. It was the custom of the king,
when issuing an edict, to send it to the Parliament of
Paris to be registered, after which ceremony it became law. Whether the Parliament could nullify an
edict by refusing to register it, had long been a
mooted question and the cause of many quarrels.
But hitherto it had been conceded that when the
Parliament refused to register, the king might per-
emptorily order the law to be placed on record in a
session called "a bed of justice;" and such had always
been the course pursued.

The new minister, Loménie de Brienne, now sent
to the Parliament several of the edicts approved by
the Assembly of the Notables. The laws for free
trade in corn, for provincial assemblies, and for the
abolition of forced labor were immediately registered.
But on the reception of the edict for the new taxes,
the rebellious spirit in the Parliament was quickly
shown. The taxes proposed were not in themselves
objectionable. The principal one was on land, which
would affect the wealthy, and do something toward
relieving the poor from their overwhelming burdens.
But the Parliament was not composed of men who were
inclined to look into the merits of the case, or to
consider it from a public-spirited point of view. They
were anxious, first, to gain popularity by the sure
method of opposing the court; and, secondly, they
selfishly opposed the new measures because it tended
to increase their own taxation. Thus, while posing
before the people in a patriotic *rôle* as opponents

of the court, they really acted in their own selfish interest. They refused to register the edicts, and denied the king's power to have them registered in a " bed of justice," — a proceeding which sapped the foundations of the French monarchy.

A clerical member declared that only a States-General could grant a subsidy or legalize a perpetual edict. This doctrine was altogether new. The States-General had not been thought of for nearly two hundred years till Lafayette proposed it, nor did the Parliament really desire to have the States summoned. Amidst great excitement the edicts were then registered in a " bed of justice " and the Parliament exiled. This despotic measure exasperated public feeling. The popularity of the disgraced Parliament was general throughout the country, and the fact that it was so little deserved shows how weary the people were of the monarchy itself, and how ready they were to applaud any opposition to the court. The situation soon became so alarming that Lafayette's proposition to summon the States-General was seen to be the only resource. The king named the year 1792 for the great event; but it was found impossible to tide over the nation's troubles until that time, and the summons was issued for May, 1789.

The French people were far from anticipating any unfavorable or dangerous results from the States-General. The announcement of its assemblage was succeeded by a period of calm and optimism. Every man looked for some advantage to himself or to the country as a result of this extraordinary measure. None was more happy in the prospect than Lafayette. With his naturally sanguine temper and unbounded faith in human nature, he was confident that the French people needed only the opportunity to become as free and as happy as any in the world. In October, 1787, he wrote to Adams: "The affairs of this country, considered in a constitutional light, are mending fast. The minds of the nation have made a great progress. Opposition is not, of course, free from party-spirit. . . . This country will, within twelve or fifteen years, come to a pretty good constitution, not the best perhaps that can be framed, but one. . . . I think a representation will be obtained in France much better than the one now existing in England."

These characteristically rose-colored views illustrate Lafayette's hopefulness and confidence wherever his cherished liberty was concerned. Yet he was not blind to the actual state of France. Writing to Washington, he described the situation with great discernment: "The king is all-powerful; he possesses all the means of compulsion, of punishment, and of corruption. The ministers naturally incline and believe themselves bound to preserve despotism. The court is filled with swarms of vile and effeminate courtiers; men's minds are enervated by the influence of women and the love of pleasure; the lower classes are plunged in ignorance. On the other hand, French character is lively, enterprising, and inclined to despise those who govern. The public mind begins to be enlightened by the works of philosophers and the example of other nations. The French are easily excited by a noble sentiment of honor, and if they are slaves, they do not like to admit it. The inhabitants of the distant provinces are disgusted with the despotism and the extravagance of the court, so that there is a strange contrast between the Oriental power of the king, the care of the ministers to preserve it intact, the intrigues and servility of a race of courtiers on the one hand, and on the other, the general freedom of thought, of conversation, and of writing, in spite of the spies, the Bastille, and the press laws. The spirit of opposition and of patriotism diffused through the highest class of the nation, including the personal servants of the king, mingled with the fear of losing their places and pensions; the derisive insolence of the populace of the cities, always ready, it is true, to disperse before a detachment of guards, and the more serious discontent of the rural population, — all these ingredients mingled together will bring us little by little, without a great convulsion, to an independent representation and, consequently, to a diminution of the royal authority. But it is a matter of time, and will proceed the more slowly that the interests of powerful men will clog the wheels." Thus thought Lafayette and many other intelligent Frenchmen before the overwhelming catastrophe which was to unsettle all theories and falsify all prophecies. To Lafayette, it seemed that a popular assembly once gathered together, all other benefits would follow naturally. As events proceeded and the political situation became more disturbed, he again wrote to Washington : " In the midst of these troubles and this anarchy, the friends of liberty strengthen themselves daily, shut their ears to every compromise, and say that they shall have a national assembly or nothing. Such is, my dear general, the improvement in our situation. For my part, I am satisfied with the thought that before long I shall be in an assembly of representatives of the French nation or at Mt. Vernon."

CHAPTER IX.

Election of Deputies to the States-General. — Their Character. —
Lafayette's Campaign. — The Meeting of the States, and the
Quarrel of the Orders. — Lafayette's Position. — His Political
Separation from Gouverneur Morris. — His Declaration of Rights.
— Threatening Attitude of the Court. — Storming of the Bastille.
— Lafayette chosen Commander of the National Guard.

THE election of deputies to the States-General proceeded in a ferment of excitement. The French
nation, which for more than one hundred and fifty
years had taken no part in its own government, now
found itself called upon to solve the difficulties which
the crown had failed to meet. All classes looked forward to the event with satisfaction and a sense of new
dignity. Regarding the issue, few misgivings were
felt. And yet the mere summoning of the States-
General in the actual condition of France was in itself
revolutionary and dangerous. The crown, in acknowl-
edging its incapacity to deal alone with the situation,
and in calling the nation to its assistance, was practically abdicating that supreme authority which had
been hitherto its essential characteristic. To the
people at large, public business had always been the
"*affaire du roi,*" with which the subject had nothing
to do. But now the public business had become the
people's business, and the people pressed forward eagerly
to assume it. The positions of deputies were ardently

sought after, and those who had no hope of election took great pride and pleasure in the exercise of the suffrage. The temper of the nation was plainly shown in the choice of deputies. Among the nobility the ancient families were liberally inclined, as a rule, and desired to send men who, like La Rochefoucauld and Montmorency, were in favor of reforms. But the new nobility, who had acquired their titles by purchase, clung to their newly gotten privileges, and bent their efforts toward sending men opposed to essential changes. Therefore the representation of the nobility was divided into two hostile camps, and what should have been the conservative influence in the Assembly was fatally weakened. While many were blind to the national interest and selfishly averse to measures which might curtail their privileges or increase their taxation, a considerable number went to the opposite extreme, — men who had served in America and adopted liberal ideas, like Lafayette, the Lameths, Beauharnais, the Vicomte de Noailles, and the Duc d'Aiguillon, who longed for substantial liberties and a share in the government of their country, who were ready to give up all privileges inconsistent with these higher interests.

The great body of priests showed their deep-seated resentment at the long experience of contempt and neglect which they had suffered at the hands of the higher clergy, by refusing to elect bishops as their deputies, and by sending curés who belonged to the third estate and were in full sympathy with it.

The representatives of the third estate were chiefly

lawyers, as these were the only men able to speak in public. As a body, they were in favor of the most radical changes; they were opposed to the crown and to the nobility alike, and were actuated by a long-standing sense of wrong. While very patriotic, they were extremely ill-fitted for the care of public interests. Knowledge of the true meaning of the word "liberty" was hardly to be found among them. They had been accustomed too long to absolute submission and to political inaction to have practical ideas regarding government. Nearly every man had his individual theory of the right social state, — an imaginary Eldorado, born of the wrongs he had suffered. At first there was no union among the deputies of the third estate. They arrived in Paris strangers to each other, with no organization or concerted views regarding their course. Much might have been done by small attentions on the part of the court to preserve among them what little loyalty to the crown yet remained. But so entire was the ignorance of the government concerning the state of the country and the temper of the people, that no effort in this direction was made. The deputies were soon united in a common defence against the contempt and tyranny which they experienced from the court.

Early in 1789, Lafayette left Paris for Auvergne, to make his campaign as a deputy. When, in the previous year, a second meeting of the Notables had been called to determine the method of assembling the States-General, the question arose whether the nobles should seek to represent the third estate. Lafayette strongly recommended this course, but was successfully opposed by Mirabeau, at whose suggestion a contrary resolution was passed. Lafayette, therefore, was elected to represent the nobles; but Mirabeau, when rejected by the aristocratic party, sought and received an election from the people.

In Auvergne, Lafayette found great confusion and jealousy among the orders and towns. The nobles, to whose suffrages he was to offer himself, were generally prejudiced against his well-known liberal opinions. Some of his acquaintance gave him to understand that if he would yield on certain points, he would be elected unanimously; otherwise, not at all. Lafayette, however, would not retreat a step from his position, and, after an acrimonious campaign, found himself duly chosen the deputy of the *noblesse* of Riom.

On the 2d of May, the deputies of the three orders went to pay their respects to the king, on which occasion the contemptuous reception of the third estate by the court officers deeply offended the members of that order. On the 4th, all the deputies marched in procession to hear Mass at the Church of St. Louis. All Paris came out to Versailles to see the extraordinary procession, — the old monarchy of France moving with pomp and solemnity to its dissolution. The third estate marched first, clad in black, containing in its ranks the men whose names call up the terrible events to which this ceremony was the prelude, — Mirabeau, Danton, Marat, Guillotin, Desmoulins, and

Robespierre. The clergy and the nobility followed in their order, bearing the outward signs of a proud supremacy which a few days more would see ended forever. The king, surrounded by the princes of the blood and the great dignitaries of the monarchy, was saluted as often by the new cry of *" Vive la nation "* as by the old one of *" Vive le roi."* The queen, already hated as the impersonation of the insolent and extravagant court, was received in significant silence.

On the 5th of May, the States-General was formally opened in the hall of the " Lesser Pleasures." The magnificence of the decorations of the hall, the splendor of the costumes worn by the court officials and the nobility, in contrast with the black coats of the third estate, made the scene extremely brilliant. The most distinguished of Frenchmen and foreigners were present, including Gouverneur Morris, the future American minister. But the speech of Necker, the great event of the day, only brought discontent. The third estate, who had come from all parts of France to seek relief from overwhelming exactions, heard only of the necessity for new taxation. Their feelings and their attitude were sufficiently shown when, at the end of the sitting, the king having put on his hat, and having been imitated by the nobility, the deputies in black asserted the dignity of the people by putting on theirs also.

May the 7th was the day fixed for the beginning of business, which meant the beginning of the great struggle between the court and the people for the government of France. The States-General had not been summoned for so long that the established method of its deliberations was a matter of conjecture and uncertainty. The great question, discussed for many months by all classes, had been whether the three orders should vote by order-or as individuals. If the first, then the nobility and the clergy could always out-vote the third estate and decide all business to suit themselves. If the second, then the numerical superiority of the third estate would give them the preponderance. This great question, on which every interest depended, was still undecided on the 7th of May.

On that day, the nobles and the clergy asserted their view of the matter very plainly by assembling in separate meetings, leaving the hall of the Lesser Pleasures to the deputies of the third estate. When the clergy and nobility had organized and elected their officers, a difference of opinion on the propriety of their course soon became evident. In the clergy, a motion to unite with the third estate was lost only by the close vote of 133 to 114. The nobles defeated Lafayette's motion for union by the more decisive vote of 188 to 47.

Meanwhile, the third estate, having assembled in its hall, realized that its importance and power depended on union with the other orders. Refusing to organize, it passively awaited the arrival of the nobles and clergy. For two weeks this deadlock continued.

Then the king ordered a conference to take place between committees of the different orders; but no compromise could be reached. Meanwhile, public opinion was inclining more and more to the side of the third estate, and rioting among the populace of Paris threatened a violent termination of the crisis. On 'the 1st of June, the third estate, weary of the struggle, and encouraged by popular support, boldly summoned the other orders to join them, declaring that in case of another refusal, they would themselves organize, not as an order, but as the States-General of France. On the 12th of June, in accordance with this resolution, they elected Bailly as their president, and called the roll of all the deputies, none of the nobility or clergy answering to their names. The next day, however, three clerical deputies appeared, and the tumultuous applause from the galleries which greeted their arrival encouraged the meeting, under the leadership of Mirabeau and Barnave, to declare themselves positively the National Assembly of France. The stupidity of the court, which afforded the opportunity for this act of independence, could find no remedy for the situation but to induce the king to suspend the meetings until a "royal session" could be held on June 22. But the taste of authority and unchecked success which had attended the progress of the third estate was already too strong to allow of delay. When, on June 20, the deputies found the hall of the "Lesser Pleasures" closed to them by reason of the preparations being made there for the royal session, they withdrew eagerly to the tennis court, and there took the famous oath never to separate till they had given a constitution to France. This momentous occasion determined the issue. The third estate had now placed itself in direct opposition to the court, and had arrayed the sovereignty of the people against the sovereignty of the king. The deputies must now win the battle or be treated as rebels.

The next day the Comte d'Artois engaged the tennis court for a game, and the meeting had to take place in the Church of St. Louis. There the commons were joined by one hundred and forty-nine clerical and two noble deputies, a defection which might have warned the court of its weakness. But the king was still so ill-advised that at the royal session, held on the 23d, he ignored what had passed ; and while promising " of his own goodness and generosity " to levy no new taxes without the people's consent, he yet commanded that the orders should deliberate separately, and that the privileges of the nobility and clergy should not be attacked. When the king with the nobles and clergy had left the hall, the third estate had to decide between submission or rebellion. But now they knew and enjoyed their power too well to retreat. " Gentlemen," declared Sieyès, " you are to-day what you were yesterday." Mirabeau defiantly stated to the master of ceremonies, who wished to clear the hall, " The commons of France will never retire except at the point of the bayonet." The king, weak himself, and surrounded by incapable advisers, could continue the struggle no longer. Forty-seven more nobles joined the Assembly, and on the 25th June the remainder followed by royal command.

During the course of this struggle, Lafayette was in a position of great uncertainty and disappointment. His instructions as a deputy of the *noblesse* of Auvergne distinctly enjoined upon to await the action of the majority of the nobles before joining the third estate. And yet his heart was altogether with the deputies of the people. To continue in the position of an opponent of progress and reform was inexpressibly repugnant to him. To resign his position as a deputy was equally so, for, as he said in a letter to his wife, " it is natural that when twelve hundred Frenchmen are working at a constitution, I should desire to be among them." Unable to rest easily in his position as an apparent opponent of the third estate, longing to take part in the efforts of the people to attain their liberty, he could see no course but to resign his present powers and to seek a reëlection as a member of the third estate. Jefferson, the American minister, and Gouverneur Morris, who had lately arrived in Paris, were watching the course of events with deep interest and from widely differing points of view. In the beginning of May, Jefferson wrote to Lafayette, advising him to disregard his instructions and to take his stand outright with the third estate, urging upon him that his liberal opinions would preclude his attaining influence with the nobility, while if he delayed too long in taking up the cause of the commons, that party would receive his advances with suspicion. Morris recommended that he should resign his seat, on the ground that his instructions were contrary to his conscience. Neither course was wholly satisfactory to Lafayette, and his difficulty was finally solved by the king's order to the nobility.

The quarrel between the third estate and the upper orders intensified the hatred of the people for the nobility and the clergy. The Revolution, as far as it had progressed, was evidently directing itself against the feudal privileges of the upper orders. Their sudden destruction, which seemed imminent, amounted to a complete upheaval of society. Such an event, not unwelcome to Lafayette, was strongly deprecated by Morris. " Jefferson and I," he wrote in his diary, "differ in our system of politics. He, with all the leaders of liberty here, is desirous of annihilating distinctions of order. How far such views may be right respecting mankind in general is, I think, extremely problematical ; but with respect to this nation, I am sure it is wrong."

From this point began the political separation of Morris and Lafayette. The American citizen, brought up among free institutions, was led by his knowledge of their nature to oppose all sudden and violent changes. The French noble, reared under despotism, could consider only the happiness of throwing off the hated tyranny of crown and aristocracy. Morris saw with extraordinary clearness what passed unobserved in the fever of French progress, that every legislative

body should be restrained by some conservative influence. In France this influence must be exercised
by the upper orders. He foresaw the terrible consequences which must result from the unopposed
career of the third estate with its new-found liberty,
and he urged upon Lafayette the preservation of some
constitutional authority for the *noblesse.* In his diary,
June 23, he says: "At dinner I sit next to M. de
Lafayette, who tells me that I injure the cause, for
that my sentiments are continually quoted against the
good party. I seize this opportunity to tell him that
I am opposed to the democracy from regard to
liberty; that I see they are going headlong to
destruction, and would fain stop them if I could;
that their views respecting this nation are totally inconsistent with the materials of which it is composed;
and that the worst thing which could happen would
be to grant their wishes. He tells me that he is sensible that his party are mad, and tells them so, but is
not the less determined to die with them. I tell him
that I think it would be quite as well to bring them
to their senses and live with them."

With such acuteness did Morris perceive the fatal
issue of passing events; with such clearness did he
appreciate the impossibility that a people which for
many generations had slavishly submitted to a cruel
despotism and was totally ignorant of political affairs
could suddenly become self-governing; in a word,
that the French nation could be changed into an
Anglo-Saxon nation. But the calm reason which he

could bring to bear on the subject was impossible to
the French themselves, and among them to Lafayette.
The whole nation was in an intense fever of excitement. To calculate the ultimate effect of what they
were doing was beyond their power. The terrible
incubus of feudality was to be thrown off; to accomplish that was the all-absorbing thought. Morris
might wisely advise Lafayette to bring his party to its
senses, but to stay the tremendous current of innovation had long become impossible, and the attempt to
stay it would be universally regarded as equivalent to
upholding the abuses of the old order.

The revolutionary proceedings of the Assembly,
which was now arrogating all power to itself, was supported by rioting in Paris and Versailles. These
disorders induced the king to concentrate troops in
both cities. But the appearance of the soldiers caused
great indignation in the Assembly, the members of
which believed that their progress was to be checked
by force. On the 8th of July, Mirabeau moved to
request the king to send the troops away. The motion was referred to a committee, when Lafayette for
the first time addressed the Assembly. "There are,"
he said, "but two motives for referring a proposition
to a committee, — when there are doubts as to the
facts in the case, or on the determination which
should be taken. But, gentlemen, the presence of
the troops about the Assembly is a fact evident to
each one of us. As to the determination to be taken
in such a case, I will not insult the Assembly by

believing that any one of us can hesitate. I, therefore, shall not confine myself to supporting the motion
of Mirabeau; I ask, instead of the reference ordered
by the president, that the chamber take an immediate
vote." These words determined the question. The
address was voted, and the refusal it met with widened
still further the breach between the crown and the
Assembly.

Soon afterwards, Lafayette presented to the Assembly his "Declaration of Rights," which became the
basis of that afterwards adopted. The Declaration
amounted to a justification of the present acts of the
French people, and in some measure to a statement
of the new social condition about to be established.
If the principles put forth were true, then the *Ancien
Régime* was unjustifiable.

"Nature made men free and equal; the distinctions necessary to social order are founded only on
general utility.

"Every man is born with inalienable and impre-
scriptible rights; such are, liberty of opinion, the care
of his honor and of his life, the right of property, the
free disposition of his person, of his industry, of all
his faculties, the communication of his thoughts by
all possible means, the pursuit of well-being and resistance to oppression.

"The exercise of natural rights has no limits but
those which assure the enjoyment of the same to
other members of society.

"No man can be subjected to any laws but those

assented to by himself or his representatives, previously promulgated and lawfully applied. .

"The principle of all sovereignty resides in the nation. No body of men, no individual, can have any
authority which does not expressly emanate from it.

"All government has for its unique end the public
good. This interest exacts that the legislative, executive, and judiciary powers should be distinct and
defined, and that their organization should assure the
free representation of citizens, the responsibility of
agents, and the impartiality of judges.

"The laws should be clear, precise, and uniform for
all citizens.

"Subsidies should be freely granted and proportion-
ally assessed.

"And as the introduction of abuses and the right
of succeeding generations necessitate the revision of
every human institution, it should be possible for the
nation to have, in certain cases, an extraordinary
convocation of deputies, of which the sole object
should be to examine and correct, if necessary, the
vices of the constitution."

Such were the political ideas with which Lafayette
started on the regeneration of his country. To us
the Declaration is a series of general truisms, but to
Europe of 1789 nearly every sentence contained trea-
sonable and revolutionary doctrine. There was a very
essential difference between a declaration of rights put
forward in England or America and one promulgated in
France. When men of Anglo-Saxon race had occasion

to assert their rights, they found no difficulty in agree-
ing upon the particular privileges which their fathers
had enjoyed before them, and which they proposed to
preserve for themselves. But the French people, as a
people, had no rights. Sovereignty, power, and priv-
ilege were derived only from the crown. Hence,
when the French had determined to be free, they had
to formulate some abstract conception of what the
word "freedom" meant, and forcibly place that conception in the room of the old monarchic principle.
Lafayette realized this necessity when he composed his
Declaration. But he has been condemned for submit-
ting it to the Assembly at a time when vigorous action, and not the discussion of abstract principles, was
imperative. But before the Assembly could act, it
had to arrive at some generally accepted, if vague,
idea of its own aims. There was hardly a deputy
who came up from the provinces without his own
peculiar declaration of abstract rights in his head, the
product of his real wrongs and the theories of Rousseau. The temperate, practical statements of Lafayette, mere political platitudes to modern ears, formed
the best basis the Assembly was likely to get for its
final declaration. The long discussion which followed was inevitable from the endless variety of political views and chimerical social theories held by the
deputies. In fact, the discussion involved the justice
of the Revolution itself. On the truth of the statements contained in Lafayette's paper depended the
question, whether the nation was rebelling against just

rulers or was changing an outgrown system of government.

The court pursued its policy of checking the progress of the Assembly and of overawing the population of Paris by the show of force. Marshal de
Broglie was appointed commander of the troops now
collecting in Paris and Versailles, and the unusual title
of Marshal-General was held before him as the reward
of success. Sheltered behind this fancied protection,
the court meditated a blow which was to put an end
to innovation, to bring the Assembly to its senses, and
to show the rebellious mob that the king alone was
the ruler of France.

When, on the evening of July 11, the news reached
Paris that Necker and his ministry had been dismissed,
it was received with incredulity followed by dismay.
The weakness of the court and the vanity of its dependence on the army were so well known that men
believed with difficulty that an act of such folly could
have been committed. Every one awaited the result
with consternation. The conflict between the crown
and the Assembly had reached a crisis; victory for
one must mean the destruction of the other. The
court had challenged the people to a trial of strength,
and the attitude of the populace left no doubt as to
its determination.

In this emergency the Assembly declared itself permanent, sat day and night, and elected Lafayette its
vice-president. This choice was dictated by the prob-
ability of an armed struggle. Lafayette was the one

man who so combined military knowledge with liberal opinions and public confidence as to fit him to command troops in the popular interest. The Assembly, in making him their vice-president, pointed him out as their choice for military command. Although Paris was in a state of violent commotion, and daily conflicts were occurring between De Broglie's troops and a mob armed with weapons pillaged in the public buildings ; although the Assembly considered the situation too serious to adjourn overnight, — the court remained in a condition of such blind security that a grand ball was given at the palace the night of July 13.

The next day, the results of the government's policy in dismissing Necker and confronting popular opinion with troops was seen in the taking of the Bastille. The storming of that fortress which had stood so long as the instrument and sign of absolute power, the furious rage and bloodthirsty violence of the assailing mob, proclaimed the answer of the people to the threatening measures of the court. It was intended to strike terror into the hearts of the king, the queen, and their counsellors, to convince them that force would be met by force. In the fall of the Bastille was typified the fall of arbitrary power and feudalism. It was a blow, the purport of which none could mistake. The Duc de la Rochefoucauld-Liancourt went out to Versailles, entered the king's bedchamber, and announced the event to him. " Why," said Louis XVI., " this is a revolt ! " — " No, sire," was replied, " it is a revolution."

Demoralizing as was this act of open rebellion, disgraceful as were the bloody murders which accompanied it, the sentiment of many men of high position did not condemn the act. It was generally accepted, among others by Lafayette, that some great blow was necessary to bring the court to its senses, and that the mob had done a service to French liberty. "Yesterday," wrote Morris in his diary, "it was the fashion at Versailles not to believe that there were any disturbances at Paris. I presume that this day's transactions will induce a conviction that all is not perfectly quiet."

The next morning the taking of the Bastille bore its intended fruit. Marshal de Broglie, who had found, instead of a loyal army, only disaffected regiments which had joined or were preparing to join the mob, sent in his resignation. The Assembly, fearing further lawless proceedings in Paris, in which it knew that not a few of its own members were taking part, was about to despatch a committee to the king to beg him to recall Necker as a means of quieting the public, when the king himself, without other escort than his two brothers, appeared before it. The king, deserted by his army, his authority now quite gone, had no means of restoring order except through the Assembly. He begged that body to undertake the work, promising to recall the dismissed ministers. Elated by this new victory, by which all real power was shown to be in their hands, the members surrounded the king with unmeaning expressions of loyalty, and

. conducted him back to his palace with acclamations. Lafayette was then despatched to Paris, with fifty other deputies, to restore order.

The deputation found the city in a deplorable condition. The shops were closed, the streets obstructed with barricades and burning ruins, while an endless conflict was going on between gangs of ruffians and citizens who were trying to keep the peace and protect property. At the Hotel de Ville were most apparent the effects of the destruction of authority. The electors of the city, the only men with any show of legal power, were practically imprisoned by the mob. Many, exhausted by long-continued watch, were asleep on the benches; others were endeavoring to satisfy with praises of the conquerors of the Bastille the ragged crowds who threatened their lives unless at once furnished with bread and arms.

But although the terrible consequences of anarchy were staring them in the face, the men who wished for the destruction of arbitrary power and the establishment of a constitution saw little evil in the prevailing disorders in comparison with the benefits which they thought would accrue to their cause from the terror thus communicated to the adherents of the old *régime.* That hated system had really come to an end from its own rottenness; but Frenchmen could not believe that the incubus which had weighed upon them so long might not be replaced. The speech which Lafayette made to the electors and the crowd at the Hotel de Ville shows how little he feared as yet from the mob in comparison to what he feared from the court. He congratulated the electors and the citizens of Paris "upon the liberty which they had conquered by their courage, upon the peace and happiness that they would owe to the justice of a beneficent and undeceived king. . . . That the National Assembly recognized with pleasure that all France owed the constitution which would assure its happiness to the great efforts which the Parisians had just made for public liberty."

While it was natural for men to believe that some such counter-demonstration as the capture of the Bastille was necessary to overcome the opposition and the military interference of the court, it was nevertheless inevitable that the impunity with which this event was allowed to take place gave an impetus to mob violence which could not be overcome during the remainder of the Revolution. Riots, under pretence of aiding the popular cause, became legalized in the public mind.

The power of the king had now passed from him to the National Assembly. But that numerous body of men, absorbed in interminable discussions on abstract ideas, was totally incapable of applying its power to the government of the country. The electors at the Hotel de Ville, on the 15th of July, resolved that there must be a mayor to direct the affairs of Paris, and a National Guard to preserve order. Dangers threatened from every quarter. When the question arose as to who should fill these offices, Moreau de Saint Méry, the president of the electors, pointed to the bust of Lafayette, which had been sent as a gift to the city of Paris by the State of Virginia, in 1784. The gesture was immediately understood, and Lafayette was chosen by acclamation. Not less unanimous was the choice of Bailly for mayor.

Lafayette was now taken from the assembly to assume the more active employment of commanding the National Guard. While the Assembly pursued the destruction of the old order and the erection of a new, Lafayette, at the age of thirty-two, became the chief depositary of executive power.

CHAPTER X.

Necessity of a Military Force to keep Order. — Formation of the
National Guard. — The King visits Paris. — Formal Appointments
of Lafayette and Bailly. — Organizing the Guard. — Murders of
Foulon and Berthier. — Lafayette resigns. — Is again appointed.
— The National Assembly. — Lafayette's Mistakes. — Condition
of France, and Position of Lafayette in the Autumn of 1789.

THE nominations of Lafayette as commander of a
National Guard, and of Bailly as mayor of Paris, by the
electors at the Hotel de Ville on June 15 was the
consequence of the, general feeling that no effective
government now existed, and that something must be
done to avert anarchy.

What was the case with Paris was the case with the
provinces. Throughout France, the deepest interest
was exhibited in passing events. In every town the
arrival of the Paris courier or newspaper was awaited
with intense anxiety. Letters or papers were read
aloud to groups of people on the sidewalk, who applauded with unreasoning enthusiasm the progress of
the Revolution. The victory of the Assembly over
the king and aristocracy led the people of the provinces to believe that their cause was already won. A
general demoralization ensued. The defeat of the
crown seemed paramount to an absolution from all
obedience to law. The populace had always been
taught to look upon the king as the government; now

that the king was publicly disgraced, authority and order seemed no longer to exist.

The news of the dismissal of Necker was received with almost as much irritation in the provinces as in Paris, and the accounts of the taking of the Bastille suggested to the rural population their answer to any attempt on the part of the crown to resume its authority. The example of rebellion thus set was speedily followed. Rioting and lawlessness soon prevailed everywhere, increased and imbittered by the scarcity of food. In the towns, bread riots became continual, and the custom-houses, the means of collecting the exorbitant taxes, were destroyed. In the rural districts, *châteaux* were to be seen burning on all sides. The towers in which were preserved the titles and documents which gave to the nobleman his oppressive rights were carried by storm and their contents scattered. Law and authority were fast becoming synonymous with tyranny ; the word "liberty," now in every mouth, had no other signification than license.

Into Paris slunk hordes of gaunt footpads from all over France, attracted by the prospect of disorder and pillage. Thus reënforced, the mob of the city broke into the arsenals, armed themselves, and overawed what authority remained. Added to these desperate characters were the members of the middle classes of violently revolutionary opinions, who assembled in the Palais Royal and incited the people to extreme measures.

The maintenance of order had' therefore become the most pressing question. Hitherto, this duty had belonged to the army. But the mere suspicion of armed interference by the government had been enough to provoke the riots which culminated in the taking of the Bastille. And, in fact, the army itself could no longer be said to exist. The soldiery participated in all the feelings of the revolutionists. Besides sharing the general hatred of arbitrary power and the desire for liberty, they had special causes of discontent of their own. To them, merit brought no promotion, loyalty no reward. None but a nobleman could be an officer. Their treatment had been very bad, and the late introduction of flogging as a punishment had increased the bitterness of feeling. The army was fast disbanding, and of what remained in the ranks only a few regiments could be trusted to obey their officers and defend the king's life. Marshal de Broglie, finding that he could do nothing with the troops at Paris and Versailles, went to the provinces in hopes of rallying an army there. But he was everywhere repulsed, barely escaping with his life. At Metz, his old garrison, he was refused even an entrance to the citadel, and the old marshal, without a soldier to command, joined the band of exiles across the frontier.

From such circumstances naturally arose the National Guard. To have an armed force under the control of the Assembly, which might protect them alike from the mercenaries of the crown and the rioting of the mob, was soon resolved upon by the leaders of the popular party. "*Gardes bourgeoises*" had already existed in France, notably in the city of Lyons, and the idea of a militia was not altogether new. On the 8th of July, when the Assembly was agitated by the sight of royal troops around it, Mirabeau moved to request the king to substitute "*gardes bourgeoises*" for the regular troops. The proposition was not then adopted, but on June 10 the subject of a militia was discussed in Paris by the electors. On the 11th, collisions between Parisians and the German troops in the pay of the court increased the public interest in the matter. On the 13th, a deputation of the Assembly represented to the king the danger resulting from the inevitable conflicts between the populace and the troops, and urged him to confide the care of the city to a militia. The king replied that the regulation of such matters belonged to him alone, and that he considered the population of Paris too large to be controlled by such means.

When this answer was communicated to the Assembly, Lafayette moved that, "fearful of the terrible consequences which may follow the reply of the king, the Assembly will not cease to insist upon the withdrawal of the troops and the establishment of the *gardes bourgeoises.*" On the same day, the electors at Paris proceeded to form such a guard on their own account. Numbers of young men enlisted, among them many rebellious members of the "*Gardes Françaises*" who had deserted their colors. The men thus collected did something toward the preservation of order on the night of the 13th, but the next day occurred the overwhelming riot, terminating in the assault on the Bastille. Then the king yielded, as he always did, too late, when it was evident that force alone had procured the concession. "Informed of the formation of a '*garde bourgeoise*,'" he said to a deputation of the Assembly, "I have given orders to general officers to place themselves at the head of this guard, that they may aid by their experience and direct the zeal of good citizens. I have also ordered that the troops at the Champ de Mars shall leave Paris." But the next day, the appearance of Lafayette at the Hotel de Ville resulted in his choice by the electors as commander-in-chief. The king was obliged to confirm this choice, and he was thus deprived even of the merit of naming the chief officer of the guard whose existence had been forced upon him.

When the deputation which had gone to Paris returned to the Assembly on the night of July 15, it could only report that it had found Paris in a lamentable condition, and that peace could only be restored by the personal presence of the king in the city. The mobs which had been concerned in the taking of the Bastille and in other acts of rebellion were still in great fear of retribution; only a visit from the king himself could assure them of immunity. These circumstances being represented to Louis XVI., he consented to visit the city on the 17th.

The 16th was occupied by Lafayette at the Paris

Hotel de Ville in preparing for the king's reception and in organizing the new militia. Then, on Lafayette's recommendation, it was determined to adopt the name of National Guard, and to invite each district of the city to send representatives to confer with the commander regarding the enlistment and organization. So intense was the excitement and the insurrectionary spirit of the time, so uncertain were the boundaries between rascality and revolutionary zeal, that it was difficult to establish the fact that the new guard was created to preserve order and not to fight the king and pillage the aristocracy. The great armed mob, now in process of organization, had to be treated with great tact, lest it should refuse to submit to authority in any shape. Thus the electors, under the lead of Lafayette, were obliged to say, " that if this gathering of armed citizens, already famous for their courage, remained without order and discipline, guided only by the impression of the moment, it would not only be exposed to losing the fruits of its efforts by confusion of movements, but that it might even, without wishing it, contain within itself the seeds of trouble and division." With such words the tumultuous mob was in-duced to submit to some discipline. The *Gardes Françaises*, who had abandoned their colors and the duty of protecting their sovereign, who were now scat-tered through the city furnishing leaders for every riot, were informed that it was decided to be proper to in-corporate in the National Guard "those brave *Gardes Françaises*, so worthy by their patriotic conduct of the gratitude of the community, but who, dispersed through the districts of Paris, feel themselves the need of being subjected to a regular discipline."

Such words used in connection with rascally vagabonds and rebellious soldiers show how great were the difficulties of Lafayette's position. He was to organize a militia, and to preserve order with it, in a city in which order was regarded as the sign of a hated tyranny; in which disobedience to every constituted authority, murder, and pillage were considered the privileges of a free people; in which to hang officials of the crown and to parade their bloody heads on pikes was applauded as the heroic act of a good citizen; in which the public sentiment openly approved any acts of violence done under the pretence of "patriotism."

This same day, while Lafayette was busy with his recruiting duties at the Hotel de Ville, he had his first real taste of the business in hand. The mob, always surging around the public buildings on the lookout for prey, had its attention directed toward an unoffend. ing abbé, named Cordier. A score of hands seized him, and the crowd was preparing to hang him then and there, when Lafayette appeared and attempted the apparently vain effort of rescue. But the mob would not be balked of its victim. At that moment, it happened that the tutor of young George Washington Lafayette had brought the boy to the Hotel de Ville to see his father; Lafayette held him up in view of the crowd, saying, " Gentlemen, I have the honor of presenting to you my son." The French mob, as ready to burst into tears about nothing as to hang an innocent man, was immediately overcome with " effusion," during the course of which emotion Lafayette and his friends smuggled the abbé out of harm's way.

Short as the time was, Lafayette succeeded in making suitable arrangements for the ceremony of the 17th. The king made his will and took the sacraments before leaving Versailles, for so far had the demoralization progressed that doubts were entertained that he would live to return. He left the palace with an escort of Versailles militia, accompanied by a deputation of the Assembly, and guarded by a few soldiers who still remained faithful. On his arrival at the gates of Paris, Bailly presented him with the keys of the city, and made a long address which contained the famous, but, for Louis, certainly unpleasant, words : " They are the same keys that were presented to Henry IV. He had reconquered his people ; now it is the people who have reconquered their king." From the gates, the king followed the streets to the Hotel de Ville through a double line of National Guards, which Lafayette had posted to insure order. The procession was joined by numbers of the newly enlisted militia, and proceeded through immense crowds of spectators. The visit of the king, illustrating the victory of the people, and involving the assurance of immunity for past excesses, caused a feeling of good-humor to pervade the crowd, and the king met with friendly glances on all sides. But it was a day of deep humiliation for him, and of lasting injury to the cause of good government in France.

Arrived at the Hotel de Ville, the king was received by the new body of electors. He was handed the national cockade, just brought into use, which he was obliged to fix on his hat. Then Lally Tollendal made his great speech, in which he repeated the nomination already made by the electors of Lafayette and Bailly. The unanimous shouts of approbation compelled the king to confirm these nominations, which, as a matter of law, no one but himself had a right to make. Louis XVI. then returned to Versailles, on the whole pleased, as the day had been less unpleasant than had been expected. But the compulsory acceptation of the cockade and the nominations meant nothing less than the extinction óf his authority. The power of the absolute sovereign of France had been reduced in a few months to the confirmation of the acts of an irresponsible gathering of his own subjects.

Lafayette's arrangements had resulted in perfect order all day, and when he reconducted the king to his carriage, the latter cordially said, " M. de La- fayette, I was looking for you to let you know that I confirm your nomination to the place of commander of the National Guard." Lafayette, dissatisfied with the manner in which his position had been conferred upon him, insisted on a regular election by the people, " from whom should emanate all power." He doubt- less felt that if his business was to control the sovereign people he had better put their consent distinctly on record. The principle that all power should emanate from the people had been impressed on Lafayette's mind in America. It was in exact contradiction to that hitherto recognized in France, which made the crown the sole source of power. The sudden transition from one to the other could not fail to demoralize a nation wholly unaccustomed to the exercise of political rights. But the circumstances of the time inclined Lafayette, like all other Frenchmen, to think only of establishing correct principles, regardless of the fitness of the people to practise them.

The four days following the visit of the king were occupied by Lafayette in perfecting a plan of organization for the National Guard. He submitted this to the authorities at the Hotel de Ville, with the celebrated speech, " I bring you a cockade which will make the tour of the world, and an institution, at once civil and military, which will triumph over the old tactics of Europe, and which will reduce arbitrary governments to the alternative of being beaten if they do not imitate it, and overthrown if they dare to imitate it." Thus, full of hope and enthusiasm, Lafayette began his career as commander of the National Guard. A glimpse of him at work in Paris is given by Morris in his diary : —

"*July 20.* Go to the Hotel de Ville, and with much difficulty find out the Marquis de Lafayette, who is exhausted by a variety of attentions. Tell him I will send his letters to America, and that he must give me a passport to visit the Bastille. Agree to dine with him, on condition that I may bring my own wine. Return home, write, and about four go to the Hotel de Lafayette. Find there madame, the Duc de la Rochefoucauld, and others. Dine. He gives me my passport. Suggest my plan regarding the *Gardes Françaises,* which he likes. Advise him to have a complete plan for the militia prepared, and to submit it to the committee. Ask him if he can think of any steps which may be taken to induce the king to con- fer on him the government of the Isle de France. He tells me that he would prefer that of Paris simply; that he has the utmost power his heart could wish, and is grown tired of it; that he has commanded absolutely a hundred thousand men, has marched his sovereign about the streets as he pleased, prescribed the degree of applause which he should receive, and could have detained him prisoner had he thought proper. He wishes, therefore, as soon as possible, to return to private life."

It is not surprising that so young a man as Lafay- ette should have been somewhat overcome by the immense power which had devolved upon him. To a Frenchman who had been brought up to look upon his sovereign as his absolute master, it was dazzling to find the situation reversed. But the task of intro- ducing discipline into the uncertain ranks of the Na- tional Guard now allowed him to think of little else. Uniforms were agreed upon and ordered, for hitherto it had been impossible to distinguish the militia from other citizens.

Lafayette recruited his army from the *bourgeois* class, for the good reason that in the fever then raging for uncontrolled freedom, that class was the only one from which the proper material could be taken. The importance of order was impressed on the *bourgeois* by the fact that they had shops and houses which they did not wish to see pillaged. The lower classes had nothing to lose ; in discouraging their enlistment in the Guard, Lafayette acted with a wisdom demonstrated by subsequent events. The inferior officers were elected, the others Lafayette selected himself, largely from among those who had served with him in America. While the acknowledged purpose of the National Guard was the maintenance of order, another object, very important in the public mind, was the prevention of counter-revolution on the part of the court, and the consequent punishment of all those who had taken part in recent events. This feeling that the Guard was to protect the people against the court was a serious obstacle in Lafayette's way. The militia were ready enough to act against aristocrats, but it was difficult to make them oppose a so-called " patriotic " mob.

The necessity for strict police measures was soon to be terribly illustrated. For a week past a large crowd composed of starving workmen, country beggars, and army deserters had thronged the streets angrily demanding food. The city was extremely short of provisions, and it was impossible to satisfy the demands made upon it. The threatening attitude of the mob became doubly serious from the fact that old restraints had been withdrawn. The police and magistrates of former times had become powerless. Lafayette said that the old resources of government were "incompatible with liberty." But no one seemed to appreciate how much more incompatible with liberty was the absence of legal restraints. Though Lafayette's revolutionary zeal blinded him to the disasters to which such insubordination must lead, he did apply himself with untiring zeal to the prevention of violence. During these days, many individuals owed their lives to his intercession, often made at great personal risk. He was still unknown to the populace, and was frequently obliged to prove his identity.

On July 22, an old man named Foulon, a member of the late ministry, who had long been the object of public dislike, and was now detested because it was rumored that he said that "the people might eat grass," was arrested in the country, and brought to the Hotel de Ville, followed by a mob who demanded his immediate judgment. Bailly, the mayor, and the electors, had no jurisdiction in the matter, and limited their efforts to the attempt to protect Foulon. The mob was growing more and more threatening, and there seemed little hope for the unfortunate man, when Lafayette, who had been informed of the tumult, arrived, stationed himself beside the president of the electors, and thus addressed the crowd : —

"I am known to you all; you have chosen me for

your general; and this honorable choice imposes
upon me the duty to address you with the freedom
and frankness which belong to my character. You
wish to put to death without trial this man who is
before you : it is an injustice which would dishonor
you, which would brand me with shame, which would
blast all the efforts which I have made in the cause
of liberty, if I were weak enough to permit it. I shall
not permit this injustice ! But I am very far from
thinking of saving him, if he be guilty. I wish only
that the order of this Assembly be carried out, and
that this man be taken to prison to be judged by the
tribunal which the nation will indicate. I wish the
law to be respected, — that law without which there is
no liberty, that law without the aid of which I should
have contributed nothing to the Revolution of the
New World, and without which I shall not contribute
to the Revolution now preparing.

"What I say in favor of forms and of law should
not be interpreted in favor of M. Foulon. My
feelings toward him are not doubtful, and, perhaps,
even the manner in which I have expressed myself
about him on several occasions would alone suffice
to take from me the right to judge him. But the
more he is presumed to be guilty, the more important it is that the proper forms should be observed
in regard to him, whether to make his punishment
the more striking, or to allow his legal interrogation
and to receive from his mouth the revelation of his
accomplices.

"Therefore, I shall give orders that he be taken to the prison of the Abbaye Saint Germain."

This well-conceived address made a visible impression on all those within hearing, and at first seemed destined to have the desired effect. But the distant portion of the crowd, excited by the cries of the increasing mob outside, continued to demand the prisoner. Foulon himself, in the midst of the disorder, attempted to speak; but at the sound of his voice the fury of the mob increased. A voice called, "What need is there of a trial for a man who has been judged for thirty years?" Three times Lafayette addressed the mob; but the staircases and hallways of the Hotel de Ville became choked with people and resounded with cries. The outside mob pressed in until the people surged against the platform on which Foulon was seated and upset his chair. Cries arose that the Palais Royal and the Faubourg St. Antoine were coming to take the prisoner. Lafayette shouted to the soldiers who had Foulon in charge, "Take him to prison." As he spoke, the crowd applauded. Foulon unhappily then applauded also. At once the cry arose that the two understood each other; the mob rushed upon the prisoner, dragged him out to the lamp-post, and was soon parading his head about on a pike.

The next day, Foulon's son-in-law, Berthier, the Intendant of Paris, was arrested in the country. Hearing of his approach, Bailly and Lafayette sent a company of volunteers under a capable officer named d'Hermigny, to meet the Intendant and protect him while passing through the city. This force brought Berthier in safety to the Hotel de Ville. Thence Bailly and the electors sent him under the same escort to the Conciergerie prison. But every precaution was in vain. Before he had gone far the mob had seized him, and his head, like Foulon's, was set on a pike. "After dinner," says Morris in his diary, "walk a little under the arcade of the Palais Royal, waiting for my carriage. In this period the head and body of M. de Foulon are introduced in triumph. The head on a pike, the body dragged naked on the earth. Afterwards this horrid exhibition is carried through the different streets. His crime is to have accepted a place in the ministry. This mutilated form of an old man of seventy-five is shown to his son-in-law, Berthier, the Intendant of Paris, and afterwards he also is put to death and cut to pieces, the populace carrying about the mangled fragments with a savage joy. Gracious God, what a people!"

Shocked by these murders and disgusted by his own inability to prevent them, Lafayette sent his resignation to the electors, and for some time persisted in his refusal to resume his office. But no other man could be found in Paris equally fitted for the place, so that on the personal solicitation of the electors and a deputation from the sixty districts of the city, he again took command.

Having got uniforms for the National Guards, and having introduced some discipline into their ranks,

Lafayette was able to patrol the streets and to close the Palais Royal, used as headquarters by violent revolutionists, so that the city presented an outward aspect of calm.

The commander of the guard was now the chief man, in the public eye, possessing executive power. The king had none, and the Assembly could only talk. To Lafayette were directed petitions and demands of every sort as to the chief authority of the nation. In this situation, when events tended to place ever-increasing power in his hands, his course illustrated the strength of his principles. He issued a circular distinctly defining his own powers as being limited to military matters, and urging the public to address itself to the municipality and other civil authorities. As Bailly said, he sought to carry out this principle throughout his tenure of office. Although Lafayette's efforts gave a semblance of order to Paris, beneath the surface unquenchable fires were raging. The scarcity of food and work increased with the demoralization of society. The idle and starving multitude were continually excited by violent speeches and incendiary pamphlets.

The National Assembly, filled with theorists who occupied invaluable time with long-winded speeches, had done nothing so far to allay the public distresses. The people needed a regular government; the National Assembly was solely occupied with discussing its abstract rights. On the night of August 4, the Committee of Researches, appointed to examine the condition of France, rendered so terrible a report that the Assembly could no longer postpone definite action. Custom-houses and *châteaux* burning, the collection of taxes almost impossible, lawlessness and terror everywhere; it was evident that something must be done to satisfy the people and to induce them to return to their ordinary occupations. In this emergency, the Vicomte de Noailles, Lafayette's cousin, who had served with him in America, mounted the tribune. He declared that the people were agitated because they were uncertain whether they were to be freed from the abuses of the *Ancien Régime*, and he urged the Assembly forthwith to terminate suspense by uprooting the oppressions of feudality. Other equally unselfish young nobles seconded Noailles. Very soon the sitting of the Assembly became what Mirabeau described as an " orgy." Every motion which called for the sacrifice of anything was carried amidst the wildest enthusiasm.

The deputies, having declared the rights of man in the morning, in the evening abolished at a blow all the ancient feudal rights, titles, and privileges of the nobility, the tithes of the Church, and nearly all recognized forms of taxation. They gave away not only what belonged to themselves, but what belonged to others. Reason had no part in their acts. It was in vain that Sieyès pointed out that the abolition of the tithes was merely a gift made to the landowners. No thought was given to what new taxes should replace the old. The peasantry naturally refused to pay what had been declared illegal, and the government was left without resources for current expenses. It was a night of generous folly, for the precipitancy of which the country must suffer. Nearly every benefit which France gained by the Revolution dated from that night. But the benefits came so suddenly that the country was thrown into yet greater disorder. The old *régime* was destroyed, but nothing new was ready to take its place. Lafayette was not present in the Assembly, his duties keeping him in Paris. But for what had been done, his approval was unqualified.

The 25th of August being the day of St. Louis, Bailly and the municipality of Paris proceeded to Versailles to pay their respects to the king. Lafayette was in charge of a detachment of National Guards, acting as escort. The condition of uncertainty on the part of the court and the public is illustrated by the fact that when Lafayette led up to the balcony on which the king stood a detachment of militia who wished to present a bouquet to His Majesty, it was generally believed that a *coup d'état* was about to take place.

Early in September, the municipality of Paris voted to the commander of the National Guard an indemnity for the expenses to which he had already been put in the public service, and also attached a salary to his office. Both of these benefits Lafayette declined, on the ground that money was now too much needed to assist the suffering classes, and that his own fortune placed him above want. A renewal of the same offers met with another refusal. Lafayette showed the same disinterestedness in money matters that had characterized his conduct in America. The first revolution had impaired his fortunes, the second was to ruin them.

A project now undertaken by Lafayette illustrates the high-minded humanity of his aims, together with his lack of judgment in State affairs. The criminal jurisprudence of France was in a state shocking to intelligent minds. Among other monstrous provisions, an accused person had neither a right to a public trial nor to be represented by counsel. Two years before, in the Assembly of the Notables, Lafayette had vainly endeavored to reform a system so unjust. Now that he had the necessary influence, he bent his efforts to attain the desired end, although advised by Bailly that the moment was not propitious. He induced the municipality to request the National Assembly to institute a more humane method of criminal procedure. The new laws were passed in October, and a strange mode of trial became lawful at a time when the dockets were overcrowded. Bailly says in his journal that he did all in his power to dissuade Lafayette from this act. While applauding the purity of his motives, he considered that the commander of the National Guard was concerning himself with matters not in his department, and of which he had not sufficient knowledge. Lafayette claimed that he could not conscientiously arrest men when he knew that they must submit to a trial no less than barbarous. On the other hand,

Bailly justly remarked that the new procedure required elections, was unfamiliar to the judges, and caused a delay in the execution of justice of about two months. During this time the prisons filled up, and the lack of trials gave to crime an appearance of impunity. Such circumstances bring out the unpractical element in Lafayette's mind which caused him to pursue an abstract good without calculating the propriety of its immediate realization.   .

At this time Montmorin, one of the king's ministers, approached Lafayette with an offer to make him lieutenant-general of the kingdom, the court seeking this means of counteracting the hostile power of the Duke of Orleans. The proposition was declined by Lafayette, on the ground that no such favor was necessary to secure his support of the king against the Duke of Orleans. He aimed at establishing a constitutional monarchy in France, and he would accept no personal aggrandizement at the expense of his principles.

October was now approaching, and with it those terrible events which were to destroy all semblance of royal authority. In these events, Lafayette's office placed great responsibility on his shoulders. The general state of France must be examined to arrive at a satisfactory explanation of what was about to occur.

The Assembly had seized upon all the functions of government, but was incapable of exercising any. It was occupied with subjects almost foreign to the present needs of the country. Nearly every influential man was absorbed in some special hobby in the way of a constitution which he wished to see tried. There were very few besides Mirabeau who could discern and endeavor to meet the wants of the nation. The deputies were occupied with ideal schemes for making the people perfectly happy in the future, regardless of the present miseries which kept all France in a turmoil. Besides, they were totally unaccustomed to the work of a deliberative assembly. A system of procedure, a regular debate, such as existed in the English Parliament, were restrictions beneath the notice of the French Assembly. The floor was a scene of perpetual noise and disorder. When a member had succeeded by main force in establishing himself in the tribune, he continued speaking until pulled or pitched out, or until his voice was drowned by shouts. Endless deputations, all useless, and many ridiculous, interrupted business at will. The proceedings of the 4th of August had plunged the country in still greater disorder. After that continued the discussion of the rights of man, and particularly of the precise words in which such rights were to be expressed. Then arose the question of the king's veto, whether it should be absolute or suspensive. This was followed by the discussion of the number of legislative chambers which should exist, — two, as in England and America, or one only. The tendency of the Assembly to take a position as opposite as possible from that of the old monarchy was shown by its determination to make the king a mere figure-head, by giving him only a suspensive veto, and to confide all power to the representatives of the people in a single chamber. The deputies were beginning to divide themselves up into something like parties. But their ignorance of parliamentary methods and their want of order prevented their attaining the dignity of a deliberative assembly. The galleries were filled with people who applauded, hissed, and threatened at their pleasure. A deputy who opposed the maddest scheme pleasing to the mob was marked out for a vengeance which became more and more certain as the Revolution progressed.

For lack of other control, the people now took the conduct of affairs into its own hands. Not to be behind Paris, the inhabitants of provincial towns stormed their court-houses, which they regarded as their Bastille, drove out the royal officers, and set up municipal governments of their own. In addition to these political outbreaks occurred bread riots, in which many officials were murdered and much property destroyed. While the mobs insisted on being fed at the public expense, they stopped the revenues by destroying toll-houses and driving away tax-gatherers. In the rural districts the peasantry gradually became acquainted with the new state of affairs, and they, too, had to assert their rights by burning *châteaux*, and refusing payment of taxes. Conflicts arose between the peasantry and the towns'-people which added new complications to the disorder. The people of France, who had been accustomed from generation to generation to rely upon the throne as the source of all authority, now found itself suddenly cast on its own resources. An illustration of the universal helplessness was the panic which went by the name of the "great fear." It was believed all over France that troops of brigands, coming from no one knew where, were on their way to pillage and kill the inhabitants. Each village or town fancied itself the special object of the brigands. The sight of a muddy courier galloping along the road was enough to call all the men to arms, and to send the women and children to the churches for protection.

In Paris the uncertainty was less, because the inhabitants were well informed as to what was going on. But there still existed the fear of a counter-revolution, and of the punishment to be inflicted by the aristocrats if they should get the upper hand again. An outward appearance of calm was maintained by the National Guard, but beneath the surface smouldered the flames of revengeful anger which only awaited an opportunity to burst forth. The public mind continued in a state of political excitement. Every man now thought himself fitted to govern his fellows. The different trades organized into political clubs, while the districts of the city held regular meetings and legislated on their own account. The projects for a new constitution, which were being discussed by the Assembly, were debated with fury in the clubs and street gatherings. Of the intelligence displayed, Morris gives us an idea: "A gentleman tells us an anecdote which shows how well this nation is adapted to the enjoyment of freedom. He walked near a knot of people collected together where an orator was haranguing. The substance of his oration was, ' Messieurs, we are in need of bread, and here is the reason : for only three days has the king had this suspensive veto, and already the aristocrats have bought suspensions, and have sent the grains out of the kingdom.' To this sensible and profound *discours*, his audience gave a hearty assent. ' *Ma foi, il a raison ! Ce n'est que ça !* ' O rare ! These are the modern Athenians ! alone learned, alone wise, alone polite, and the rest of mankind barbarians ! " In addition to the demagogues who kept the people in a fever of unrest, were the cheap newspapers which fanned public excitement by inflammatory tirades against authority.

Between France and anarchy, in the autumn of 1789, there was no barrier but the National Guard, and that barrier was unequal to the strain upon it. The new militia was only beginning to accept the restraints of military discipline and to inspire confidence in its ability to preserve order. The. ranks were made up chiefly of civilians in uniform who intended to obey whenever the orders conformed with their own views. While ready to stop the pillage of a shop, injuries to aristocrats or their property did not seem of equal importance. They had no idea of the strict discipline which compels blind obedience to a commander. They regarded themselves as volunteers who should be treated with due consideration, and required to act only in accordance with their political opinions.

In the middle of September, when Lafayette was dining at Jefferson's house in company with Morris and the Duc de la Rochefoucauld, Lafayette observed that some of his troops wished to march to Versailles to urge on the Assembly the passage of measures then before it. Morris was amused at what he called this " rare situation," and asked Lafayette if his troops would obey him. Lafayette replied that they would not mount guard when it rained, but he thought they would readily follow him into action. No reply could have been more French, nor, so to speak, more Lafayette. Troops which considered it part of their business to instruct the legislature, and who would mount guard in fair weather only, were not a safe reliance for their chief. But Lafayette's unbounded confidence in human nature and the French character caused him to revert to the happy thought that the gallant fellows had plenty of pluck.

Like every French movement, the organization of the National Guard had to be crowned by a grand ceremony, which affected everybody very much for a moment, and was forgotten the next. All the flags were carried to Nôtre Dame in procession, and there solemnly blessed by the Archbishop of Paris on September 24. The ceremony was imposing, and an eloquent discourse was duly preached; but it was all show, and added nothing to the stability of the men.

Lafayette's own position in these times has been

left on record.   He was an unqualified revolutionist, as far as the destruction of the *Ancien Régime* was concerned ; so much so as to say of the soldiers who had deserted their ranks in the royal army, that "the true deserters were those who had not joined the standard of the nation."   But his revolutionary intentions went no further than the abolition of old abuses and the establishment of a constitutional monarchy.   To a friend he wrote : "Do not calculate my power ; I shall make no use of it.   Do not calculate what I have done ; I wish no recompense.   Consider public utility, the good and the liberty of my country, and believe that I shall refuse no burden, no danger, so long as at the moment of calm I can become again a private individual.   .   .   .   Such is the manner in which I shall always act.   If the king refuse the constitution, I shall fight him.   If he accept it, I shall defend him."

CHAPTER XI.

The Populace demands the Presence of the King and the Assembly in Paris. — The 5th and 6th of October. — Lafayette's Conduct and Responsibility.

As winter approached, the population of Paris became more restless and ungovernable. The discredit into which the old monarchy had fallen was indicated by the names M. et Mme. Veto, now attached to the king and queen. The ruling thought of the middle and lower classes became a determination to have the king and the Assembly in Paris under their own control. The scarcity of food was a perpetual temptation to pillage much dreaded by the *bourgeois*. They knew little enough of economic laws to suppose that the Assembly could create abundance by legislation if they could only be made to follow out the ideas of the Parisians. At Versailles they only talked ; once in Paris, they could be forced to pass the desired measures. The *bourgeois* were also in constant dread of an anti-revolutionary movement from the provinces in favor of the king. From Versailles, he might be carried off to an interior town where a centre of resistance might be established.

The lower classes were equally desirous of getting the king in their power. For generations they had remained in a state of ignorance nothing short of brutal. To their minds the king was the fountain of good and evil. The laws which oppressed them were the king's laws; the tax-gatherer who pursued them from village to village and from attic to attic did his work in the king's name. On the other hand, every occasion for public rejoicing was purposely associated with the sovereign. Abundant crops were ascribed to his goodness, public relief came from his treasury. He was naturally regarded by the masses as an individual of almost supernatural powers, who could command famine or plenty at will. Shut up in his palace at Versailles, the aristocrats were forcing him to oppress the people. Surrounded by patriots in the Tuileries, the tables would be turned.

In this state of the public mind, an incident occurred at Versailles which roused the populace to immediate action. The palace guards at Versailles had lately received the addition of a force known as the Flanders Regiment. The court, pursuing a natural policy of self-preservation, made every effort to win the attachment of the new troops. The use of the great hall of the palace was granted to the body-guards to give a banquet to their newly arrived companions of the Flanders Regiment. At the conclusion of the repast, Louis XVI., Marie Antoinette, and the royal family appeared in a gallery overlooking the hall, where they were enthusiastically received with the now rarely heard and doubly welcome cries of " *Vive le roi*" and " *Vive la reine.*" Somewhat carried away by these demonstrations, the king and queen descended into the hall and mingled with the Guards. The latter, excited by wine and their feelings of loyalty, carried their marks of affection for the royal family beyond the bounds of prudence. The tricolored cockades were thrown away, white ones mounted in their place, and the whole assemblage, animated by a generous impulse in favor of their unhappy sovereign, united in the celebrated refrain, " *O, Richard! Oh, mon roi, l'univers t'abandonne!* " The movement continued the next day, when the ladies of honor pinned white rosettes on the men's coats, and it was claimed by the popular party that National Guards with tricolored cockades were insulted.

The news of these incidents was speedily carried to Paris and much exaggerated by the revolutionary newspapers. It was sedulously represented to the people that while they starved in Paris, wines and delicacies were lavished at Versailles upon soldiers who longed for the opportunity to fire upon patriots. It was claimed that the Flanders Regiment was only the first arrival of the troops who were coming to Versailles to overthrow the Revolution and restore the old order.

The plans already begun in the districts of Paris immediately took shape and acquired an overwhelming impetus. By the 4th of October, street gatherings and tumults announced the approach of some unusual event. Lafayette perceived the threatening aspect of the populace, and took the precautionary measure of stationing a detachment of National Guards on the road to Versailles. But a number of deputies of the

Assembly, always jealous of the least use of a military force, made so strenuous an objection to the presence of the Guards that the Assembly ordered their withdrawal. As a matter of fact, the presence or absence of the Guards would have been of little consequence the next day, as the National Guard ranged itself distinctly on the side of the mob. Throughout Sunday, the 4th, Lafayette doubled his patrols and prevented violent outbreaks. But such means were impotent to avert the impending catastrophe. The idea occurred to the hungry and angry masses that while the National Guard might prevent the men from acting, they would not interfere with women. In Versailles, there was feasting and trampling on the national cockade ; in Paris, the stronghold of patriotism, there was starvation. If the men could do nothing, the women could.

At about six o'clock in the morning of October 5 the tocsin sounded through the city, and crowds of ragged men and women poured from the adjoining streets to the space in front of the Hotel de Ville. There were only a few clerks and National Guards in the building at that hour. The mob soon forced its way inside, spreading itself through the rooms and corridors, demanding bread, and seeking some victim for its fury. This was found in the person of an inoffensive abbé, whom the people proceeded to hang from the highest pinnacle of the roof. Lafayette was sent for as soon as possible. Meanwhile, Maillard, one of the conquerors of the Bastille and a mob leader, who had higher game in view than a wretched abbé, adopted a stratagem to get the crowd out of the building. Seizing a drum, he beat upon it, shouting, "To Versailles!" This being what the rioters wanted, they hastened to fall into line behind him, leaving the abbé half hung on the roof, and soon emptied themselves into the square. There they found the Place de Grève and the adjoining streets packed with women who answered their shouts of "To Versailles!"

The female gathering was begun by a fishwoman, who beat a drum in a poor quarter of Paris, and was speedily joined by others. As the women marched to the Hotel de Ville, their numbers were steadily increased by willing recruits, and all women walking in the streets or so imprudent as to show themselves in the windows were forced to fall in. Even ladies, in the course of the morning, were taken from their carriages and impressed. The crowds of shrieking women, of whom the majority were the refuse of the Faubourg St. Antoine, ranged themselves under the leadership of Maillard, and ceaselessly repeated the cry, "To Versailles!"

Lafayette arrived at the Hotel de Ville just after its evacuation, and a consultation took place between himself, Bailly, and the municipality. Lafayette's first step was to despatch couriers to Versailles to warn that city of the tumult, to inform the authorities that the cries of the mob had changed from "bread" to "To Versailles," and that preparations must be made to repel an invasion.

From nine in the morning till four in the afternoon

Lafayette struggled with the crowd to prevent a general march to Versailles. The women went on under the leadership of Maillard; but the square and the adjoining streets were filled with men and National Guards vociferously demanding to be led in the same direction. Early in the morning Lafayette had gone out and had forbidden the National Guard to move. But while he was within the Hotel de Ville with the municipality, deputation after deputation entered to induce him to yield to their demands. "General," said the grenadiers, "we do not think you a traitor; but we think the government betrays you. It is time that this end. We cannot turn our bayonets against women crying to us for bread. The people are miserable; the source of the mischief is at Versailles; we must go seek the king and bring him to Paris. We must exterminate the Flanders Regiment and the body-guards, who have dared to trample on the national cockade. If the king be too weak to wear his crown, let him lay it down. You will crown his son, you will name a council of regency, and all will go better." Lafayette's remonstrances and personal appeals only met with the reply, "General, we would shed the last drop of our blood for you; but the root of the mischief is at Versailles; we must go and bring the king to Paris; all the people wish it." The mob and the military having become one, no means of control was left but persuasion. The tumult increased as the day advanced. Bailly went out and addressed the crowd, but without effect. His words were drowned by the

cries of " To Versailles ! " For eight hours Lafayette
commanded and exhorted by turns. The departure
of the women could not be prevented. The only
force which could have opposed them was itself clam-
oring to march. To the regular soldiers and National
Guards at Versailles it belonged to control the women
when they should arrive. Lafayette's object was to
keep the mingled masses of citizens and National
Guards in front of the Hotel de Ville from leaving
Paris and taking possession of the king and the
National Assembly. Several times, as he rode about
exhorting the Guards to return to their duty, muskets
were levelled at him. On all sides continued the cry,
" To Versailles ! " Finally, toward four o'clock, the
situation became untenable. Armed crowds began to
start on their own account for Versailles, dragging cannon. National Guards surrounded Lafayette, declaring their intention to march and take him with them.
Discipline, never much regarded among them, was
now altogether relaxed. Many persons advised Lafayette to yield, on the ground that only his presence
at Versailles could prevent mischief there. Lafayette
sent an aide-de-camp to the municipality to ask for
orders. A letter was returned to him, passed from
hand to hand over the heads of the crowd, in which
the municipality directed him to proceed. After giving orders to a detachment of National Guards to
remain in the city for patrol duty, he set out for
Versailles, preceded and followed by an immense con-
course of civilians, military, and miscellaneous rabble.

Lafayette has been blamed by historians for not having marched to Versailles much sooner, and also for having gone at all. As commander of the National Guard of Paris, his manifest duty was to remain in the city to control the outbreak there. To the regular troops and National Guard of Versailles it belongèd to check an invasion by a mob which had escaped the authorities in Paris. That he did all that an individual could have done to prevent the march of the mob is shown by the fact of his having detained the angry and determined crowd for eight hours with no other means than his voice and personal influence. When he did lead the march to Versailles, it was at the command of the mayor and municipality, who saw that it was impossible to avert the catastrophe, and hoped that Lafayette's presence would lessen its evil results. Morris summoned up the events of the day as follows : —

" *October 5.*   Go towards Chaillot to see what is doing, but am stopped at the Pont Royal. Go into the Tuileries. A host of women are gone towards Versailles with some cannon. A strange manœuvre ! Walk up to Mr. Short's. He is just going out to dine. We return together to the Place Louis Quinze. This tumult is the continuation of last night. A wild, mad enterprise ! Go to the arsenal. Admitted with difficulty. They are at dinner. Madame Lavoisier is detained in town, as all carriages are stopped and the ladies obliged to join the female mob. . . . Lafayette has marched by compulsion, guarded by his own troops, who suspect and threaten him. Dreadful situation ! Obliged to do what he abhors, or suffer an ignominious death, with the certainty that the sacrifice of his life will not prevent the mischief."

Meanwhile, the couriers despatched by Lafayette brought to Versailles the news of the coming invasion. The Assembly, as usual, took no action. It had arrogated to itself all authority, but its unwieldy size and unregulated character prevented it from exercising any power at critical times. Thus, in the beginning of the Revolution, the mob was suffered to rule unchecked and to learn to place its wishes above all law and authority. Messengers were sent from the palace to recall the king, who was hunting in the Versailles forests, as it proved, for the last time. He returned to find the palace prepared for a siege, the court-yards filled with body-guards, the Swiss, and the Flanders Regiment.

Toward four o'clock the mob of women, led by Maillard with his drum, made their appearance. Hungry, bedraggled with mud, wet by the rain which had fallen all day, they spread themselves over the city, entirely unopposed. Although their approach had been long known, and the city had a large body of National Guards, no steps had been taken to control them. Many went to the Assembly, filled the galleries, and shouted to the deputies to pass laws at once to lower the price of bread. A large number made their preparations to pass the night in the Assembly chamber, and the place soon became a pandemonium. The deputies contented themselves with suspending business and declaring the sitting permanent. Thus, their chamber, instead of being defended from such indignities, became the lodging-place of the scum of Paris. Several members accompanied a deputation of the women to the king. These were received by Louis XVI. with great kindness, and on their return gave so favorable an account of their experience that their companions wanted to tear them to pieces on suspicion of treachery.

Within the palace prevailed terror and confusion. The royal family finally determined to leave Versailles, the carriages were ordered, and the body-guards held in readiness as escort. But when the carriages crossed the court-yard from the great stables, their purpose was perceived, and the National Guards themselves seized the horses' heads and turned them back.

While the mob thronged about the palace insulting or firing at the Guards, filled the Assembly chamber, and dictated to the deputies the measures they should pass, not the slightest attempt was made by those in authority to stem the tide of riot. Many individuals whose office and influence gave them the power, at least, to modify the disorder were practically the accomplices of the mob. The Assembly was waiting that day for the king's sanction to the Declaration of Rights, and many prominent deputies secretly welcomed the prevailing anarchy in the expectation that the fear thus inspired would hasten the king's acceptance. Their expectation was realized. But

when President Mounier returned to the chamber
with the royal assent, he found it the scene of a general riot, a fat fishwoman haranguing the crowd from
his own presidential chair. Such now was the state
of France. The Assembly had robbed the king of
his authority, and now the populace seized that of the
Assembly. The mob might be pushed from the floor,
but henceforth it would rule from the galleries. Mounier could not restore enough order to announce the
king's recognition of the rights of man, and the deputies occupied themselves with the effort to collect
enough bread to satisfy the hunger of their constituents.

Thus passed the evening till eleven o'clock, when
Lafayette arrived with the National Guards and the accompanying crowds from Paris. On the way he had
ranged the rougher elements of the procession between his advance and rear guard, in order to keep
them under control. Halting the troops near the
Assembly, he made them renew their oaths " to the
nation, the law, and the king." These were taken, as
usual, with enthusiasm and without the least appreciation of their binding force. Having given orders to
his staff concerning the disposition of the men as they
arrived, Lafayette, accompanied by two commissioners
of the city of Paris, proceeded to the palace to receive
the orders of the king. At the gates, the Swiss guards
refused him an entrance until he announced his purpose to enter alone. He found the interior of the
palace crowded with courtiers. As he passed through
the chamber called the *" œil de bœuf "* a voice ex-

claimed, "Here is Cromwell!" to which Lafayette replied, "Cromwell would not have entered alone." The king received him with cordiality in public, directed him to provide for the exterior defence of the palace, but declared that he would rely entirely on his own guards for the protection of the interior.

Lafayette then occupied himself with the disposition of the troops during the night. Seven hours of slow marching in the rain had fatigued them extremely. Versailles was already overcrowded, and the men were obliged to bivouac where they could. Lafayette stationed a battalion of National Guards beside the building occupied by the body-guards, to protect them. He established a system of patrols throughout the city, and placed strong guards around the palace, the positions of which were agreed upon between him and Count d'Estaing, who commanded in the interior. These measures occupied him till about one o'clock in the morning of the 5th. At that time the Count de la Marck and the Abbé de Damas, having entered the palace from curiosity, found Lafayette, an aide-de-camp, and the commander of the body-guards discussing the measures which had been taken. Soon afterwards a body-guard entered hastily, announcing that the quarters of the guard were threatened with an attack from the mob. Lafayette immediately descended to the court-yard, entered La Marck's carriage, and was driven in the direction of the body-guard's building. The carriage was stopped before it left the court-yard by drunken men armed with pikes, whom

Lafayette quieted. The party soon met other crowds, and La Marck, not relishing the idea of being mixed up with the mob, conducted Lafayette to a point near his headquarters and left him to pursue his journey on foot.[1] The threatened attack on the body-guards proved to be only a rumor, and the battalion already stationed to protect them was sufficient for the purpose. Lafayette says in his Memoirs that at two o'clock all was quiet about the palace and the guards duly mounted. At three o'clock the city seemed entirely tranquil, and the Assembly adjourned. The exhausted crowds from Paris had sought rest where they could, and filled the churches, barracks, and stables. Lafayette called on M. de Montmorin, discussed the situation with him, and then passing through the latter's garden he reached the Hotel de Noailles, where he had established his headquarters. He received the reports of his aides-de-camp and gave his final orders. It was then about three o'clock in the morning.

For twenty successive hours Lafayette had been occupied with the most fatiguing duties. On foot or on horseback, without a moment's rest, he had harangued the mob over and over again, given all the orders, and attended to all the business of that eventful day. As he told M. de Montmorin, he could hardly stand on his legs. His enemies have tried to

---

[1] Correspondance entre le Comte de Mirabeau et le Comte de la Marck, l., 116. Mémoires de Lafayette: Récit des Événements du 5 et 6 Octobre.

make it a crime that he should then have gone to sleep, and to fasten on him the name of General Morpheus. The only evidence on the subject is that of Lafayette himself. He says that he was preparing to take rest when interrupted by the commotions of the early morning. It is a puerile question at best, and cannot affect Lafayette's reputation. After twenty hours of intense effort, exhausting to both mind and body, when his staff had received their orders, the guards mounted, the streets patrolled, and the whole city sunk in sleep, it would have been his duty to seek sleep himself. There was every reason to believe that the coming day would call for quite as severe a drain on his strength, and it was his business to prepare himself for it. The Hotel de Noailles was close to the king's palace, and Lafayette was, therefore, at the post of danger.

By five o'clock in the morning, groups of men and women whose quarters had not been temptingly comfortable had gathered in the streets. A crowd which happened to collect in front of a small gateway of the palace became engaged in a wordy quarrel with a few body-guards posted within. The defence of this gateway did not belong to the National Guards; it was one of the interior posts in charge of the king's own troops. The gateway was a sort of back entrance to the palace, and on account of its small size and distant position had received only an insignificant guard. The wet and hungry crowd, becoming exasperated in its altercation with the soldiers, made a sudden rush at the gate. The fastenings, which were insecure, immediately yielded, and the mob at once filled the inner court, called the Cour des Marbres. Thence the palace was open to the invaders. Streaming up the stairs and through the corridors they killed the few body-guards who opposed them, fighting step by step and from door to door. They would have reached the queen's apartments before she could escape, had not two body-guards, covered with wounds, defended the door until a reënforcement of their comrades dragged them in. The queen had just time enough to put on a dress and escape into the king's rooms with her shoes and stockings in her hands. When the mob forced its way into her room it left no doubt of its intentions by running pikes through her bed, howling for vengeance. As usual with French rioters, the death of their enemies was not enough. The murdered body-guards were decapitated and their heads set on pikes.

As soon as the news of this attack reached Lafayette, he sent two companies of grenadiers with orders to clear the interior of the palace. On his arrival, soon after, he found the interior in the possession of his National Guards; but without, in the court-yards, surged and howled the crowds who had come from Paris the day before. Lafayette attempted to disperse them, but he was met only with cries of "To Paris!" and with threats against the royal family and the body-guards. The inmates of the palace could see the wretched populace parading the heads of their victims in triumph, and making signs to all who appeared at the windows that a similar fate awaited them. Within reach of the sound of the ceaseless yells, "To Paris !" a consultation was held by the king and the few officials who dared to remain near him. It was decided that Lafayette should announce that the king would go to Paris that afternoon. This concession to the demands of the mob was, of course, the destruction of all authority. But such was the general demoralization that no power existed to prevent the catastrophe. The king could not rely on his own troops for defence, for they, though devoted, were few, and the populace would be too glad of an excuse to exterminate them to a man. Lafayette had seen too much of his National Guards during the last twenty-four hours to have any hope that they would obey him in opposition to the mob. Finally, the Assembly, the self-constituted source of national power, had not the capacity, even had it the will, to resist the riotous assemblage which imposed its commands alike on the sovereignty of the crown and the sovereignty of the people's representatives.

Lafayette appeared on the balcony of the palace and announced the king's determination. This being well received, he attempted to turn the current of ferocious anger which animated the crowd. At his request, the king accompanied him out on the balcony and was greeted with shouts of " *Vive le roi !* " Lafayette then addressed the queen: " What are your intentions, madame? " — " I know the fate which awaits me," she replied, "but my duty is to die at the feet of the king and in the arms of my children." — "Well, madame, come with me." — "What ! alone on the balcony?   Have you not seen the signs which have been made to me?" — "Yes, madame, but let us go."   The queen first appeared with her children, but the crowd cried, "No children ! " and these were sent back.   To harangue the vast and noisy mob was impossible.   Lafayette did the only thing which could have the effect he desired : taking the queen's hand, he bowed low and kissed it.   The vacillating French mob, always ready to go from one extreme to another, immediately set up a shout of "Long live the general ! Long live the queen ! " and for the time its murderous intentions were forgotten.

The king approached Lafayette and asked what he could do for the body-guards.   Lafayette called a guard, fixed a tricolor cockade on his hat, and, leading him out on the balcony, embraced him before the mob.   This scene was greeted with yells of "*Vive les gardes du corps!*" and peace was made.

Then ensued the long procession to Paris, in which fifty thousand persons participated.   In the general demoralization, Lafayette was the only individual who possessed even a show of authority.   All orders were issued in his name.   Even the passports for the members of the royal household had to be signed by him. The king did not leave the palace till half-past one, but the procession had been going on for hours before he started.   Lafayette sent on the populace first as far as possible. The crowds straggled to the city, carrying loaves of bread stuck on bayonets, intermingled with the heads of the murdered body-guards, and scream- ing, " *Vive la nation!* " The popular idea of the object and results of the tumult of the last two days was indicated by the frequent cries, " We have the baker, the baker's wife, and the baker's boy ! "

The king's carriage proceeded at a walk, protected by the body-guards, who, in their turn, were protected by the National Guards. Still the mob surged up to the carriage doors with imprecations and impudent shouts of triumph. On the road the procession passed a country-house where the infamous Duke of Orleans had posted his family, to view in comfort the humilia- tion of his king and queen. Lafayette rode beside the royal family. At Paris, enormous crowds lined the streets. Bailly, who met the king at the gates, and who always managed to say the wrong thing when addressing the king, made a speech beginning, " What a glorious day is this ! " The exhausted oc- cupants of the royal carriage were obliged to proceed to the Hotel de Ville, there to endure more patriotic speech-making, before they were allowed to hide their misery in the Tuileries.

Thus ended the days of October 5 and 6, in which the old French monarchy was dragged in the dust without a hand being raised to save it. It must be said that an edifice so rotten was hardly worth propping up. The proud doctrine of Louis XIV., *L'État c'est moi*, had borne its legitimate fruit of tyranny and oppression. Now, a long-suffering people, goaded beyond endurance, cried in its turn, *L'État c'est moi!* and visited the sins of *Le Grande Monarque* upon his descendant.

Regarding the part which Lafayette acted in these events, two views until lately have been common. The adherents of the *Ancien Régime*, the Orleanist faction and English Tory writers maintained that Lafayette had planned and carried out the whole proceeding to increase his own power. As the investigations of a hundred years have failed to furnish a scrap of evidence in support of this view, it has no longer any intelligent exponent. On the other hand, the partisans of the Revolution and some American admirers of Lafayette have exaggerated his influence for good on the 5th and 6th of October, and have made too much of his efforts to protect the lives of the royal family.

The events of these two days were not caused by the machinations of any set of individuals. They were brought about by an irresistible current of popular passion. The populace of Paris, the National Guards, a considerable portion of the *bourgeois*, animated by a single impulse, overbore every obstacle. They acted in the name of the sovereign people, and there is no doubt that the people of France approved their acts. The Assembly, although warned in advance, not only made no effort to resist the attack, but gave that attack a tacit approval by its obedient removal to Paris. The *bourgeois* who had not marched to Ver-

sailles acquiesced in the acts of those who had. The
news of what had taken place was received with
approval in the provinces. There is no doubt that
Lafayette detested the total disregard of law involved
in the forcible removal of the king and the Assembly.
He strove as long as possible to avert the calamity,
but he was powerless to stem the current of revolutionary passion. It was not a proud position for him
to be the commander of troops on whose obedience he
could not rely. On the other hand, it is not fair to
place too much responsibility for the victory of the
mob on Lafayette's shoulders. The nobility, the
boasted support of the throne, was incapable of afford-
ing to its sovereign any assistance in his peril. On the
morning of the 6th, when Lafayette rushed into the
inner apartments of the palace, one of the grand officers of the household, fearing lest the general should
transgress a rule of etiquette by entering without invitation, hastened to him with the words, " Sir, the
king is pleased to grant you *les entrées du cabinet.*"
The old monarchy had changed the feudal chiefs into
courtiers, and now looked in vain to them for assistance.
The movement of October 5 and 6 was the work of an
ignorant populace ; but it had the connivance and
assistance of the National Assembly and the great
bourgeois class. On them the responsibility must
eventually rest, and they were to pay dearly for their
alliance with lawlessness. From the moment that
Paris forcibly ingulfed the king and the Assembly,
the destinies of France fell more and more into the

hands of the least worthy of her citizens. Mirabeau, alone among prominent Frenchmen, discerned the dangerous tendency of events. Lafayette, noble-minded but unpractical, still trusted to see realized the dream of his life, — a constitutional government for France.

www.ingramcontent.com/pod-product-compliance
Lightning Source LLC
Chambersburg PA
CBHW020858020726
47497CB00005B/1460